we both have secrets

BOOKS BY EMMA ROBINSON

The Undercover Mother

Happily Never After

One Way Ticket to Paris

My Silent Daughter

The Forgotten Wife

My Husband's Daughter

His First Wife's Secret

To Save My Child

Only for My Daughter

To Be a Mother

My Stepmother's Secret

Please Take My Baby

She Has My Child

All My Fault

The Favourite Child

we both have secrets

emma robinson

bookouture

Published by Bookouture in 2025

An imprint of Storyfire Ltd.
Carmelite House
50 Victoria Embankment
London EC4Y 0DZ

www.bookouture.com

The authorised representative in the EEA is Hachette Ireland
8 Castlecourt Centre
Dublin 15 D15 XTP3
Ireland
(email: info@hbgi.ie)

Copyright © Emma Robinson, 2025

Emma Robinson has asserted her right to be identified
as the author of this work.

All rights reserved. No part of this publication may be reproduced, stored in any
retrieval system, or transmitted, in any form or by any means, electronic,
mechanical, photocopying, recording or otherwise, without the prior written
permission of the publishers.

ISBN: 978-1-80550-008-7
eBook ISBN: 978-1-80550-007-0

This book is a work of fiction. Names, characters, businesses, organizations,
places and events other than those clearly in the public domain, are either the
product of the author's imagination or are used fictitiously. Any resemblance to
actual persons, living or dead, events or locales is entirely coincidental.

For Nina
From Jander to Jumping
Thank you for your unwavering support

PROLOGUE

Before I begin, you have to understand how much I love you. You might question that once you find out what I've kept from you, but it's true. I couldn't have asked for any more from you. You've been a wonderful wife to me and an even better mother to our girls.

I also want to say that I am sorry. Deeply sorry. What I'm about to say is going to blow our lives apart. But there's nothing else for it. I've tried so hard to keep it from you, not wanting to cause you pain. But I can't hide it any longer. I wasn't made for a double life.

You deserve the truth. But I don't know if there's any coming back from this, Ellen. And I'm terrified that you won't ever forgive me...

Torn hurriedly from his notebook, Robert's letter was damp and creased in Ellen's hand, its words burned into her brain. As she stood alone on the beach, all she could see were family groups sprawled out on the sand. Happy holidaying parents and children, spending time with one another. It felt like a blink ago that this was them. Robert, Ellen, Grace and Abigail. How had she got to here? Searching for her husband to beg him to tell her the truth.

And their girls. She felt a stab of pain in her stomach at the thought of having to tell them that their parents' marriage was over. All she'd ever wanted for them was a stable home life, parents who were always there for them. Hadn't she even sacrificed her own career because it would have taken her away from home?

But as the tears started to pool in her eyes she had to acknowledge that the timing of this wasn't a coincidence. Abigail leaving for university was the beginning of the end for their family. She had hoped that this might be the start of a new adventure for her and Robert.

He had clearly been thinking the opposite.

ONE

TWO DAYS EARLIER

Maybe this holiday was – as Robert had warned – a truly terrible idea.

Almost at the end of the three-hour flight to Malaga and, so far, they'd barely spoken other than to ascertain which tasteless sandwich to order from the in-flight menu. Robert was deep in a thriller novel and Ellen was flicking through the magazine she'd picked up at the airport. It was just reminding her why she didn't buy these things. Everyone was young and beautiful and it was a mirror to the fact that she was no longer either of those.

Bored with being made to feel inadequate, she stuffed the magazine into the seat pocket behind the airline brochure and safety leaflet and pulled out a packet of Mint Imperials, offering one to Robert. 'It'll be strange to see Lucy again, won't it?'

Robert kept his thumb in his book as he took a mint. 'I still don't really understand why we're going. We haven't been in touch with Lucy for over twenty years. Don't you think it'll be a little strange to be staying in her house?'

Between him fielding last-minute work calls and her dash to the shops for a suck-it-all-in swimsuit and beach towels she wouldn't be ashamed of, they'd only briefly spoken about the trip since she'd booked the flights yesterday. 'I know what you're saying, but it felt like fate, her daughter being in the same halls as Abigail.'

Last week, she'd moved their youngest daughter Abigail into her university accommodation and the whole thing had been decidedly surreal. Neither she nor Robert had been back to Canterbury since they'd graduated in 1998. It had changed a great deal since then – Abigail's room was more mid-price hotel chain than student digs, with a hefty rent to match – but she'd still experienced the bittersweet nostalgia of being back on that campus where she and Robert had met and fallen in love.

Robert frowned. 'Well, Lucy was a student there, the same as us. Maybe she waged a campaign to influence her daughter like you did with Abigail.'

His gruff tone was softened by a raised eyebrow, which made her laugh. 'Emily was so much like Lucy. We'd only been there about fifteen minutes when she stuck her head around the door and introduced herself. She asked Abbie about a million questions, which is what led to me telling her that we'd been students there and that's how I found out she was Lucy's daughter. I couldn't believe it when she told me her mother's maiden name and we put two and two together.'

She was sure she'd told him all this already. Did he ever actually listen? Robert opened his book again and scanned the page for his place. 'And two and two made her tell Lucy about you, which is why we're now on a plane to stay with her in Malaga.'

'We did say that we were going to have a few days away once Abigail started university. Lucy's invitation came at the right time.'

She refrained from adding that she'd dropped enough hints to Robert that she wanted him to be the one to book something this time. For her, last week had consisted of packing and checking lists and last-minute trips to IKEA for kitchen supplies for Abigail – but he'd done nothing. He also hadn't been the one who'd had to drop her off and then drive away with her stomach doing flips-flops at the significance of leaving her. Yet again, he was away with work. Something that was happening more and more lately. For someone who said he didn't enjoy his job in medical sales, he was spending a lot of time doing it.

This time, he folded the corner of his page and closed the book on the tray table. 'Still, it's a bit weird, isn't it? Hello, we haven't spoken in over over twenty years, but would you like to fly out to Spain tomorrow and stay in my house?'

Glad she had his attention, Ellen shifted in her seat so that they could have a proper conversation. 'It wasn't quite like that. I told her that we'd booked the week off work but hadn't planned anything yet and, anyway, it's not as if she's a stranger. We were all really good friends back then, weren't we? And she obviously wanted to reconnect or why would she have asked Emily to get my number from Abbie?'

Robert frowned at the cover of his thriller, which featured a man with rolled up shirt-sleeves walking off into a bright-orange sunset. 'It would've been nice to have at least discussed it before you immediately booked our flights.'

She turned back to stare at the seat in front of her. 'I thought it would be a nice surprise.'

A strident voice boomed from the intercom. 'Cabin Crew, seats for landing.'

In baggage reclaim, it was busy and uncomfortable. Small clumps of people shuffled around, waiting for the luggage carousel to creak into action, restless for their bags to arrive so that they could begin their holiday. Young lovers holding hands and sharing headphones, families trying to keep excitable toddlers close, and then couples like them, whose children had flown the nest.

6 EMMA ROBINSON

Though she'd expected to feel a little lost without Abigail in the house, Ellen still hadn't been prepared for the scale of the seismic shift of her last child leaving home. Canterbury was less than two hours away from them in Sussex, but it might as well have been on the moon. Once she'd dropped her off in halls, Ellen had come home and stood on the threshold of Abbie's bedroom, strewn with the clothes she'd decided against taking. Already, she missed her like a limb.

Arms folded, feet wide apart, Robert was waiting to pounce on their luggage as soon as it appeared. In his crumpled linen jacket and dark-blue jeans, he looked like one of the characters from his novel. A diplomat, maybe. She leaned towards him and nudged his elbow. 'Lucy has a pool. You love swimming.'

Sighing, his arms dropped to his sides and he let his head hang in either irritation or apology. 'You don't need to keep selling this to me, Ellen. I know I've been a bit grumpy, I'm sorry. It just feels awkward to me. If you and Lucy were such good friends, why haven't you been in touch all this time? But I said I'd come. And I'm here.'

He was here physically. But there was such a distance between them lately. All they talked about was the girls, or work, or which of the bins needed putting at the end of the driveway this week. One of the reasons she'd picked that magazine up at the airport was the headline on the front: 'Recapture the Romance'. That's what they needed to do. And surely a few days together in a beautiful house in the sunshine was the place to do it?

Finally, the baggage reclaim belt groaned into action and Robert moved closer to search for their cases. He wasn't wrong to ask why she and Lucy hadn't stayed in touch all this time, though. Despite rolling it around in her mind as she'd tried to get to sleep last night, she didn't have an answer. After graduation, they'd promised to keep in touch, but their lives had gone in different directions. Now they were here, she felt a little nervous about seeing Lucy again. Twenty-seven years was a long time. What if they had nothing in common?

'Here's the first one.' Robert pulled out the telescopic handle of her suitcase and rolled it towards her before returning to look for its pair.

A series of dings on her phone meant that it had finally connected to a Spanish network. One was a message from Lucy to say that she was already at the arrivals gate and looking forward to seeing them. Last night, Ellen had searched through a cluster of ancient boxes in the garage to dig out some old photographs of their three years at university, thinking it would be fun to bring them. Back then, Lucy had been stunningly beautiful, getting so much attention that the rest of the girls in their group might as well have been invisible. She'd also tried to stalk her online to find out what she looked like now, but couldn't find her on Instagram or Facebook and had been too embarrassed to ask her to text a picture. Surely she'd be able to recognise her?

The second suitcase wobbled its way onto the conveyor belt, the grinding gears of which made Ellen wince. She was still worried about the clothes she'd packed. According to BBC Weather, the sunshine in Malaga was going to be glorious. But that meant shorts and t-shirts and – most terrifyingly – swim-suits. Grace, her elder daughter, had offered to lend her a bikini yesterday and she'd almost choked on her cheese and pickle sandwich at the very notion.

Robert walked the second suitcase towards her. 'Shall we go?'

All around them, holidaymakers chattered excitedly. In contrast, Robert was in practical mode, striding towards the exit. The closer they got to seeing Lucy, the more nervous Ellen felt. Had it been madness to book those flights yesterday after one telephone conversation? What if they had nothing in common after all this time? Memories of university would last them an evening, but they were going to be there for three nights. However nice the house and pool and weather, if they had nothing to say to one another, it would be a very awkward holiday. What if Robert was right and this was a truly terrible idea? She reached for his hand. 'You will try and enjoy yourself, won't you?'

He frowned and, for a brief moment, he looked as if he might be about to say something serious, but then his face cleared and he smiled. 'I'll do my very best.'

As they emerged into the sunlit hall, she scanned the barrier. Trying not to get in the way of the people behind them, she slowed her steps and attempted to see past the friends and families throwing their arms around one another, reuniting in rich melodious Spanish, looking for a familiar face.

And there she was. Lucy. Tanned, slim, wearing a cream fitted suit with a black silk blouse, cut low enough to show a glimpse of cleavage. In all her imaginings, Ellen hadn't expected her to look that glamorous. Why hadn't she taken Grace's advice to wear something more stylish for the flight?

Lucy waved and the slim diamond bracelet at her wrist caught the light coming through the large glass windows. 'Robert! Ellen! Over here!'

Several of the cab drivers draped along the rail holding placards with the names of their clients looked appreciatively in her direction. Clearly, she was still turning heads. Robert picked up speed and was at the barrier just before Ellen. Lucy threw her arms around him and said something in his ear which was lost in the voices around them. Then she turned to Ellen with a perfect smile and pulled her into a brief expensively scented embrace. 'I'm so pleased you've both come.'

Over Lucy's shoulder, the look on Robert's face was pretty unreadable. Maybe it was just nerves about this impulsive reunion, but there was something in his eyes that made Ellen feel strangely uncomfortable.

TWO

As Ellen had anticipated, Lucy's home was absolutely incredible. Just outside the main centre of Malaga town, on a road that was just starting to turn up into the hillside, Lucy's pale-blue Renault pulled through black wrought-iron gates onto a square courtyard in front of the prettiest house Ellen had ever seen. Two floors of smooth white stucco walls, a tiled roof and, behind a pretty tinkling fountain, a large archway led the way to a heavy wooden front door.

'Wow.' She saw her envy reflected in Robert's eyes. 'This is some place.'

Pulling the brake hard against the slight incline, Lucy pushed her sunglasses up onto her head and squinted through the windscreen at the house. 'One of the perks of being married to a property developer. It was just a shell when we found it. Come and see inside.'

Thick and fragrant, the afternoon air was too hot for the jeans Ellen had worn for the flight and her t-shirt clung to her back. Aside from unbuttoning the neck of his shirt, Robert looked as fresh as Lucy. He'd always thrived in the heat.

Inside, a cool marble floor and air conditioning provided a

welcome relief but Ellen couldn't wait to peel off her damp clothes and take a shower. Lucy threw open a set of dark wood doors into a granite-topped kitchen. On the counter, an emerald-green bottle rested in a bucket of ice, accompanied by three crystal glasses. 'Cava. From Joe's special collection. We have to toast your visit properly, after all. I'll pour us a glass and then show you both to your room.'

Further down the cool hall, two white doors opened onto a large, airy room. A double bed in the centre with crisp white linen looked cool and inviting. Along one wall, a cherry wood dressing table with a large mirror. Lucy strode across the room and opened French windows onto a balcony that looked out onto a large azure pool. She turned and smiled. 'Will this be okay?'

Ellen couldn't remember the last time they'd stayed somewhere this nice. 'It's wonderful. I might never leave.'

Lucy was back across the room and almost to the door when she paused beside Robert and touched him lightly on the arm. 'Why don't you both get your swimming costumes on and join me by the pool when you're ready. Take your time.'

Robert had definitely cheered up since the flight and it wasn't just the effects of the sunshine. 'I don't need asking twice.'

With a polite smile, Ellen nodded, but she was far less keen on the idea. She could already imagine how much better Lucy was likely to look than she would squeezed into her new 'bodyshaping' suit.

As soon as the door was closed, Robert started unbuttoning his shirt, his stomach toned and his chest muscular from his recent visits to the gym. 'That pool looks amazing. Exactly what I need right now.'

Five minutes ago, she'd wanted to cool off, too. But watching him undress, she wondered if they could take their time as Lucy had suggested. Have a few moments to themselves first. Maybe even take a shower together. Feeling the flush of anticipation, she pulled her own top over her head and dropped it onto the bed.

But when she turned around, Robert had already pulled on his trunks and was at the door. 'Shall I meet you out there?'

She swallowed down her disappointment. Turned away to hide the embarrassment that her thoughts had been so different from his. That he wasn't even going to wait for her. 'I'll be out in a minute. Don't you want the suncream?'

He shook his head. 'I'm getting straight into the pool. Bring it with you and I'll put some on when I get out.'

She resisted the urge to tell him that he would need it on before he got in the water. She wasn't his mother after all.

Speaking of being a mother, she sent both girls a quick text to let them know she and Robert had arrived safely. Then she took a couple of photos of the room and added them to the thread. Within a few moments, she got a love heart from Abigail and then her phone rang with a FaceTime call from Grace.

'Hi, Mum. The place looks great, is that your room?'

'It is. And we've got a balcony that overlooks the pool. Your dad is already out there.'

She wandered over to the window and pushed back the light gauzy curtain to see Robert below, chest deep in the pool, with his forearms resting on the marble tiled edge. Beside him, legs dangling in the water, a glass of Cava in hand, Lucy was enviably slim and toned. She clearly had no need for a swimsuit with panels to keep her sucked in. With a large brimmed hat shading her face, she could've stepped straight from the pages of Ellen's magazine. Ellen thanked her lucky stars that she'd also grabbed the matching cover-all along with her new swimsuit, hoping its sheer fabric would float over her curves rather than accentuate them.

On the phone screen, Grace frowned at her. 'Why aren't you down in the pool with Dad?'

Though she missed the days of toothy toddlerhood, there were many advantages to having a daughter in her mid-twenties, not the least of which was having someone more than willing to give you honest fashion advice. 'I'm trying to get up the confidence to let anyone see me in my new swimsuit. It was the only one in my size and I'm worried it's a bit low cut.'

Grace rolled her eyes. 'Show me.'

She pressed the screen to change the camera to looking outwards and – holding it aloft – stood in front of the mirror. Staring critically at herself in the black costume, she could see the flesh bulging from the elastic at the top of her legs. But she was more worried about the amount of skin that was exposed. 'What do you think? Too much chest? Tell me the truth.'

'Don't I always? You look great, Mum. Your boobs look great.'

Obviously that meant she was showing too much of them. She pulled the top of the swimsuit upwards. 'You should see Lucy. She looks about a decade younger than me. She probably thinks I'm a complete frump.'

On the screen, another eye-roll from Grace. 'You need to stop worrying what other people think, Mum. You look great, honestly.'

Ellen sighed and dropped down onto the end of the bed. 'Well, either way, I need to get out there. I told your dad I was only going to be a couple of minutes.'

She glanced out of the window again. She couldn't make out Robert's face, but she heard the splash of him moving his arms and legs in the water and the tinkle of Lucy's laugh. That was the thing with Robert, he never wanted to go anywhere, or see anyone, but when he did, he was the life and soul of the party.

Grace was clearly bored of the swimsuit conversation. 'Anyway. Back to me. I wasn't going to call and tell you this when

WE BOTH HAVE SECRETS 13

you were on holiday, but then you texted me and I assumed it would be okay.'

The hairs on the back of Ellen's neck rose with a kind of motherly sixth sense. What was she going to say? *Please let it be something positive.* 'It's always okay for you to call me. What's up?'

'Well, Max has got to go on a last-minute business trip to Dubai. Someone from our office was supposed to go but they've come down with a bug. So, they've asked Max to go. This Friday.'

She could tell by the excitement in Grace's voice what was coming next. 'And?'

'And he's asked me to go with him.'

Of course he had. 'That's lovely, sweetheart, but how will you get the time off work so quickly?'

Grace scrunched up her nose. 'Okay, I know that you're not going to approve of this, but I think it's genius. I can call in sick on Friday morning with the same bug that Jack – he's the one who was supposed to go on the trip – has. It'll be totally believable.'

Ellen wasn't so sure about that. 'But what if work find out, Grace? You could lose your job.' Still at the window, Ellen watched as Lucy slipped effortlessly off the side of the pool into the water with barely a splash. Still wearing her wide-brimmed hat, she obscured Robert from Ellen's view.

There was a big sigh on the other end of the phone. 'I knew you'd think it was a bad idea. But we've planned it all. We won't put anything on social media about being there. Max doesn't like me putting anything on social media anyway. So it'll all be off the radar. I won't even be flying with him because he's going first thing in the morning and he's flying Business Class. I'll fly later in the day after I've called into work and told them that I'm sick. No one knows about us at work anyway, so it'll all be fine. No one will suspect a thing.'

Could she not see all the red flags that Max was practically waving in her face? 'You still haven't told anyone at work about the two of you? Not even the girls you live with?'

Another sigh. 'We've talked about this before, Mum. It'd be really awkward for me at work if people knew we were together. He and his wife only separated last year. People would think badly of us.'

The more she heard about Max, the more Ellen suspected that he and his wife were not separated at all, but she knew better than to repeat this theory to her eldest daughter. She saved her compliance and forgiveness for her boyfriend: Ellen was in the wrong whatever she said or did. 'I just think it's a big risk to your job to be doing this.'

Grace pouted. 'Well, I thought you'd be excited for me. Haven't you always told me that I should travel and see the world?'

She had said that, but she'd meant for her daughter to forge her own path, not trail behind someone else. Particularly someone who, whether he and his wife were genuinely separated or not, was still technically married. Saying all that to Grace was out of the question. 'Just think about it before you make a decision.'

'I will. And then I'll send you a picture of me in Dubai.'

The patio around the pool was warm – even through her sandals – and, now that Ellen wore only the diaphanous cover up and her swimsuit, the heat of the late afternoon was far more pleasant. Trying her best to appear more confident than she felt, she headed for the sunbeds on the other side of the pool.

Robert was frowning at something Lucy was saying. As she got closer, he looked up and gave her a wave. 'I was wondering where you'd got to.'

'Grace called. I'll fill you in later.'

Lucy turned in the pool, the ripples caused by her movement circling outwards. 'I was just telling Robert how good he looks. Very fit for a man his age.'

Given how long it was since they'd spent time together, this seemed more than a little forward. She wasn't wrong, though. Robert did look good. His dark hair was still thick with only a touch of grey and, though he was slim, his body still had the same definition it'd had more than twenty years ago. 'Yes, I'm a lucky woman, aren't I?'

Due to the hat and sunglasses, it was difficult to read Lucy's expression, but her voice had a definite edge to it. 'You *certainly* are.'

At university, Lucy had always been the flirtatious one. She'd thought nothing of walking up to a group of boys in a bar and beginning a conversation. When you looked like she did, you didn't often have to worry about encountering rejection. It was just her way, to talk to people like this. It wasn't something Ellen should be worried about.

Right now, she was more concerned about what was going through her husband's mind. Robert was a man, after all. And it was impossible not to look at her and Lucy and find Ellen lacking. Which is why she had no intention of removing the dress and getting in the pool. Instead, she slid onto the sunbed and lifted her legs up onto the footrest, trying as best she could to arrange herself into a flattering posture.

Robert called out to her. 'Are you not getting in? It's lovely in here.'

She smiled at her husband and shook her head. 'No, I'm fine here for a bit. You enjoy it.'

Fully expecting him to launch himself into lengths of the pool – he usually couldn't keep still for a moment – Ellen was surprised that he stayed where he was, the only movement an occasional kick of the legs. Meanwhile, Lucy swam back and forth in front of him, her voice too low for Ellen to catch.

For a brief moment, the sun disappeared behind the one cloud in the sky and a shadow passed across the patio. Ellen shivered. When was the last time that Robert had looked at her the way he was looking at Lucy? And what was Lucy up to? It was Ellen who'd made the arrangement to come out here, but Lucy seemed to have eyes only for Robert. Had it been him that she'd actually wanted to see? Was Ellen being paranoid or was she keeping her voice purposefully low enough for Ellen to be excluded from their conversation?

THREE

'I can't believe we're all here together.'

After they'd made the most of the October afternoon sun, Ellen and Robert had unpacked and taken showers while Lucy prepared dinner. With just the three of them around the table, the setting was uneven. Robert and Ellen this side and Lucy on the other. She stretched across the table with her wine glass to chink both of theirs.

Robert sipped at the dark-purple Rioja. 'Well, the wine is definitely a lot better than the mouthwash we drank in those days.'

Lucy reached forward to clink his glass again. 'That is very true. And we are definitely better dressed. Did you actually own any other clothes than that checked shirt and grey jumper?'

Ellen followed Lucy's appraising eye to her husband who'd changed into linen trousers and an open-necked white shirt. Even those couple of hours in the pool had brought a sun-kissed glow to his face. Hers felt tight and dry.

Lucy leaned back in her chair with a gleam in her eye. 'It feels like a lifetime ago that we were all there. Well, it was a lifetime – your daughter's lifetime. Wasn't she born about three months after we left?'

Was she making a little dig? 'Five months. Nearly six.'

To this day, Ellen could remember the cold fear that had coursed through her when she'd seen that thin blue line on the pregnancy test. Her periods had never been particularly regular so it was only when she'd started to feel really sick that she'd considered the possibility. Even then, she hadn't really believed that it was pregnancy causing her early morning trips to the shared bathroom.

'Quite a good way to take the best-looking guy in our year off the market before the graduation ball. Well played.'

Lucy raised her glass and laughed at her own joke and Robert joined in. Ellen tried to show she'd taken it well, but it was hard not to feel the sting. Robert had been absolutely incredible back then. After the shock of her news, he'd taken her into his arms and told her that they were always going to end up together anyway. 'This is just a little earlier than planned.' For the last twenty-seven years she'd hoped that he'd really meant that. That they would have been married whether there'd been a baby or not.

'Gosh, we were young back then.' Lucy toyed with the glass in her hand, swirling the Rioja around so that it lapped the side of the glass, leaving a red stain. 'Do you remember the parties we used to have after the bar closed on campus? You would make those ridiculous cocktails.'

The last comment was directed at Robert. Ellen was surprised. What cocktails?

But Robert was grimacing. 'Goodness, yes. We'd buy anything cheap from the supermarket and mix those concoctions. I'm surprised we didn't make ourselves ill. Sometimes they had lumps in where the creamy ones had curdled.'

Lucy laughed. 'They were crazy, crazy nights. Have the two

WE BOTH HAVE SECRETS 19

of you been recapturing those days now that your girls are out the door?'

No. They hadn't. Any hope Ellen had had all these years that they would make up for the missed opportunities in their twenties once their children were older had not materialised. These days, Robert seemed more interested in work than in her. 'Not yet. But Abigail's only just left.'

She took a large gulp of Rioja, the wine jammy and thick on the back of her tongue. Lucy raised a manicured eyebrow. 'Really? I assumed that you two would be love's young dream again.'

This was starting to get a little too close for comfort. Lucy seemed happy to slip back into the intimacy of their college days, but Ellen wasn't ready to open up about her marriage, her worries, her life. Especially with Robert sitting there. 'Well, maybe this lovely place will inspire us. Have you had the house long?'

Lucy sat back in her seat and looked around her. It really was a beautiful room. White marble beneath their feet, a glass table top and black leather chairs were bathed in light from the floor-to-ceiling windows, sharing the last of the early evening sun. 'We've been here a couple of years. Joe will get itchy feet soon and move us somewhere else. It's always best for me to not get too attached.'

She sounded wistful, but Ellen saw the pleasure in her eyes at the concept of going somewhere new. Maybe this was the way to avoid getting bored of your life; not staying in the same place for too long.

Robert cleared his throat. 'He must be pretty successful at it? Joe? To afford somewhere like this as a second home? Along with your place in Hertfordshire?'

How did Robert know where their other home was? Ellen didn't remember Lucy mentioning it? It must've been when they were in the pool earlier.

Lucy shrugged. 'Yes, he does really well. But he works hard for it. He's away a lot. Sometimes at the last minute. You must know how that is with all your trade shows.'

How had they got this much information about each other after only fifteen minutes alone in the pool? 'How often are you in Hertfordshire?'

'Usually I'm there most of the time. But now Emily has left for university, there's no need for me to be there so I'll probably spend most of my time here. That should curtail Joe's activities.'

Though she was clearly joking, there was an edge to her laugh. Ellen had assumed her husband would be here already. 'Will Joe be home soon?'

'He's away tonight. Work. He was planning on being here when you arrived and then he was needed to sort out some issues with the builders he's using in a new complex a few hours up the coast. Downside of the job, unfortunately. Hopefully, he'll be here in the morning. How's your job in the lab? I still can't believe you're an actual scientist.'

Ellen wasn't sure that she'd call it that. 'It's a lot of repetitive testing, to be honest. But the hours have worked well around the kids.'

'You must be the only one of us actually using your degree. Don't suppose you need much chemistry for medical sales, Robert?'

Ellen almost winced. Though it was well paid, Robert didn't enjoy what he did. Travelling the country, selling pharmaceuticals to NHS trusts. A ping from Ellen's phone interrupted her train of thought. It was Abigail.

Hope you're having a nice time, Mum. I'm going out tonight with Emily Meads. She's found a bar in town and we're going as a group. Love you! xxx

WE BOTH HAVE SECRETS

She waved her phone at Lucy. 'Our daughters are going out together tonight, apparently.'

Lucy's laugh was deep and husky. 'I apologise in advance.'

Her words prickled in Ellen's ears. 'What do you mean?'

'I'm joking. But Emily is a little wild. I hope Abigail is able to say no.'

She couldn't have made Ellen more concerned if she'd tried. If Emily was wild, then Abigail was tame. One of Ellen's biggest concerns about her going to university was her ability to make friends. She was so quiet and introverted. Plus, all she heard from her own friends with daughters at university were the horror stories about drinks getting spiked and young women being vulnerable. She couldn't bear it if something happened to Abigail. 'It's so scary, isn't it? Them being away on their own. No one to check if they get back safely each night?'

Until Robert reached over and placed his hand over hers, she hadn't realised that she was gripping a white linen napkin with her fingers. 'She'll be fine, Ellen.'

It was easy for him to say that. Boys had a very different experience of nights out than girls did. He'd been amazed when Grace and Abigail first started to go out alone and she'd passed on all the tips she had at her disposal: keep your keys in your hand in case someone grabs you and you need to fight back; cross the road to see if the man walking too close behind you follows; never ever leave a friend behind.

Lucy frowned and her smile turned up on one side in gentle mockery. 'Surely you've been through all of this with your elder daughter?'

Ellen shook her head. 'Grace didn't go to university. She did a degree-level apprenticeship with a bank in the City.'

At the time, she'd been disappointed that Grace wouldn't get the whole experience of going away to university. But there'd been relief, too. While Grace was working – and studying – she'd lived at home, where she'd been until a year ago when she moved into a house share with two other girls from work.

Nodding slowly, Lucy reached over for Ellen's plate, clattering it onto her own before reaching for Robert's. 'Very sensible. No debt. My elder daughter was studying for years. It seemed never ending. And now we're starting all over again.'

That was the first time she'd mentioned any other children. 'You have another daughter?'

'Yes. Charlotte.'

Lucy picked up the bottle on the table to refill Ellen's glass. When she held it up to Robert, he shook his head, so she poured the remains of the wine into her own glass. Was Ellen imagining the look that just passed between Robert and Lucy at the mention of her eldest daughter?

Lucy pushed her chair back and rose, holding the plates. 'How about we take dessert out onto the patio? It's still warm enough, I think. Shall we have coffee too? Decaf for you, Robert?'

This was one too far. Ellen fought to keep her voice curious rather than accusatory. 'How do you know that Robert takes his coffee decaffeinated?'

Was that the slightest blush on Lucy's cheek? 'You must've told me. Or Robert did? Or a good guess, maybe. Go on outside, I won't be a minute.'

It was too petty a thing to make a scene about, but all of these side remarks were beginning to add up. As soon as they were out of earshot, seated around a small metal table near the pool, she asked Robert, 'How did Lucy know you drink decaffeinated coffee?'

He shrugged. 'I don't know. We were talking about healthy eating earlier while I was in the pool. Maybe I mentioned it?'

It was possible, but unlikely. And she wasn't about to start a discussion on the way he and Lucy had been acting today when she could reappear at any moment. She shivered. Now the sun had lost its strength, there was a chill in the air. 'I'm going to get a cardigan from our room. Do you want anything?'

Robert was gazing past the pool at the sea in the distance. Without turning to look at her, he shook his head. 'I'm fine, thanks.'

The patio door was still open, so Ellen didn't make a sound as she entered and walked towards her bedroom. From the open kitchen door, she heard a loud ringtone – a Killers song maybe? – and heard Lucy pick up.

The corridor past the kitchen was long enough that she heard her answer and ask how things were going with whoever it was on the other end of the line. It wasn't as if Ellen was eavesdropping, but when she was almost at her bedroom door, she heard the words that confirmed that she was right to be suspicious. Lucy's voice was low, but perfectly clear.

'Yes... He's here... No, she doesn't know anything.'

And then she closed the kitchen door.

FOUR

Ellen had been barely a minute grabbing her cardigan from the wardrobe but, as she returned to the table, Lucy was already emerging from the kitchen with a tray of three small custard desserts, which she held aloft. 'Catalan Cream.'

With no time to tell Robert what she'd overheard, Ellen retook her seat with a tight smile. Forcing herself to take the same tiny spoonfuls as Lucy made her more frustrated by the second, fueling her anger. By the time Lucy pushed her bowl away and suggested more coffee, Ellen was ready to explode. 'Actually, I think I'm ready for bed.'

Lucy's shoulders dropped in disappointment. 'But it's still early. And you're only here for three nights. We need to make the most of your time.'

If it hadn't been for the overheard conversation, Ellen might've felt guilty. 'It must be the flight, and the wine. I'll be much livelier after a good night's sleep.'

Lucy had turned to Robert then. 'You're not going to go, too? Shall I put on more coffee?'

Over her shoulder, Ellen shot him a look that dared him not

WE BOTH HAVE SECRETS

to come with her and he got the message. 'Do you know what, I'm tired, too. Let's save the coffee for breakfast.'

As soon as the door was closed to their bedroom, she was on him. 'What was that all about?'

He looked genuinely confused. 'What?'

He could play dumb all he wanted. 'You and Lucy. The flirting.'

A bemused smile played at the edge of his mouth. 'Flirting? Are you serious?'

She wasn't going to be put off. 'In the pool earlier, you were pretty cosy just the two of you.'

Unbuttoning his shirt, Robert sighed. 'We weren't *cosy*. You didn't want to get in the pool. And I was trying to compensate for the fact you were acting so strangely. What were you doing, just sulking on the side like that?'

A lump rose in her throat. Did he really have no idea? 'I wasn't sulking. I just felt... left out.'

Even to herself, she sounded pathetic. But wouldn't it be even worse to have to say the truth. I felt fat. I felt frumpy. And old. And, yes, left out next to Lucy and her slim body and stylish hair and expensive clothes.

Robert threw his shirt over the back of a chair and pulled on the pyjama top she'd left on his side of the duvet. 'Can we just go to bed? You said that you were tired.'

Anger and frustration made her snap at him. 'I only said that to get out of there. I know something strange is going on. I overheard Lucy talking about us on the phone. She said *he's here* and then *she doesn't know anything*. What do you think that means? What don't I know?'

Robert shook his head at her like she was a small child having a tantrum. 'You don't even know that she was talking about you. She was probably talking to her husband. About one of their daughters, maybe? It's been an emotional few days,

Ellen. And you're tired. Everything will look better in the morning.'

He sounded so reasonable that she began to doubt herself. His explanation was more likely. Could she have misunderstood? Still, she wasn't ready to give in. 'Well, the two of you were still very flirty.'

Robert was the most amenable of men, but even he had his limits. 'Now you're being paranoid and I'm too tired for this. You do remember that I didn't even want to come on this holiday? You were the one who pushed for it, you were the one who said I would enjoy it once I got here and now you're criticising my behaviour? Because I'm talking to our host? I'm going to sleep.'

With that, he threw back the cover, got into bed and turned away from her.

As she stared at his unmoving shoulders, hot tears collected at the back of her eyes. Why couldn't she tell him how she felt? He was her husband. They'd slept next to each other for the last twenty-seven years. He knew her better than she knew herself and yet... something had changed between them recently. If only she could put her finger on when it had started, maybe they could claw it back.

Was it the so-called empty nest syndrome? They'd had children pretty much their whole married life. They'd never learned to be together without children. Now, with Abigail leaving home, going to university, they were forced to look at one another again. What if he looked at her and didn't like what he saw? Being here with Lucy, she wasn't sure that she liked what she saw, either. She couldn't even blame having children on the fact that she'd let herself go, because didn't Lucy have two daughters at pretty much the same age as her? What happened if their relationship didn't outlast their youngest daughter leaving home?

She slipped her pyjamas out from underneath the pillow on

her side of the bed. Even they seemed further evidence of her lack of style. She didn't imagine for a second that Lucy wore grey jersey pyjamas that had begun to go bobbly through being washed so often. Lucy would probably wear silk and lace, short and sheer. And her husband would not be snoring with his back to her.

Slowly, she laid herself next to Robert, already knowing it would be impossible to sleep. The fresh white sheets were pleasantly cool, but his body was hot and made her feel lonelier than ever. She opened her Kindle, but after rereading the first sentence five times, she gave up on that and picked up her phone. Doing what she swore she wouldn't once Abigail was at university, she checked her location. She wasn't back at her halls of residence. In fact, she wasn't on campus at all.

She's eighteen. She's sensible. She needs her freedom. She repeated the mantra to herself but it was no use. Ellen's heart thudded in her chest at the memory of Lucy describing her own daughter as a 'livewire'. Where might Emily have taken her? Would Abigail stick to her own plan to 'never have more than three drinks a night'?

She closed her eyes. Why had she looked? Now she wouldn't be able to settle until she was sure that Abigail was safely home. Although even being back at the campus wouldn't be evidence of her safety. There'd be parties in their halls and who knows what might happen?

This wasn't normal, was it? Obsessing about where her daughter was and what she was doing. Abigail wasn't Ellen and this wasn't 1997. Her daughter was far more prepared for university life than she had been. But she was wide awake now and there was no use laying here tossing and turning. All she'd achieve would be to wake Robert and he'd remind her of her promise not to use the tracking app to torture herself. Her mouth and throat were dry. Maybe a glass of water would help.

The marble floor was cold on her feet and, as she padded to

the kitchen, she saw the blue electronic glow of a phone before she saw Lucy on a stool next to the breakfast bar, drinking a glass of wine in the kitchen. She looked up and smiled, her face half in darkness. 'Can't sleep?'

After pretending to be tired, Ellen didn't want to admit to insomnia. 'Actually, I was going to get a glass of water. Is that okay?'

Aside from the phone, the only other light in the kitchen came from a strip beneath the wall cabinets. Lucy's eyes were in darkness and difficult to read. 'Of course, help yourself. The glasses are in the top cupboard, next to the refrigerator.'

Neatly lined up on the second shelf, the glasses were made of heavy crystal – very different from the mismatched selection that would've been on offer in Ellen's kitchen. Was everything in this place perfect? She let the water run a little until it was cold, filled her glass and turned back to Lucy. 'You're up late.'

Lucy waved her phone. 'Texting with Joe. He's out to dinner with some clients.'

Ellen's own phone was still in her hand and, when she checked again, Abigail was still out. 'Does he work away a lot?'

Lucy sipped at her wine. Even this small movement was measured, controlled. 'Yes. Before Emily started university, there were a lot of flights back and forth.'

The mention of university and Emily made her check her phone again. No movement. 'Is that difficult? Being apart so much?'

Lucy shrugged. 'A little. But I have a pretty full life.'

There'd been no mention of a career, so Ellen wondered what her life was full of. 'Don't you worry about him? Being away on his own, I mean.'

'Are you asking me if I trust my husband?' Lucy stared at her as if she had grown a second head.

'No. No. Sorry. I just mean... that your lives are so separate. Doesn't it cause problems when you're together?'

WE BOTH HAVE SECRETS 29

Even in the darkness, she could see the depth of Lucy's frown. 'What kind of problems do you mean?'

From the look on Lucy's face, Ellen realised how rude she was being. 'Sorry. You must think I'm being awful. It's just... well, in the past, Robert travelled a lot with work, but he almost always came home at the end of the day, whatever time it was. But lately, business has been harder to come by and he's had to widen his sales territory. It means he's away more. And for longer. It's a change. We're having to adjust.'

When they were younger, she'd sit up and wait for him. After children, she would go to bed but make him promise to wake her when he got in, wanting to know that he was home and safe. These days, she was more likely to be alone in their king-size bed while he was in a budget hotel hundreds of miles away.

Lucy's smile was as inscrutable as the Mona Lisa's. 'I don't think it matters if your husband works across town or across the country. If you want your marriage to work, you need to make sure you create something that he wants to hurry back to.'

She swept an arm to take in the beautiful kitchen – its clean, expensive, luxurious gleam – and then swept the same arm down her own body, before laughing. Not knowing the Lucy of now, Ellen really didn't know how much was a joke and how much was serious. She had certainly created something beautiful, both in her home and in herself.

Standing here in the middle of Lucy's life, the difference between the two of them was in stark relief. What about *her* life? What had Ellen and Robert created? She couldn't help but worry that their life – potentially even Ellen herself – weren't enough for Robert now that the girls had left home. Is that why he was away so much lately?

She hadn't realised that she'd checked her phone again until Lucy remarked on it. 'Are you waiting for a message?'

Her cheeks warmed, embarrassed to admit that she was

checking up on her daughter. 'Just looking to see that Abigail is back in her halls. I like to know that she's safe.'

Lucy raised an eyebrow. 'Surely you're not tracking her? She's eighteen. She shouldn't be home this early. They're supposed to be out every night enjoying themselves for the first few weeks. It's when they'll make their friends. You remember what we were like?'

Ellen remembered exactly what they were like. That was the problem. With relief, she saw Abigail's icon moving in the direction of home.

At the same time, Lucy's phone buzzed with a message and she turned it over. Smiled. 'That's Joe. Dinner was a success. He'll be here tomorrow afternoon.'

For a moment, this seemed like an opportune moment to ask about Lucy's call earlier. But Robert's words came back to her. Was she just being paranoid? 'Great. I'm going to get back to bed. I'll see you in the morning.'

As she made her way to her bedroom, Ellen wondered what Joe would be like. In her mind he was handsome and fit and successful. Once he was here, surely Lucy would no longer be paying Robert quite so much attention. Still, Lucy's words were ringing in her ears. 'You remember what we were like.'

She did remember. All too well.

FIVE
1995

Ellen had never met anyone as cool as Lucy in her whole life.

It had taken days to decide what to wear for her first day at college. She was desperate to wear something that would portray her as the person she wanted to become. Not the bookish, quiet girl who hadn't had a proper boyfriend and had only been abroad once on a school trip to France. Remade with contact lenses and a pair of jeans she'd had to work a month to afford, this was her opportunity to be confident and outgoing and make a huge group of friends who would be in her life forever.

Having missed the first couple of days – her beloved Nan's funeral coinciding with the middle of induction week – Ellen had been worried that it would be difficult to fit in. Both parents had made the trip to drop her off. Though her mum had tried to hide it by rummaging in her large baggy handbag for a packet of Polo mints, she'd cried when her dad had shepherded her out of the door so that Ellen 'could get herself settled'. It was either that, or her dad's quick dry kiss on her forehead – *see you soon then, love* – that'd made her stomach lurch with the realisation that they were leaving her here, alone. What'd felt like the beginning of a new life – and adventure – now felt scary and bigger than she could manage.

Two minutes later, there was a knock on the bedroom door and she opened it to find a girl wearing a sheepskin jacket over a white shirt and pair of washed-out jeans. A cigarette hung from her bottom lip and her bitten-down nails were painted black. 'Hi. I'm Lucy. We're going to the bar. Do you want to come?'

Gratefully, she'd grabbed her bag and followed Lucy and the two other girls she'd picked up on the way. All of them spoke like they'd just been out riding their horses so Ellen kept her conversation to a minimum, remembering her English teacher mother's admonitions to enunciate the ends of her words, in the hope that she wouldn't stand out as different.

'Let's head to the SU. I think the boys said they were going there.' Lucy was clearly the leader of this little group already and Ellen was more than happy to fall in and follow to whatever the 'SU' was.

It turned out to be the Students' Union Bar. A huge cacophonous space full of Doc Marten boots, tartan shirts and baggy jeans. Everyone seemed to be drinking from pint glasses. The air was damp with the smell of spilled beer and body odour.

'I'll get a round.' Lucy was already halfway to the bar. She hadn't even asked what everyone wanted to drink.

Ellen shuffled from foot to foot as she listened to the other two girls discussing the places they'd been that summer – their parents' houses in France or Spain – and the schools they'd come from – private and expensive – and the people they knew who'd been to this university or others. Her cheeks had burned when she admitted she'd spent the summer working in a department store, had attended her local state school and that she was the first person in her family to go to university at all.

It was a relief when Lucy came back holding two brimming pints of beer, followed by a guy she'd corralled into carrying the other two. Ellen hadn't drunk a whole pint of beer before, she wasn't even convinced that she even liked the bitter taste of it, but she accepted it gratefully and tried not to care when the hapless boy slopped it over her fingers.

Lucy held hers aloft. 'Cheers, everyone. Here's to a great first term.'

Over the next few days, Lucy took Ellen with her wherever she went. Whether it was to sign up for societies at the Fresher's Fayre, or to register for their library cards or just to the bar to meet up with the new friends that she seemed to acquire as easily as breathing.

Everyone loved Lucy, including Ellen. How could you not? She wore her beauty easily and could make a second-hand shirt and her latest boyfriend's jeans look suitable for the front cover of a fashion magazine. Ellen was dazzled by her. In a group of wealthy, confident – sometimes arrogant – students, she wasn't scared of anyone. And she frequently told Ellen how she should be the same. 'Who cares what school they've been to or what their daddy earns. You are just as good as they are.'

It was easy for her, of course. Because she *was* one of them. She didn't have to suffer the snide comments they made about some of the other – perfectly nice – students on their courses or in their accommodation. Ian, in particular, liked to make comments about the 'state schoolers' and how inferior he found their depth and breadth of knowledge on his chemistry course.

Like Lucy, Ellen was studying biology. Having been at the top of her class – of her entire year – at school, it was a hard lesson to realise how she was just another bright kid here. Worse, because her school had – albeit successfully – taught to the exam, there were whole sections of knowledge to which those students who'd been to grammar and private schools had already been exposed and which she knew nothing about. She hated it when Ian said that a private education was 'just better', but she couldn't argue with it.

They weren't all like that, of course. Otherwise, she

wouldn't have stayed friends with them. Lucy wasn't like that. And nor was Robert.

She hadn't really noticed him at first. He didn't push himself forward like Ian and some of the others. Though he moved in the same circles – he played rugby, had been to a well-respected boys' school and spent every winter skiing in France – he also had a softer side. He sang in the choir and had spent a month of his summer volunteering at a school in Kerala, India. One day, it must have been in the spring term of her first year, some of the louder members of the group were taking part in a drinking competition and he'd rolled his eyes at Ellen over the top of their heads. From that moment, she'd got a funny feeling in her stomach every time she saw him.

Not that they got together in that first year, though. There wasn't time for that with Lucy taking her here, there and everywhere. She had mentioned to her once that she was attracted to Robert, but Lucy had shaken her head. 'You can't go out with someone from the group. It's rule number one. What would happen if you broke up?'

It'd made sense. The last thing Ellen wanted was to end up on the outside of that friendship. So she'd stuck to the rule for the whole of the first year.

Even when Lucy didn't.

SIX

Ellen had had a terrible night's sleep. Even after she'd waited to watch Abigail return safely to her halls of residence on the phone screen, she'd lain awake wondering about where she'd been and reflecting on her own evening here in Spain. When she'd finally slept, it was fitful and full of dreams of Robert and Lucy laughing and drinking and ignoring her. Which is why she'd ended up sleeping later than she usually did.

When she woke up, the bed was empty and, on the side table, a scribbled note.

I'm going for a walk on the beach. Didn't want to wake you.

After waking so often, how had she slept through him leaving? He must've crept around like a mouse, not wanting her to wake up and join him. This walking was a new thing, too. Often at home – when he *was* home – he'd take himself off for a stroll in the evening, just as she wanted to settle down and watch something on the television. As if he was avoiding her.

Poised and fresh, Lucy was in the kitchen, taking warm pastries from the oven, their sweet bready aroma filling the air.

'Perfect timing. I thought we could have breakfast out on the patio?'

'That sounds lovely, but Robert isn't here. He's gone for a walk.'

As she lifted the pastries into a linen-lined basket, Lucy smiled. 'I know. I saw him as he left and gave him a map. I think he was going to the beach so he'll be gone for another hour at least, I'd guess.'

It was distinctly uncomfortable that Lucy knew more about her husband's whereabouts than Ellen. That they'd been up and chatting while she slept through it. Wearing a white crochet dress over a swimsuit, Lucy looked at least a decade younger than Ellen and was in full make-up already. 'Have you been for a swim?'

'Yes. Thirty lengths every morning. It's marvellous exercise. Do you work out?'

Ellen had started and given up on more exercise classes than she could name. She always meant to keep at it, but the sheer repetitive routine of them left her unenthusiastic until lethargy eventually won. She crossed her fingers behind her back. 'I enjoy yoga.'

Lucy grinned. 'Wonderful. Me, too. I have a spare mat, maybe we can do a sun salutation together?'

Clearly, that had been the wrong thing to pick. 'Hmmm. Maybe. Can I help you carry some of this outside?'

At the centre of the breakfast table, a heavy mason jar full of pink and yellow wild flowers with dark-green stems contrasted the white linen and pale-blue sky. Both their delicate scent and the perfectly thrown-together arrangement could only be achieved by careful selection. Lucy had already laid the table with heavy white pottery plates, artistically mismatched coloured glass tumblers and a glass jug of freshly squeezed orange juice. Ellen felt slovenly for having slept while all of this was being prepared. A lukewarm sun slipped across the back of her neck as she set down the basket of freshly baked croissants that Lucy had given her, each one a perfect crescent.

'I assumed you were coffee rather than tea?' Lucy came from behind her with a steel coffee pot and a jug of cream.

'Yes. Coffee would be great, thanks.'

Beyond the low wall surrounding the property, the sea was as smooth as turquoise glass and the morning sun was starting to warm Ellen's face as she slipped on her sunglasses. She had to relax. She was here in this beautiful place with the potential to reconnect with an old friend. She needed to stop this petty jealousy and enjoy these few days. 'You really do have a lovely home here.'

Lucy placed the coffee pot on an iron rest and then slipped into the seat opposite. 'Thanks. But I can't take the credit really. It's all Joe. He has an eye for things. He sees an old wreck of a building and can picture it once it's restored. He looks at the bones, he always says.'

Lucy picked up the basket and offered Ellen a croissant, which she placed on her plate. 'What time will he be here today?'

'Lunchtime, hopefully.'

Ellen was curious about the man who had tamed Lucy into this level of domesticity. 'Have you been together a long time? I don't even know when you got married.'

As Lucy poured coffee into two white cups, a rich nutty aroma filled the air between them. Before she replied, she pushed a cream jug in Ellen's direction. 'We got married when our daughter was two. Our elder daughter that is. She's a doctor, actually. We're very proud.'

She threw the last statement away as if it were a self-deprecating joke, but Ellen could see from the sheen in her eyes that the pride was real. 'That's amazing. You deserve to be proud. How old is your daughter?'

38   EMMA ROBINSON

Lucy sipped at her black coffee before she replied. 'Charlotte is twenty-five. My millennium baby.'

Behind her sunglasses, Ellen frowned. Twenty-five? That was only a year younger than Grace. 'So you must've had her only a year after we left university?'

That year had been a blur for Ellen. She'd graduated with a small bump hidden under her black gown and then she and Robert – with a lot of help from their shocked but supportive parents – had moved into a small two-bedroom house. Motherhood had hit her like a steam train: Grace had been a fitful sleeper and a fussy feeder. Likely because Ellen was twenty-two and didn't know what the heck she was doing.

'Yes.' Lucy picked up a croissant from the basket and pulled a tiny piece from one end. 'I was travelling when I found out I was pregnant.'

Ellen had a vague memory of Lucy planning a trip in their final year. At the time, she'd tried to persuade Ellen and Robert to go with her, but – even before they'd discovered the pregnancy – they were both looking for graduate positions and Ellen wouldn't have had the money to take time out. 'Do I know Joe, then? Was he at the university with us? Or did you meet him while you were travelling?'

Lucy looked over Ellen's head and smiled. 'Just in time for breakfast, Robbie. How was your walk?'

Trying not to let that long-forgotten pet name grate on her, Ellen turned to greet her husband. His crisp white t-shirt and linen shorts were an odd choice for exercise. He didn't even look out of breath.

He took the seat beside her and poured himself a glass of orange juice as if it was a regular everyday activity to sit down to breakfast together. 'It was good. The sea looked amazing this morning. There were some young families on the beach already. It made me think of when we used to take the girls to the south of France and Abigail would wake up with the dawn.'

WE BOTH HAVE SECRETS

It was a lovely memory. Although it was hard work at the time having a toddler who thought sleep was for wimps. They'd take it in turns to be the one to take Abbie out of the house so that she didn't wake an eight-year-old Grace. 'I remember it well.'

Lucy was quick to prick the bubble of their pleasant reminiscence. 'You always did love travel, didn't you, Robbie? With that and your studious nature, I always envisaged you carving out a career finding cures for tropical diseases.'

Like many people from his background – those that didn't have to worry about money – Robert had taken a gap year before starting university and had pretty much covered three continents. 'Well, sometimes life has other plans. I'm a drug runner now.'

This was the joke Robert often made about his job in medical sales, but Lucy didn't laugh. 'It's such a shame you had to take that job.'

All three of them knew the reason that Robert had to start work immediately after university, but he headed off the awkwardness by turning the subject to Lucy. 'How were your travels after you left? Did you get to Thailand?'

She grinned at him. 'Yes. It was just as fabulous as you said it was. We had this amazing beach hut on Ko Phayam.'

Robert practically jumped out of his seat. 'June Horizon? Incredible, isn't it? And did you get to Vietnam?'

This was the most animated Ellen had seen Robert in months. She knew as well as Lucy that he'd always loved to travel, and they'd been on some great holidays with the girls, but the months he'd spent backpacking in Latin America, Asia and Australia had been something she'd always envied.

Lucy held up her hands. 'Oh my goodness, you are NEVER going to guess who I saw in Vietnam. Do you remember that guy who fell asleep in the hallway? That first day of Fresher's Week?'

Robert rubbed at the stubble on his chin before a smile spread over his face. 'That was the first night, wasn't it? We were trapped in that room for ages.'

Ellen tried to get involved. 'Who was that?'

Flushed with the pleasure of a shared memory, Robert turned to her. 'I must've told you. Some guy got really drunk on his first day and fell asleep in the hallway outside my room. We couldn't get out until he woke up.'

He definitely hadn't told her that story before, because she would have asked what Lucy was doing in his room on the first day. 'Goodness. Would I have met him?'

But Robert had turned back to Lucy. 'How did you recognise him?'

'I didn't. There was this hostel and he was there and we got talking and just worked it out. He was hilarious about it. I got a photo with him and I was planning to send it to you like a postcard when I got home and had the film developed but...'

How might she have ended that sentence? *But you had a baby by then. But we'd fallen out of touch by then.* Robert hadn't picked up on the passive aggression. He was shaking his head, lost in memory. 'Good times.'

Ellen was tiring of this nostalgia trip. 'Sounds like you had a great time on your travels. Grace might be going to Dubai soon, actually.'

In the middle of taking a croissant from the basket Lucy offered him, Robert banged his forehead with the heel of his hand. 'I forgot to tell you. Grace called when I was walking back. She was a bit upset.'

Ellen's heart sank. 'Upset? Why? What's happened?'

He shook his head slowly. 'Nothing to panic about. I think it's something to do with her boyfriend. She was calling me to see if I was with you. You weren't answering your phone.'

Her mobile was in her bag, underneath the table. But when she checked it, the battery had died. 'What did she say? Have

WE BOTH HAVE SECRETS 41

they had an argument?' Though she'd hate for her daughter to be upset, having him out of her life would be a good thing in the long run.

'Something about him standing her up last night, I think.'

Grace was an adult, but Ellen still couldn't bear to think of her being upset so she pushed her chair back to leave. 'I'll go and stick my phone on charge and send her a message to check she's okay.'

Robert seemed unconcerned. 'Finish your breakfast. I spoke to her about it and she's fine now.'

She could just imagine that conversation. Robert was a great dad, but affairs of the heart were not his forte. 'I'll just go and put my phone on charge, anyway. I won't be a minute. Sorry, Lucy.'

'No problem. I'll put some more coffee on while you're gone.'

As well as wanting to plug in her phone – and send Grace a quick text message – Ellen was more than ready to take a break from listening to Lucy and Robert's shared history. They had only known each other for a couple of days before she'd arrived on campus. Listening to Lucy, you'd have got the impression that they'd known each other years longer.

Hearing that Lucy had gone ahead with her travel plans also made Ellen curious about the birth of her elder daughter. On her way back to the bedroom, she ran the numbers in her mind to work out how quickly Lucy must've met Joe – and fallen pregnant – to have a twenty-five-year-old daughter. Was she being purposefully vague in avoiding Ellen's question about when and where they'd met? Either she'd met him on her travels or when she was still at the university. Though she couldn't remember a Joe in their crowd, it was possible that he was a friend of a friend. Could it be that she and Robert knew him already?

SEVEN

After plugging in her phone, Ellen sat on the bed and waited for the home screen to come back to life so that she could send Grace a quick text.

Robert maintained that Grace was old enough to sort out her own relationship problems, but he had no idea what it was like for Ellen. If something was going on with either of the girls – big or small – she couldn't rest until she knew what it was and had tried to help. No one tells you when you have a child how you feel every emotion of theirs like it was your own. Worse, if they were going through something upsetting, she'd wish she could take it from them and carry the feelings herself.

As soon as the screen lit up, she wrote a quick text to Grace.

Everything okay?

Though she waited a few moments for a reply, there was nothing. Just in case, she turned the ringer up to full volume and left the bedroom door open.

At the breakfast table, Robert and Lucy were deep in conversation. Whatever they were discussing, it clearly wasn't small talk. Lucy – leaned forward in her seat – was waving her arms around. Robert faced away from Ellen, but she knew him well enough to intuit that his straight back and folded arms meant that he didn't like whatever Lucy was saying.

As soon as she saw Ellen, Lucy dropped her arms to the table and smiled. 'Did you find your charger?'

'Yes. Phone's plugged in. Everything okay here?'

Robert turned in his seat, his face flushed. 'Of course.'

Before she could probe further, they heard the crunch of the gravel at the front of the house and the roar of a throaty sports car engine. Lucy put her hand to her ear. 'That'll be Joe.'

Joe Meads had thick dark hair and the kind of tan that came from being outside a great deal. He wore a light-grey suit with a black shirt, button opened at the neck. He was very handsome. If anyone had asked Ellen, she would've guessed he was Spanish, so his clipped English accent was almost a surprise. 'Ellen! So great to meet you at long last. Lucy has told me so much about you.'

He kissed her on one cheek, then – when he went in for the second cheek – they bumped noses. He laughed, but she was mortified. 'Has she?'

Why would Lucy be telling him so much about her? And what was she telling him?

Joe's greeting for Robert was very different. 'Robbie! Hi, how are you?'

He grasped Robert's hand to shake it, then placed his other hand on Robert's shoulder. There was something terribly familiar about his greeting. Robert's response was similarly warm. 'I'm good. Your place is fantastic. Thanks for having us here.'

'Sorry, have you two met before?' She looked between them. Robert's expression didn't change but Joe looked confused.

'Of course they haven't.' Lucy swept between them and kissed her husband – once on each cheek, much more smoothly than Ellen had managed – before holding out her arms. 'Now we're all here, shall we go out for a drive? Show Robert and Ellen the sights and sounds of Malaga?'

'Great idea.' Joe picked up his brown leather travel case from the floor. 'Let me take this up to our room and have a quick shower and then we'll head out. A couple of hours doing the tourist thing and then we'll take you to one of our favourite places for lunch.'

They'd only just finished breakfast, although, she noticed, Lucy hadn't actually eaten anything. Robert was nodding. 'I need a shower, too. Ten minutes?'

As soon as she and Robert were back in their room, she was going to ask him what was going on. It was clear that he and Joe knew each other, so why were they lying to her? But then Lucy took her arm. 'While the boys are making themselves pretty, come and talk to me while I clear away the breakfast things.'

She could hardly make her excuses without it looking like she didn't want to help Lucy, so she followed her, filing away her annoyance for later when she and Robert were alone.

In the kitchen, Ellen insisted that Lucy allow her to stack the dishwasher. 'You've been waiting on us since we got here. Let me do something.'

As she perched on one of the bar stools, Lucy held up a perfectly manicured hand. 'If you insist.'

Turning the coffee cups over onto the top rack, Ellen kept her voice light. 'Joe seems really nice. Really friendly. It was almost as if he'd met Robert before.'

She turned to catch Lucy's reaction, but she merely shrugged. 'That's just how he is. Best friends with everyone he meets. He's been excited to meet you. If you space those mugs out a little, you'll be able to get the glasses in between them.'

Did she think Ellen had never stacked a dishwasher? She took the glasses from the counter and slotted them in. 'We'll have to stop talking about university days now he's here or he'll feel left out.'

Lucy didn't take the hint. 'Oh, he won't mind. He's always interested in stories from my youth. It's been fun talking about old times. I can't believe that our youngest daughters are now the same age as we were then.'

Several times since she'd dropped Abigail off, Ellen had told Robert that she was worried about their youngest daughter being away from home. If Grace was sunshine and showers, Abigail was a temperate spring day. From a young age, she'd had a small group of friends who were her absolute world. They did everything together. Frequently, Ellen and the mothers of the other girls would remark on how lucky they were that the girls were all happy to spend their evenings at one another's houses rather than out on the town. Now, she worried that Abigail had been too protected and cosseted. How was she going to cope out in the world on her own? 'It is weird. I look at Abigail and she still seems a child to me. But I felt so grown up when I was her age.'

Looking down into her mug, Lucy nodded. 'Yes, me too. But we weren't really, were we? We both got cheated out of a lot of our growing up years, having our children so young.'

Though Ellen knew that lots of people would assume she felt the same, it hadn't been true. Grace's conception was a shock, but she had loved every minute of making a home with Robert. 'Maybe. They're worth it, though.'

Lucy pushed the side plates across the counter towards her. 'I think I enjoy being a mother a great deal more now that the girls are older. It's so much easier than running around after a toddler and dealing with puberty.'

She laughed as if she was making an obvious point but, again, Ellen didn't really agree. Slotting the plates onto the lower part of the dishwasher, she had a sudden memory of a chubby two-year-old Grace sitting up in her high chair in their tiny first house. 'I don't know. I often find myself wishing they were babies again and I could keep them safe.'

She closed the door of the dishwasher and turned to see Lucy raising an eyebrow at her. 'Really? But they're both doing fine, aren't they?'

For all her irritation with Lucy earlier, it would be good to talk to another mother about her concerns about Max. 'I'm worried about Grace. Her boyfriend is really unreliable. I'm worried he's messing her around.'

Sometimes she wondered if being so young when she'd had Grace had been detrimental to her daughter. She'd always done the best she could as a mother, but had she made mistakes with her as a parent? She was so beautiful and clever and funny and kind that both Ellen and Robert were so proud of her. Why, then, did she want to waste her wonderful self on this man who treated her as if she was disposable?

Lucy pulled a face. 'He's the one that upset her earlier?'

'Yes. And it isn't the first time he's reduced her to tears, either. They've only been together for just over a year and, in that time, he's let her down on her birthday, twice cancelled dinner to meet me and Robert and once booked a week away in Italy with friends without even telling her.'

Every part of Ellen wanted to shake her daughter and tell her that she was being a fool for putting up with it. And Lucy's face showed she agreed. 'It's so hard to watch, isn't it? And I'm assuming you have to tiptoe around and not tell her what you think?'

'Exactly.' That was the problem with adult children. You couldn't risk going so far that they'd push you away or stop talking to you. When Grace spoke to her about Max, Ellen's job

WE BOTH HAVE SECRETS 47

– she'd learned to her cost – was to listen and say just enough to be invested, not so much to sound judgemental.

Lucy was nodding. 'I know what that's like.'

It was a relief to talk to someone who understood. 'Has your daughter had any awful boyfriends?'

Lucy's laugh was hollow. 'Let's just say that it hasn't been plain sailing.'

Her support encouraged Ellen to go further. 'Grace's boyfriend has told her that he's separated from his wife but I'm not convinced. He won't let Grace tell anyone they're together because he says it'll be awkward at work. But that sounds really suspicious to me. I think he could still be married.'

Lucy didn't appear remotely shocked by this. 'That is a tricky one. But what can you do? You can't control who they fall in love with, can you? Any more than we could control who we fell in love with.'

Ellen wasn't so sure about that. Robert had been her first proper boyfriend and she'd known what a good man he was before they'd even shared their first kiss. 'If I try and give any advice at all, Grace won't listen. She always tells me that I've got no idea what it's like to be single at her age.'

This accusation had been levelled at her many times in the past. Partly because she and Robert had settled down so young that neither of them had run the gauntlet of dating in their twenties. But mostly, she'd realised, because neither of the girls saw her and Robert as actual people. They were just Mum and Dad. Had arrived on this Earth at forty-odd years old and didn't understand what it was to feel uncertainty or worry. Or jealousy.

Again, Lucy was nodding her understanding. 'Charlotte has said the same thing to me. And they're right. More's the pity.'

More's the pity? 'Goodness, I'm glad I didn't have to do that. The more I watch what Grace goes through, the more I think I swerved a bullet by meeting Robert when I did.'

'Really?' Lucy raised an eyebrow. 'You don't wish you'd played the field more before you settled down? Travelled the world? Kissed a few frogs?'

'Absolutely not.' Ellen hadn't ever felt like she'd missed out on anything. Thanks to supportive parents, she'd been able to work and raise her family. If anything, she'd enjoyed being a young mum. But the look on Lucy's face right now suggested that she didn't believe her. That she must've wanted more from her youth, just as Lucy had.

The glint in her eyes was similar to the sparkle in Robert's a short while ago as he'd talked about Thailand and Vietnam over the breakfast table. She hadn't seen him so alive in months. Hearing Lucy talk about her regret at missing out on her 'growing up years' she was beginning to wonder if Robert felt the same.

EIGHT

Though Ellen knew nothing about cars, even she could tell that Joe's sports car must be top of the range. Robert travelled up front with Joe while Lucy sat with her in the back on the soft cream leather seats. With the roof down, and the sun shining on them like a blessing, they felt like celebrities as Joe took them on a whistle stop tour past the major attractions of Malaga: the cathedral with its missing tower, the bullring, the Roman theatre and Alcazaba, the hilltop fortress. All the while, he called back over his shoulder with an encyclopaedic knowledge of each of these places. 'Alcazaba is known as Little Alhambra because it has a very similar artistic and architectural style. They were both built in the Nasrid period.'

Ellen didn't like to admit that she didn't know where or what Alhambra was, much less the existence of a Nasrid period. It almost made her laugh to see Robert nodding along as if he had a clue.

Lucy leaned in. 'You'll notice, all of Joe's commentary is about the outsides of buildings. He can't help himself. Is there anywhere you'd like to stop and actually, you know, see inside?'

This spark of the old Lucy – funny, acerbic, dry – made Ellen smile. 'Actually, I wouldn't mind going to the Picasso Museum.'

'It's in the central part of the town and you'd have to queue for hours, it's always packed.' Joe called back from the front. 'It's nice enough, but they don't have any of the major works. Are you a big fan?'

In truth, Ellen could probably count on one hand the Picassos she could name. 'Not especially. If there's likely to be a long queue, I'll leave it.'

The restaurant Joe chose for lunch was on a steep incline on the way down from the Castillo de Gibralfaro. Set back from the road, its white painted columns gave it the look of a castle itself. The table cloths were thick and white, the cutlery and glasses heavy and expensive. A waiter greeted Joe at the door like an old friend and showed them to a table at the front where the tall glass windows looked out onto an aquamarine sea.

Joe filled their glasses with water from a cobalt-blue carafe as they read through the heavy leather-bound menus. Everything was, of course, in Spanish, but even Ellen could guess-translate enough of the words – pescado, salmon, sardinas – to see that there was an awful lot of fish: a food of which she wasn't particularly fond. She scanned through anxiously for something she both recognised and wanted to eat.

Joe lounged back in his seat with the easy air of a man who was at home in places like this. 'It's incredible that your daughter is at the same university – in the same halls – as our Emily, isn't it?'

In one way, it was a big coincidence. 'Yes. Although, we all went there, so I guess that narrows the coincidence down slightly.'

Joe had an intense way of looking at the person he was speaking to as if they were the most fascinating person on the planet. It was charming, but also a little intimidating: Ellen really didn't have anything that interesting to say.

'I told you that.' Lucy shook her head at him. 'You know that we were friends back then. Really good friends.'

There was something in her tone which Ellen couldn't detect. *Really good friends.* Joe shone his beam around to his wife and lay his arm lazily across the back of her chair. 'Of course, my darling. Back when you were young and almost as beautiful as you are now.'

Lucy rolled her eyes at him, but she clearly enjoyed his words. And who wouldn't? Ellen couldn't remember the last time that Robert had spoken to – or looked at – her like that.

Robert clearly had the same thought. 'Come on, mate. You're showing me up with all this romance.'

Joe laughed. 'Let me order some wine. White okay for everyone? Do you have a preference?'

Once the sommelier had been consulted and a bottle carefully selected and ordered, he turned his gaze back to Ellen. 'So, how come you all lost touch?'

For a few moments, no one spoke. Possibly because, like Ellen, neither Robert nor Lucy knew quite what had happened between them all.

They'd been really good friends. In their last year, when they were working hard and partying harder, it'd always been Robert and Ellen, Lucy and Ian. Ian and Robert were on the same course and – in the beginning – he'd seemed like a good guy. He and Lucy weren't exactly a great influence on one another. Often, they would be out until the small hours when they had an assessment the next day.

Joe was looking at her, waiting for an answer. She had to say something. 'Well, we got married and had Grace and I suppose we were just doing different things.'

It hadn't been quite like that, though. From the moment

she'd told Lucy that she was pregnant, things had shifted between them. For a start, Lucy had been incredulous that she was actually going to go through with the pregnancy.

'But you're only twenty. You've got your whole life ahead of you. Why are you going to have a baby?'

She'd understood the question. It had been a pretty shattering shock to her, too. But once she and Robert had talked it over – late into the night over mint tea in his halls – they'd both felt pretty good about it. 'I think we can do this. I think it's going to work out okay.'

'But you're going to miss out on so much. What about getting a job? Travelling? Being young?'

She was being thrown into adulthood pretty fast, but she wasn't too bothered about the travelling and she'd definitely gone off the idea of partying. 'I am disappointed I can't look for a job straight away, but once the baby is here I'll be able to start my career. Robert will support us until then. And our parents are helping out.'

Lucy had been angry then. 'You're going to regret it. You and Robert will be tied together forever, whatever happens between you. If you have a baby, that's it. Connected for life.'

It had been a very odd thing to say. Especially as the prospect of being connected to Robert for life was exactly what she'd wanted.

Lucy looked at her now with an expression that was difficult to read. If she didn't know better, Ellen would have called it dislike. 'The two of you just disappeared out of circulation.'

'Well, we did have a baby. And you were travelling, don't forget.'

She'd assumed that Lucy had gone travelling with Ian but now she wondered if that was the case. And she didn't want to be the one to bring his name into the conversation. If Lucy and Joe had met soon after graduation, she wasn't sure where Ian would fit into Lucy's history.

WE BOTH HAVE SECRETS

'Ah yes—' Joe leaned towards Lucy '—the famous world travels. I'm quite jealous that I didn't get to know you during that time. I think we would've had a blast.'

He leaned towards her and she met his kiss. The chemistry between them was palpable. How wonderful it must be to have someone so attentive, so obviously in love with you. How long had it been since she and Robert were like that? In fact, had they ever been like that? Having met so young, they'd almost grown up together. But even so, they'd allowed themselves to get stuck in a rut.

Joe turned back to them both with a smile. 'So, what stories can you tell me about my wife back in her student days?'

Lucy held up a hand. 'Don't you dare!'

They all laughed and then the waiter arrived to take their order. Lucy amazed Ellen by ordering in fluent Spanish. Of course, she lived here part of the year, it made sense that she'd learned the language. Somehow, her accent made her sound – and look – even sexier than she had before.

Robert clearly thought so, too. He couldn't take his eyes off her. When Ellen stumbled over her own pronunciation of her order – she'd only chosen vegetarian paella, for goodness' sake – she felt even more foolish. Her face burned with the embarrassment of being corrected by the waiter like a child. She looked such a fool.

Compounding her embarrassment, her phone chose that moment to ring in her bag and she fumbled to grab it and stop it from echoing around the restaurant. It was Grace. *Not more problems with Max.* But she couldn't ignore her daughter, could she? 'Sorry, I just need to take this.'

She could hear Robert apologising for her as she left the table.

The air outside was thick and warm after the air conditioning in the restaurant. Grace started speaking as soon as she picked up. 'Mum? I just saw your message. Sorry if I worried you. I was upset because I'd booked a hotel for me and Max last night and he didn't turn up. I got myself in a state thinking he might be with another girl, and then he text me just after I spoke to Dad to say he'd had to take a friend home who wasn't well and... well, anyway it doesn't matter now. He actually sent me a huge bouquet of flowers just now to say sorry.'

Ellen knew that she was supposed to be impressed by this, that the main reason for this call was that Grace didn't want her to think badly of her boyfriend. 'So he just left you in the hotel all night on your own worrying about him? A bunch of flowers doesn't make up for bad behaviour, Grace.'

Immediately, Grace's tone changed. 'I know that, Mum. But it was just a misunderstanding. He was looking after his friend.'

In isolation, that might have been forgivable, but this wasn't the first 'misunderstanding' that Grace had swept under the carpet. 'You need to make it clear that you can't be treated like that. You need to know what you're worth, Grace.'

'I do know what I'm worth. You just don't like Max. If you got to know him better, you'd see how lovely he is to me. He does love me.'

This wasn't the time to get into this. 'I need to go back into the restaurant. I'm glad you're okay.'

After ending the call, Ellen sank down onto a low wall for a moment. This was how it had always been. From the first day that Grace had been peeled from her to start school as a tiny little girl, Ellen had been on the rollercoaster that was her emotional life. She would listen to her problems – bad grades, bad friends, bad boyfriends – and absorb every nuance of pain. Then, when Grace's mood had flipped back and she was on her merry way, Ellen would be left to haul herself out of the pit of despond.

From her seated position, she could see back into the restaurant through the window. Lucy was telling a story and Robert was laughing in a way she hadn't seen in a long time. He'd been so different since they'd arrived. And where was Joe?

The door opened and Joe appeared with a vape in his hand. He winced at her. 'Don't judge me. I know what I look like with this thing, but I've promised Charlotte I'll give up smoking and this is step one.'

She held up her hands. 'No judgement. Are they rehashing old times in there? Did you want to escape?'

He sucked on the sleek silver pen and blew out a sweet-smelling vapour. 'I don't mind the stories. I'm sure that Lucy is enjoying talking to people who don't want to discuss square footage and the cost of roof tiles.'

So, he was loyal as well as loving. 'Lucy said you had to work away a lot? Properties in lots of places. That must be difficult.'

His gaze was no less concentrated when there were only two of them. The look on his face went down to her toes. 'Lucy is a very good wife. I am very lucky. We have an understanding. Come on, let's go back inside and see what story they're up to in there.'

Ellen felt decidedly unsettled by his words. An understanding? What did that mean? Lucy had said that Joe was away a lot with his work. Was he implying something else too? Did he have permission to see other women? If that was true, it cast his over-attentiveness in a new light and, suddenly, she didn't feel as envious of Lucy as she had minutes before.

She looked back through the window at Robert and Lucy and shuddered at the expressions on their faces. Did this 'understanding' stretch to Lucy's behaviour, too? Was her flirting with Robert more serious than Ellen had assumed?

Maybe it was time to take the advice she'd just given to Grace and know her own worth too. For the last twenty-four hours, she'd felt like the least interesting person in the room. That had to stop. At dinner tonight, that was going to change.

She was going to get dressed up and show Robert that she could look just as good as Lucy.

Whether it was intentional or not, all of Lucy's anecdotes had centred on memories that didn't include Ellen. Well, Ellen had some anecdotes of her own that she could recount for them all. Tonight, she was going to remind Robert of the woman he fell in love with on that night all those years ago.

NINE
1997

In their second year, they all moved off campus. Ellen and Lucy shared a house with two girls who Lucy had met by chance at the housing office while scanning the noticeboards for available private properties to rent. Surprised, but flattered, that Lucy would rather share with her and two strangers than go in with the two other girls in their group – who were staying in a serviced apartment in town that Ellen would never have been able to afford – Ellen didn't even mind that their new house-mates complained constantly about the heating and the hot water system. Robert lived with Ian and three other boys in a house that Ian's parents had actually bought outright – *'It's such a good investment to have a house in a student town'* – and they were only two streets away. Having seemed to have forgotten her 'don't screw the crew' mantra, Lucy and Ian were now an item and she spent pretty much half her life on his lap. Every Friday and Saturday night they would end up back at the boys' house after a night in town. Sometimes Lucy would come home with Ellen, often she wouldn't.

Robert was different from the rest of them. Aside from his well-spoken accent there was nothing to give away the fact he came from a wealthy family. He wore jumpers with holes in the cuffs and jeans that didn't fit quite right because they'd been handed down from his older brother. He was a scientist, but loved to read novels. Quiet, but full of knowledge. The last to push himself forward, but the first to reach out if you'd had a bad day.

That's why, when he offered to walk her home that first time, she hadn't allowed herself to believe that there was anything else in it than him being a perfect gentleman. As she was pulling on her coat to leave alone, Robert had insisted he walk her back. 'It's after midnight, you can't go on your own.'

'But it's only two streets away. I'll be there by the time you find your trainers.' Truth be told, she was equal parts excited and terrified at the prospect of being on her own with him. What if she said something stupid? What if she couldn't think of anything to say at all?

But, in the end, it'd been as easy as talking to her friends back home. He was funny and interesting and asked her lots of questions about herself. He was impressed – rather than mocking – of the fact that she had been the first person in her family to go to university. When he'd said, 'they must be very proud of you,' her cheeks had warmed with pleasure. Despite the fact that they were both walking as slowly as was possible without stopping, they reached her house less than ten minutes after leaving his. She wondered – hopefully – whether he might kiss her goodbye. But, after waiting for her to open the door, he'd given her a mock bow and left. She'd been too embarrassed to ask him to come in, even though she hadn't wanted their time alone to come to an end.

It was the third time he walked her home that she'd plucked up the courage to ask him in. 'My mum sent me a tin of hot chocolate. If you want to come in, I could make us some?'

'That'd be great. Thanks.'

Over two steaming mugs, they'd whispered so as not to

WE BOTH HAVE SECRETS 59

wake up her other two housemates. He made her laugh, impersonating one of his tutors who spoke so slowly that he sent the students to sleep and she told him all about the small town she'd grown up in. Then they discussed their friends. 'You and Ian are pretty close, aren't you?'

There was a lot about Ian that she wasn't keen on, so had been quite pleased when he'd shrugged. 'Not especially. He's okay, but he can be a bit of an idiot at times. He and Lucy seem pretty loved up. Has she said how it's going?'

It seemed like a strange question to ask. 'She's pretty happy, I think. I haven't seen as much of her in the last few weeks.'

He looked down at his hands, then back up at her. 'And how about you? No one you're interested in?'

She felt her face colour with the intensity of his eyes on hers, her stomach flutter with hope that this was going somewhere. 'Well, that would be telling.'

Shuffling forward in his chair, one of Robert's knees slipped between hers, he was close enough that she could smell the sharp notes of his aftershave. 'But you might be interested? For the right person?'

Chest tight with apprehensive excitement, she nodded. 'For the right person, yes.'

He leaned in towards her. 'And could that right person be me?'

She bit her lip, giggled. 'I think it could be. Yes.'

And then he kissed her.

For the next hour, they couldn't keep their hands off of one another. All the times she'd dreamed about him were nothing compared to the reality of being in his arms, his hands in her hair, lips pressed to hers. When he had to leave – *because if I don't go now, I never will* – it was like pulling apart two strong magnets, and she lay in bed that night with her arms wrapped around herself thinking only of him and his promise to see her again tomorrow.

When Lucy came home late the next morning, Ellen couldn't wait to tell her what had happened. But her response hadn't been what Ellen was expecting. Considering that Lucy had her own boyfriend, Ellen had hoped that she'd be pleased for her.

'Robert? You and Robert?'

It was difficult to decipher whether her expression was disbelief or disgust. Ellen had chosen to read it as surprise. 'Yes. And I'm really happy about it. I think he's really nice.'

She thought he was a lot more than that. He was sexy and funny and clever and kind. It was almost unbelievable that someone like him would even look at her. But he had, and she wasn't about to let Lucy make her feel anything less than ecstatic about it.

Narrowing her eyes for a moment, Lucy seemed to be reading her face. Then she shrugged. 'Well, good luck with that.'

From that moment on, something shifted in their friendship. It wasn't that Ellen was one of those girls who got a boyfriend and dropped her friends, far from it. No, the shift was in Lucy. Looking back, that might have been the reason that Ellen didn't go to Lucy on the night that she and Robert had their one and only terrible argument. Maybe she knew that Lucy wasn't the person to give her the right guidance. Lucy had never given any encouragement to Ellen and Robert's relationship, and had even – during one of the many periods that she and Ian had broken up – tried to suggest that getting tied down to one man was a waste of their college years. Downing shots of something sickly sweet, she'd slurred at Ellen that they would both be better off without them.

It was only a short time later that she'd realised how true those words had been.

TEN

In front of the mirror in their bedroom, Ellen's earlier resolve to look as good as Lucy weakened. Make-up was not her forte. For years, she'd been rubbing in some tinted moisturiser and a few licks of mascara and that was her done. Occasionally, if she had a night out for a Christmas party or when she and Robert had a rare dinner on their own, Abigail would insist on 'doing your face for you' and she'd succumb to having the full works before wiping half of it off in the car.

When they lived together in that draughty student house, she and Lucy would always get ready together for a night out. The two of them in one of their rooms, a bottle of beer each, music pumping from a portable radio as they took it in turns in front of the mirror. Getting ready was often more fun than the night out itself.

Twenty-seven years on, she stared at her face in the oval mirror of the dressing table. How different it was now to back then. She pulled the skin around her eyes taut with her forefingers. Was that girl still in there somewhere?

Rooting around in her make-up bag, she found a rich pink lipstick that Grace had insisted she buy months ago. Rarely wearing lipstick, it'd always felt too much and she'd never tried it. Maybe tonight she could get away with it.

Make-up done, she stood in front of the wardrobe. There wasn't much to choose from. She'd only brought one nice dress with her and that was only at the last minute. It was a navy wrap dress with capped sleeves. Though the cut was flattering, the neckline was deeper than she was comfortable with and she usually wore a vest top beneath it to cover her exposed skin. Tonight, though, she forced herself to be bold. Perhaps it would give Robert something to look at other than Lucy.

Standing in front of the mirror, still uncertain whether she was brave enough to show that much cleavage, Ellen jumped at the sound of the bathroom door cracking open. Following a billow of steam, Robert emerged with one towel around his waist, rubbing his hair with another. As he turned in her direction, he actually stopped in his tracks and looked at her, really looked at her. 'You look great.'

He looked great, too. Those extra trips to the gym had tautened his stomach and the peppering of grey in the hair on his chest actually made him more attractive. She felt her face redden. 'Thank you.' She brushed at her dress. 'It's old.'

His eyes didn't leave hers. 'I didn't mean the dress. I meant you. You seem... different.'

At least he'd noticed. 'I feel different.'

Outside on the patio, Joe was lighting candles on the table and he held out his arms at the sight of them. 'Who is this vision I see before me?'

He stepped forward to greet Ellen and, this time, she was ready for the kiss on either cheek. 'Where's Lucy?'

'Last-minute call from our younger daughter put her behind so she's still getting ready. It takes a while, apparently. Rome wasn't built in a day and all that. Makes me glad I'm a man when I see all the work you have to do.'

After his comment about his 'understanding' with Lucy, Ellen felt differently towards Joe, but she let the 'have to' slide. 'Is everything okay with Emily?'

Joe rolled his eyes. 'Some drama or other. I'm beginning to understand that she loves it. Not made for the quiet life that one. Like her mother.'

Like her mother. Lucy had been pretty wild back in the day. Perhaps that's why Ellen had been drawn to her. Before going away to college, Ellen's life had been pretty small and sheltered. Growing up in a village in Suffolk, having to get a bus to her nearest school, holidaying in Cornwall where her godparents lived. Meeting Lucy on the first day was like being taken up by a whirlwind and never knowing where or when you might land. Until she did land. Hard.

Right now, she was more concerned about whether Emily's drama involved Abigail in any way. She tapped Robert's elbow. 'I might give Abbie a quick call.'

Robert frowned at her. 'Leave her be, Ellen. If she wants us, she can call us. She needs some space.'

Her cheeks warmed at the exasperation in his voice. Maybe it wasn't just Abigail who needed space.

When Lucy swept outside in a cloud of expensive perfume, Ellen realised that she needn't have worried about whether her dress was too low cut; Lucy's neckline was deep enough to make Ellen's positively demure. 'Sorry about that everyone. Daughter Two needed some motherly advice.'

Ignoring Robert's warning glance, Ellen had to ask. 'Is she okay?'

Lucy waved away any concern. 'She's fine. Something to do with a boy as usual. She wears her heart on her sleeve, that one.'

A boy? That was another thing that worried her about Abbie. At eighteen, boys hadn't really figured in her life other than as friends. She could imagine that any daughter of Lucy's was rather more worldly than that. 'Did she mention Abigail?'

Lucy smiled. 'Yes. They seem to have sparked up quite a friendship. Funny, isn't it?'

Ellen assumed that she'd meant 'funny' as in it being a coincidence. Because surely their daughters would be likely to get on if their mothers had been friends? After all, she and Lucy had been opposites, too.

Joe was filling glasses with another bottle of Cava. 'Shall we have a toast? To old friends and new?'

Robert held up a hand. 'Just a tiny glass for me.'

She'd just accepted a large glass from Joe as he said it. She was pleased for him that he was enjoying a new regime of healthy eating and exercise, but he had a way of making her feel guilty for everything she ate or drank lately. In fact, she'd taken to hiding crisps and chocolate in the bottom drawer of her dressing table. Stuffing the wrapping to the bottom of the waste bin when she was done so that he wouldn't see it.

Lucy held up her glass. 'To old friends and new.'

In the end, dinner was really good fun. Seeing how in love Joe and Lucy were, Ellen pushed her suspicions and jealousy from her mind. It must be the worry about Abigail starting university that was bringing up old long-buried feelings from the past. Of course Robert was looking at Lucy, she was a beautiful woman. But tonight, she felt beautiful, too. Not used to drinking very much, the sparkling Cava went to her head quite quickly, especially as Joe was adept at refilling her glass without her noticing. She had no idea how many she'd had. Lucy seemed different, too. If she squinted her eyes for a moment, she could let the years fall away and they were a foursome again, laughing and joking and teasing one another. Except this was better because they didn't have a 9 a.m. lecture the next day. And Joe wasn't Ian.

Memories of happy, innocent times flowed with the Cava,

WE BOTH HAVE SECRETS 65

and Ellen was eager to spill them. 'Do you remember that time you burned those croissants and set off the fire alarm at three in the morning?'

Lucy's laugh was deep and throaty. 'How was I to know you weren't supposed to put croissants in the toaster?'

Joe leaned back in his chair and appraised his wife. 'Croissants in a toaster? How did you even get them in there?'

She winked at him. 'With a lot of determination.'

Ellen smiled at the memory. They had been happy times. When no one had needed her and everything seemed possible. She wouldn't change her life choices for anyone – it'd brought her two beautiful girls – but it was a halcyon era. 'Would you like to go back? Do it all again?'

Lucy looked horrified. 'Absolutely not. Although I'd quite like the skin I had then. And the ability to eat whatever I wanted without putting on an ounce.'

Without thinking, Ellen glanced down at Lucy's plate. She'd eaten about a third of her chicken and the potatoes were barely touched. Her own plate was almost clear.

'On that note, shall I bring out dessert?' Joe raised an eyebrow.

Lucy wrinkled her nose. 'Not yet, let's have it with coffee later, shall we?'

'Let me clear away the plates.' Ellen stood so that she couldn't be talked out of it. Even if no one else noticed the disparity in her and Lucy's appetites, she didn't want the reminder under her nose.

The Cava had made her legs a little wobbly, so she didn't chance more than hers and Lucy's plates to begin with. The door to the patio was open, so she stepped up carefully into the kitchen. She slid the plates onto the counter top and turned to go back for the others. As she turned, she almost screamed in surprise. Standing beneath the archway that led to the hall, a young woman around Grace's age looked equally surprised.

The girl recovered herself first. 'Sorry! I didn't mean to make you jump. I wasn't expecting anyone to be home.'

Lucy stepped into the kitchen and solved the mystery. 'Charlotte. What are you doing here?'

Charlotte stepped forward and kissed Lucy. 'I could ask you the same question. I was under the impression that you were going back to England this week?'

'Last-minute change of plan.' She nodded towards Ellen. 'We have our friends here. This is Ellen.'

Charlotte gave her a little wave. 'Hello. I'm Charlotte.'

Lucy's elder daughter looked a lot like her, Ellen should've guessed immediately. 'Hi, it's nice to meet you.'

Carrying the remaining two plates, Robert appeared behind Lucy. 'Where do you want these...'

He trailed off as he looked at Charlotte. There was a look of shock on his face. which he almost imperceptibly changed to one of bland indifference. 'Hi. I'm Robert. You must be Charlotte?'

Did she glance at Ellen before she replied? 'Yes, I'm Charlotte. Nice to meet you, Robert.'

The air in the room seemed to drop by a couple of degrees and there was an awkwardness that hadn't been there five minutes before. What the hell was going on?

ELEVEN

After all the hellos were over, Lucy brought out dessert and Joe followed with the coffee pot.

Charlotte was absolutely beautiful. Long dark hair and lightly tanned skin that almost glowed in the candlelight. She was the image of Lucy at the same age. Sipping at her espresso, she winced. 'Wow, Dad. That is a strong blend. Where did you get that?'

Joe beamed. 'It was a gift from one of my clients. She has it shipped from Columbia.'

Lucy rolled her eyes. 'These two and their coffee. I'm sure it runs in their veins.'

It was so strange seeing Lucy with a daughter not much younger than Grace. In fact, Charlotte's confidence and maturity actually made her seem older. It was still so curious to Ellen to think that Lucy and Joe had had a daughter only a year after her and Robert.

Charlotte turned towards them with an apologetic smile. 'I'm really sorry that I've crashed your holiday. I was given a few days off work unexpectedly so I thought I'd grab the opportunity to get some sun. I should've checked.'

'It's fine. We love having you here.' Joe reached over and squeezed his daughter's shoulder. 'We don't see enough of you.'

'Are you very busy at work?' Ellen knew that she was a doctor, but not what kind. Or even if she worked on a hospital ward or a GP surgery.

Charlotte seemed to be measuring her words with the same level of care she used with the sugar spoon to sweeten her coffee. 'Yes. I'm working with a consultant who is in a lot of demand. I'm learning lots but it's a tough schedule.'

'Joe got her the placement because he found a house for the consultant over here and he mentioned there was an opening for a junior doctor on his team.'

Charlotte blushed and looked cross. 'Gee, thanks Mum. Great way to make me sound like a nepo baby.'

Lucy looked horrified. 'No, I didn't mean it like that. I just...'

For the first time since they'd arrived, Lucy was wrong-footed. There was a part of Ellen who was enjoying it. Even perfect Lucy could be cut down by her own daughter. Girls could be tough.

'Anyway,' Charlotte continued, 'I don't really get any holiday as such because there's always something going on. But my boss has to fill in at the last minute at a conference in the US and he told me to take a break. So, here I am. All I want to do is curl up on a sun lounger with a book. But I can go and stay in a hotel so that I'm not raining on the party here?'

Immediately, Joe shook his head. 'No, don't be ridiculous.'

Ellen joined in. 'Of course you must stay here. This is your home. It will be lovely to get to know you.'

She expected Robert to echo her words, but the only accompaniment was the whisper of an evening breeze through the Oleander trees in terracotta pots outside the door. Neither he nor Lucy said anything. Why were they not making Charlotte feel at ease about staying?

WE BOTH HAVE SECRETS   69

. . .

At the edge of Lucy and Joe's property, just beyond the pool, was a long waist-height railing. Once their meal was over, with a glass of wine in one hand, Ellen held onto this railing with the other and looked out, past the other houses and the trees and shrubs and out to the wide blue sea.

She felt the railing move beneath her hand and glanced across to see Charlotte looking at her. 'Do you mind if I join you? My mother is just about to rope me in to helping to load the dishwasher.'

Ellen smiled. 'You sound just like one of my daughters. Of course, it would be nice to have your company.'

They both turned to look towards the shore. Charlotte sighed. 'It's beautiful, isn't it?'

As dusk crept over the horizon, a soothing stillness settled. For a moment, Ellen allowed her mind to rest. 'It really is. So peaceful, too. You're very lucky to have this place to escape to.'

'I know. Every single time I come, I resolve to do it more often. It's like all my troubles melt away when I look at that sea. It makes me feel... insignificant. But in a good way. Does that make sense?'

'It does.' Ellen felt the same when she looked up at huge mountains or down into deep valleys. Feeling physically small seemed to make your problems shrink, too. 'Your job must be all-consuming?'

Charlotte tilted her head as she considered the question. 'It is. I love it, but it does kind of take over everything. And erratic shift patterns do nothing for your social life. What about your daughters? One of them is at university with Emily?'

'Yes. Abigail. She's my youngest. Then I have an older daughter, Grace, who is about a year older than you. She works in the City for a financial firm. Just in the admin department.'

She felt bad for downplaying Grace's job. But the truth was, she had no real idea what Grace did. It was pretty well paid, as far as she knew. Enough that she'd been able to rent a small house in Walthamstow with two other girls from work. Still, she couldn't help feeling that Grace was staying at that company because Max worked there, too.

Charlotte pulled her long dark hair over her shoulder and twisted it around her finger to form a thick rope. 'And you went to university with my mum? I bet you've got some stories to tell about that.'

Raising an inquisitive eyebrow, Charlotte looked – in that moment – terribly familiar. Although she was the image of a young Lucy, there was something in her expression that came from something, or someone, else. But it was gone before Ellen could put a name to it. 'Yes, we had some good times. But it was so different then. I know I'm going to sound about a hundred years old, but no one had mobile phones or used the Internet. We were kind of cut off in our own little bubble.'

It was true. When she'd left home and gone to Canterbury, she'd barely spoken to her parents for weeks on end. Sometimes she'd use the payphone on the ground floor of her building to call home and check in, but that was as far as their term-time communication went. It was so different now with her ability to call Abigail whenever she wanted. When she could see where she was by checking an app on her phone. Did this connectivity make her worry less, or more, than her own mother had?

'Mum often says that they were the best years of her life. Apart from having Emily and me, obviously.'

Charlotte laughed and, again, Ellen was struck with the feeling that she'd met her before. But that wasn't possible. Until yesterday, she hadn't even known that she existed. She liked her, though. There was an ease about Charlotte that was very attractive. She had her mother's good looks, but she wore them with the indifference of youth. There was a charm in her friendly, easy manner that Ellen would imagine drew people in.

WE BOTH HAVE SECRETS

71

'Having children is a wonderful thing, but it definitely comes with more worry than you realise. It doesn't matter how old your babies get, it still feels as if they shouldn't be out in the world without you.'

'You must've been pretty young when you had your daughter?'

At a year younger than Grace, Charlotte seemed little more than a child to Ellen. But, by her age, Ellen had already been a mother for five years. It made her realise how young she'd really been. How had her own mother felt? 'I was. Your mum was, too.'

Charlotte nodded. 'Yes. It was good, though. Having a young mum. I liked it. She was always more glamorous than everyone else's mother.'

Ellen could imagine that. She didn't envy the other women at school pick-up having to stand beside Lucy every afternoon. 'It's nice to hear that you felt that way.'

Charlotte's smile was infectious. 'I really did. And she could remember what it was like to be young. She wasn't as strict as some of my friends' parents. It must be good for you, too, having your children early, because you're still young enough to enjoy the freedom now that they've gone.' She nodded back in the direction of the house. 'I know my parents are.'

Ellen glanced back in the direction of her nod and saw Robert deep in conversation with Lucy. Even after all these years, she still found him attractive when she saw him across the room like that. Was she enjoying her freedom now? Somehow it didn't feel like that. 'I suppose you're right. Maybe Robert and I should be planning our next adventure.'

An unreadable expression flashed across Charlotte's face and she drained the last of her wine. 'I'm going for a top-up. Can I get you anything?'

For no discernible reason, the air had changed between them and it wasn't only the temperature of the sea breeze that swept over the wall. Ellen shivered. 'Actually, yes. I will. But let me go and get the wine, you stay here and relax for a while.'

She took Charlotte's glass and made her way back around the other side of the pool, so that she could approach Robert and Lucy without them seeing her. As she got closer, she could hear snippets of their conversation.

'Like I said, I'm sorry. I had no idea she was going to come.'

That was Lucy, obviously talking about Charlotte. Why would she apologise to Robert about that?

'The thing is—' As if he'd sensed her approach, Robert looked up and stopped mid-sentence. 'Ellen. I was just about to join you.'

Standing close to the lantern above the door, guilt shadowed his face. Lucy turned to see Ellen and plastered on a smile. 'Do you need more wine? Is that my daughter who's sent you in so that I don't commandeer her into the kitchen?'

Whatever they were discussing, they clearly didn't want her to know. 'Just a top-up for both of us. What are you guys talking about?'

'Daughters. Families. The usual thing. I hope Charlotte isn't telling you any grisly work stories?' As she spoke, Lucy took the bottle from the ice bucket beside her and refilled both glasses as smoothly as the words she used to brush away Ellen's question.

'No. Not at all. You should both come over. The sunset is glorious.'

Not waiting for their reply, she made her way back to Charlotte. Why was Lucy so apologetic about Charlotte's arrival? What difference did it make to Robert?

As Charlotte turned with a smile to take the glass from Ellen, her expression itched at Ellen's mind. She looked so very familiar.

TWELVE

It was another hour before Ellen and Robert made their way to bed. Joe had been unrelenting in persuading them not to leave and – at one point – had even suggested they stay up to see the sunrise, before Lucy had dragged him off to their room.

Now Robert sat on the edge of the bed, pulling off his shoes, seemingly oblivious to the cauldron of anger that was about to come his way. He chuckled softly to himself. 'Joe's a character, isn't he?'

She had no time for more small talk. 'How do you know Charlotte?'

He didn't turn to face her. 'What do you mean?'

'Exactly what I said. It's clear that you've met Charlotte before. And possibly Joe, too. What's going on, Robert?'

Now he did turn towards her, his face in profile. 'How much wine have you had?'

'I heard you, talking to Lucy. She was apologising to you for Charlotte turning up. Why would she do that?'

He twisted his body so that she could see his whole face. He was looking at her as if she was crazy. 'She was apologising because she'd invited us to stay and hadn't realised that her daughter was going to turn up. I told her that it didn't matter at all, because it doesn't, does it?'

Of course it didn't matter if Lucy's daughter joined them, but he was avoiding her question. 'Why was she apologising to you? And why is she paying you so much attention?'

Robert rubbed his eyebrows with his finger and thumb. 'You are imagining things. Yesterday you said I was paying her too much attention and now you're saying the reverse. I need to go to sleep, Ellen, I'm exhausted.'

Ellen could've screamed. She was not imagining things. From the moment they'd arrived, there was another layer of communication between Robert and Lucy that she wasn't privy to. 'Don't try and pull the wool over my eyes. Every time I turn my back, you and Lucy are whispering about something and then, when I come close, you change the conversation.'

Robert rolled over and looked at her, his face dark and unreadable. 'You always do this. I said it wasn't a good idea to come and then you push push push until you get your own way and then, what a surprise, I was right.'

His tone took her breath away. He never spoke to her like that. Robert was the most easy-going man in the world. They rarely argued about anything. 'I always do this?'

He closed his eyes as if he was trying to make her go away. Took a few deep breaths before he spoke. 'I didn't want to be here. It wasn't a good idea.'

Her nagging suspicions told her that this was more than just him not wanting to take a holiday. 'Was there something between you and Lucy. Years ago. When we were at college? Before you and me, I mean.'

Lucy had known Robert before Ellen. They'd taken some of the same classes, so she'd met him there. If Ellen remembered rightly, he'd also been her lab partner that first term.

Like a politician, he continued to evade her questions. 'How is this relevant now?'

It wasn't a no. 'Answer the question. Was there ever anything between you and Lucy?'

'It was university, Ellen. Those first few weeks were a free-for-all. I think we kissed at a party early on. It was nothing. Really.'

The image that flashed into her mind made her nauseous. 'How come you've never told me that?'

'Because it's not important. We're talking about twenty-eight years ago, Ellen.'

'But, at the time, why didn't you tell me? Neither of you ever said anything.'

She remembered Lucy reacting strangely when she'd first got together with Robert. How she'd told her that he was boring and not the kind of guy she should be with. With this new information, Ellen wondered whether that had been jealousy talking.

Even with a few glasses of wine inside her, she knew that she had to choose her words carefully. There was so much bubbling beneath the surface that she didn't intend to voice. Instead, she retreated into a temporary silence while Robert got ready for bed.

Though it was only destined to make her feel worse, she checked her phone to see where Abigail was. For a moment or two, she thought it mustn't be working. Abigail's icon had completely disappeared. She shut it down and re-opened it. Still the same thing, no icon.

Heart in her mouth she called her daughter. Even if her phone had run out of battery, her icon would still be displayed at the last place she'd been. There was no possible explanation except that...

'Hello? Mum? Is that you?'

Her daughter's words sounded slurred. Behind her Robert turned in amazement. 'What are you doing, Ellen?'

She ignored him and spoke to Abigail. 'Yes. It's me. You

disappeared from my phone. I wanted to check that you were okay?'

There was an exaggerated groan at the other end. 'I'm at a party, Mum.'

She sounded drunk. Ellen wanted to ask her who was there with her, whether she was accepting drinks from people she didn't know, how she was getting home. 'That doesn't explain why you disappeared from the app. Is your phone working?'

That was a stupid question when she was speaking to her on it. Abbie got uncharacteristically angry. 'I deleted it, Mum! Because I'm eighteen and you don't need to know where I am.'

And she hung up.

For a moment, she was about to call back, until Robert spoke. 'Ellen, what were you thinking calling Abbie like that when she's out with her friends?'

She was so hurt it felt raw. With his pragmatic approach to life, she didn't expect him to understand. 'I was worried. Do you know she's deleted herself from the tracker app?'

His laugh was hollow, unkind even. 'I don't blame her. For goodness' sake, Ellen. You need to stop worrying about what the girls are doing and where they're going. It's becoming an obsession. You've got to let them live their lives. We should be living our own lives.'

His anger stung. They never argued like this. But she'd never felt as unsure of him as she had in the last few days. 'But we aren't living our lives, are we? You're working all the time. When you're home, you're constantly preoccupied. And then... the way you've been around Lucy...'

Robert groaned. 'You're drunk, Ellen. Let's just go to sleep. You'll feel better in the morning.'

Behind her, she felt the mattress move as he got into bed, but she couldn't face even turning to look at him. What had happened to them? What was going on here?

If the roles were reversed right now, she'd be asking him

WE BOTH HAVE SECRETS 77

why he was still sitting there, frozen in place, rather than coming to bed. She wouldn't have been able to fall asleep as he had. But Robert was soon softly snoring and she was left adrift, not knowing what to do with the conflict of emotions firing in her chest.

What was going on?

Though her mind was still fuzzy with the wine that Joe had poured into her glass all evening, Ellen tried to remember how Lucy and Robert had been around one another at university. Had there ever been a sign that something might've been going on back then?

She suddenly remembered the photographs she'd brought with her. To keep them flat, she'd tucked them inside the cover of a paperback which had sat, unread, on the dressing table. Thanks to their smartphones, her girls probably had more pictures of one night out than she had for her entire three years at university. This handful of snapshots was all the more precious for that.

The top one was from their first year, before she and Robert were together. He was to the right of the picture next to Lucy. Ellen was on the far left. She'd forgotten how handsome he was back then, but also how young they all looked. In her memories of those days, they'd been adults. Now, looking back from two decades on, she could see that they weren't much more than children.

From the background, and the smoke around their heads, they were clearly in a bar and Robert was very close to Lucy; their shoulders touching. Had something been going on between them then? Though Ellen and Lucy had been friends since their first meeting, in the early days there'd been evenings when Lucy had been out without her. Had some of those nights been spent with Robert? In a bar? In his room?

Dropping this photo onto the bed, she looked at the second. Ellen and Lucy with the other two girls they'd hung around with. What had happened to them? For the first year, they'd been super tight with Lucy – hanging on every word she said and copying everything that she did – then, with no real explanation, they'd disappeared from their lives. At the time, she hadn't really minded. But now she wondered if they knew something she hadn't.

Robert had kissed Lucy. It was before he was with her. It wasn't a big deal. But if it really was 'nothing' like he'd just said, why had it never come up before? Back then, when they'd first got together, there was no good reason for him not to tell her that something had happened between them. Or for Lucy to do the same.

Why had they kept it a secret?

THIRTEEN
1999

The cause of the argument had been ridiculous. It was the same old story. With the distance of age and experience, she could see how insecure she'd been. Back then, however, she'd just felt not good enough.

Robert had gone to a school far better than hers. His had been expensive, secluded, full of people with money and connections. Lucy had come from the same world; they even knew some of the same people. That was the way of it for them: everybody knew everybody, whether it was a friend of a friend or cousin of a cousin.

Of course, it wasn't Robert's fault that Ian was always so dismissive about state school education. Or that there'd been a girl who'd laughed about people from council estates. But every comment was another brick in which Ellen built the belief that she and Robert were from such different worlds that they were never going to last. That he would eventually realise that he was much better suited to one of the private school girls and would leave her behind.

Ellen had been waiting for him on a bench outside the chemistry building when she saw them coming towards her,

Robert and a girl from his class. The girl, pretty and blonde, was throwing her head back and laughing at something he'd said, then touching his arm in the same way Lucy did. Intimate. Proprietorial. When they drew level with her, she could hear the clipped vowels that told her everything she needed to know about where this girl was from. Unfortunately, where she was going – due to Robert's kindness – was to join them at the bar for a drink.

Ellen had behaved badly from the beginning. In truth, she'd been in a funk of a mood. Due to a delay in getting her grant for that term, it was the third week in January and she was skint. She'd spent the last hour worrying about having to ask her parents for more money that they didn't have but would somehow find for her. It was bad timing. As soon as the girl disappeared to the bathroom – and she and Robert were on their own – she made a stupid petty comment. 'How soon can we shake her off?'

Robert was surprised, as he should be; this was not the type of comment she usually made. 'What do you mean? We haven't got anywhere to be, have we?'

Irritation made her mean. 'No, but she's a bit of a bore. Blathering on about her big house in the country and how many horses she has.'

A cloud passed over his face. 'That's not fair, Ellen. She wasn't boasting or – what did you call it? Blathering? – about her house. That's just how she lives. She's really nice when you get to know her.'

Was it his defence of another girl or the fact he'd been dismissive of a slang word she'd used. 'Oh really? And you've got to know her, have you?'

She hadn't realised that her voice was getting louder and Robert made the mistake of telling her to quieten down. 'Everyone is looking at you, Ellen. You're making a fool of yourself. This is not how to behave in public.'

The dry tinder of her anxiety about money, stoked by her jealousy, meant a spark of anger ignited in a moment. 'I'm so sorry. We haven't all had the privileged upbringing you have. Maybe you would be better off with someone like her.'

This statement got to the very heart of her fear about Robert. That they were so different that, one day, he would realise she wasn't what he wanted and their relationship would implode.

By the look on his face, that moment might have been right then. 'I'm not having this conversation, Ellen. You are being cruel and unpleasant and I don't know why. You sound more like Lucy than yourself. I'm going to go.'

The girl from his class reappeared from the toilet and he strode across the bar to intercept her. Who knew what he'd told her, but he must have saved Ellen's blushes, because she waved and smiled before she followed him out, leaving Ellen sitting in the student union bar nursing the last quarter of a pint of snakebite and black.

For a while, she sat there angry, shredding a damp tissue into small pieces. Why had he just left like that? Surely, he could see how upset she was? This was the end of it, wasn't it? She'd known it was going to happen. How little it had taken for him to leave with another girl.

But then she started to replay the conversation in her head. And she realised how petty and horrible she'd been. Robert was the last person to make her feel as if she was lesser than their other friends. She'd done that to herself. What an absolute idiot. She had to find him and apologise before it was too late.

When she left the bar, it was around 4.30 p.m. and already getting dark. Becoming more anxious by the minute, she looked everywhere for him. The library, the courtyards, anywhere she could think of that he might go. This was before anyone had a mobile phone so she couldn't call his friends to see where he was. And he wasn't anywhere to be found. All the while she couldn't shake the idea that she'd been a total nightmare and then let him leave with a really pretty girl. If he ended up with her, she'd have no one to blame but herself.

When she couldn't find him, she went looking for Lucy to spill everything that'd happened. That morning, Lucy had told her she had a paper due tomorrow and was planning to set up camp in the library until it closed at ten o'clock. But she wasn't on the sciences floor when Ellen looked. And she wasn't getting a coffee in the café. Or in any of the other places she liked to hang out when she was kidding herself that she was 'taking a break' rather than getting her work done. She must've gone home. Just when Ellen needed her most.

All the while, she still hadn't seen Robert, or the girl he'd been with, anywhere. Where was he?

She headed back to the bar one last time, hoping against hope that he had cooled off and come looking for her. Standing just inside the door, she was scanning the room when she felt a hand on her shoulder.

FOURTEEN

The next morning, it felt like a brass band had taken up residence in Ellen's head. She closed her eyes against the bright sunshine leaching through the blinds into the bedroom. Why did she drink so much last night?

Yet again, Robert's side of the bed was empty. She reached across and felt the cold sheets with her arm. This holiday was supposed to have been the beginning of their new life – child-free and ready for their next adventure. Was this all they had to look forward to?

She rolled over onto her side and squinted at her mobile screen. It was nearly nine. She needed to get up. Lucy would be out there creating some kind of breakfast magnificence and she couldn't be up late a second time. Carefully, so as to minimise the jangling cymbals in her brain, she eased herself from bed and into the shower. Raising her face to the hot water, she tried to wash away the memories of the night before. The argument with Robert and the outburst from Abigail. Was it the drink she'd had that'd made her behave that way?

The horrors. Wasn't that what her neighbour called it? The hangover-induced anxiety that you'd said or done something terrible the night before and everyone hated you for it. Except that she really had roared at her husband, made him angry and had – possibly – made a complete and utter fool out of herself in front of the others. It had been impossible to keep smiling as if nothing was wrong.

Because something was *definitely* wrong.

Roughly, she massaged shampoo into her hair, pressing her fingers firmly into her tender temples. No matter how hard she tried to forget, she just couldn't shake the suspicion of Robert and Lucy's clandestine conversations. For all of Robert's attempts to disregard her questions as paranoia, it was clear that there was something going on. For a start, why had he never told her that he and Lucy had hooked up before she met him? And then there was his reaction to Charlotte's arrival. There'd been shock all over his face, pure and simple. Not surprise at seeing someone new, shock. Did he know Charlotte? Had he met her before? Was there something really really awful unfolding here that no one was honest enough to tell her?

Rinsing her hair, she closed her eyes against the power of the water. It wasn't the steam that burned her face, this heat came from within. Fuelled by anxiety and confusion and desperation for the truth, a Molotov cocktail of shame and anger almost consumed her.

Twisting the temperature dial to cold, she gasped as the icy water dropped like hailstones on her head and shoulders. Joe's words from yesterday echoed in her ears. His casual reference to Lucy. 'We have an understanding.' Was he trying to tell her something that she hadn't been ready to hear?

She bent over in the shower, blood rushing to her brain. She was going to be sick.

Unloading the dishwasher, Lucy was humming to herself in the kitchen. In a long white linen shirt, cinched in at the waist with

WE BOTH HAVE SECRETS   85

a silver belt that matched her flat strappy sandals, she looked as fresh as a daisy. She'd easily drunk as much wine as Ellen last night – and had eaten only half as much – how did she do it?

When she turned to face her, Lucy smiled like an indulgent parent. 'Good morning. I didn't wake you for breakfast. Robert said you needed to sleep in.'

However she felt, Ellen needed to keep cool and calm until she knew for sure what was going on here. Digging her nails into the palms of her hands, she forced a smile. 'Yes, I think I had a little too much of the Rioja. How are you so bright and breezy?'

Lucy shrugged. 'More used to it maybe? How do you feel about doing some shopping today? We could take a walk towards the cathedral, there are a lot of great clothes shops here. We have this chain of vintage clothes shops and you can pick up some really special things there.'

It would be nice to find something to take back for the girls and it might be the perfect opportunity to get to the bottom of what was happening here. 'That sounds great.'

Robert emerged from the patio, his tan already deepening. Abigail was like him, she only needed to be in the sun for a couple of hours before she was complaining about tan lines. Grace would complain in the other direction: on their holidays, she would bemoan the fact she had inherited her mother's skin which was pale and then red.

However annoyed he'd been last night, Robert was clearly intending to pretend that all was well. 'Good morning, wife. How's your head?'

She groaned. 'Not good.'

Lucy opened the huge American-style fridge and extracted orange juice. 'Hang tight. I've got a great hangover cure.'

An hour later, after juice, toast and eggs sprinkled with some kind of dried herbs and chilli flakes, Ellen did feel a little more herself. While she ate, she'd watched Lucy and Robert closely for any signs of intimacy, but there were none. On the contrary, Lucy seemed more focused on Joe, who was pacing up and down outside and talking animatedly in Spanish into his mobile phone. Whoever he was speaking to, Lucy seemed unhappy about it. Ellen was desperate to ask her about this 'understanding' that she and Joe had. But it wasn't a conversation to be had in front of Robert in the bright light of the morning. If at all.

Yawning and stretching, Charlotte wandered into the kitchen in a sun dress and bare feet. With a face free of make-up and her hair in messy waves, she looked like a goddess. Beside her, Ellen felt Robert stiffen. Charlotte reached up into a cupboard for a glass. 'I haven't slept like that in months. There's something in the air here. I feel like a new woman.'

Lucy picked up the juice and filled Charlotte's glass. 'Good. You work too hard. You need to build in more time for rest.'

It was strange seeing Lucy in mother mode. Her own face was already made up in a subtle but effective finish which made her look closer to her daughter's age than Ellen's. Was it any wonder that Robert was paying her a lot of attention?

'Yes, Mother. I promise I will spend the next two days lying around doing nothing apart from reading and eating.'

'Actually, we're going shopping today if you want to come?'

Charlotte had her head in the fridge, looking for something to eat. 'All of you? Even Dad?'

'Dad can't, I'm afraid.' They all turned in the direction of Joe's voice. He waved his mobile at them. 'There's an issue with the builders at the house in Playa Blanca. I need to be fielding calls for the next hour or two until I get it sorted out. Sorry, everyone.'

Lucy's voice was as tight as her lips. 'You said you were going to keep today free.'

He skirted the kitchen counter to pull her to him and kiss

her cheek. 'I know, sweetheart, but it can't be helped. You know what it's like.'

Lucy didn't respond to his kiss. Instead, she looked at Ellen and Robert. 'Well, we might as well get going before the day heats up.'

Robert rubbed a hand over his chin, scratchy with the last day's stubble. 'Actually, I might stay here, too. I don't want to be the only man crashing the retail party. I've brought a book with me that I want to get back to.'

Lucy did not look pleased. 'Just the three girls, then.'

Charlotte yawned. 'Do you know what, Mum. I think I'll go back to my room for a bit. I really am exhausted. Sorry.'

'Just the two of us, then.' As she turned to Ellen, Lucy's eyes weren't looking for a debate. 'Make sure you've got Robert's credit card and I'll take Joe's.'

Now that Robert and Charlotte were both staying here, Ellen felt uncomfortable about going. But – she'd been so effusive earlier – how could she say that without sounding suspicious?

The central pedestrianised area of Malaga was stunning. The grey pavements had the same kind of tiles as the forecourt of an expensive hotel. Tourists thronged the streets with bags of purchases, others sat outside cafés and restaurants or perched on the blocks of stone that formed benches in the centre of the street. The air was sweet with ice cream and happiness. It really was a beautiful place.

Even with everything going on, she had to acknowledge this to Lucy. 'I hadn't realised that Malaga was like this, I think I just thought it was a beach resort.'

Lucy nodded. 'Me too, until Joe brought me here the first time. I just fell in love with it.'

Ellen could see why. There were so many places to eat and

the buildings were beautiful. She'd read in the guide book that Picasso was born here and she still hoped to visit the museum with Robert before they left.

But he was at home. With Charlotte. A girl the same age as his daughter, so why did it bother Ellen so much? What was happening to her?

'Is Joe always as busy as this?'

'Yep.' Lucy pulled a face. 'He takes on more projects than he can actually do on his own and then refuses to delegate. I tried to instigate a rule that when he was home, he would be present, but...'

She held out her hands as if to say that the evidence was there. In that moment, Ellen felt a little sorry for her. But she was curious about what he'd said yesterday. About their understanding. And whether this concession stretched to Lucy, too. 'Do you have... friends here that you can be with when he's not around?'

Lucy scanned her face, then looked into her eyes as if she was about to tell her something, then changed her mind. 'Yes. I have friends.'

'Good friends?'

That was as intrusive as Ellen was able to get. If Lucy didn't want to tell her about any other men in her life, she could hardly ask her outright. 'Yes. Good friends.'

Lucy led the way into an expensive-looking boutique and Ellen followed. A stylish young saleswoman nodded a welcome at Lucy as they entered. As they wandered in silence for the next few minutes, the air conditioning was cool on Ellen's skin. Just as it seemed they were about to leave, Lucy plucked a dress from the rack and held it out to her. 'This would be stunning on you.'

The dress was black and fitted with tiny cap sleeves. It was not something Ellen would have chosen for herself in a million years. 'I'm not sure.'

'Come on. At least try it on.'

There was an eagerness to Lucy which took Ellen back over twenty years ago to when Lucy would be persuading her to go out to the bar or wear a shorter skirt or have one more drink. Now, like then, she capitulated. 'Okay. But I'm not buying it.'

Lucy led the way to the changing room which was a curtain pulled over a small cupboard and waited outside.

The changing room was small and the strip of mirror showed every lump and bump on Ellen's body as she peeled off her top and unzipped her skirt. 'It's a shame that Charlotte didn't come with us. She seems a lovely girl.'

The pride in Lucy's voice came through the coarse blue curtain. 'She is. I worry that she spends too much time at work though. She should be enjoying herself in her twenties. She's always known what she wants to do, and she's focused on getting there. My other daughter is a different proposition.'

Ellen tried to work out whether to step into the dress or pull it over her head. With little room to manoeuvre in here, she decided to try the former. 'Not as focused?'

Lucy laughed. 'That's one way of putting it. Flighty is another. She's like her father. Everything is about having a good time. But she lacks his work ethic, unfortunately.'

The dress got as far as Ellen's thighs before she realised that this wasn't going to work. 'Are you worried about her at university?'

'No. She'll be fine. Girls their age are far more able to navigate their lives than we were. I don't know if it's the Internet or what it is, but they just seem more aware of how to deal with things. Mind you, she tells me way more than I ever used to tell my mother. She'll come home from a party and tell me who is doing what with whom and I sometimes want to tell her that I really don't want to know. I think my mother's hair would've turned white overnight if I'd done that.'

Somehow, Ellen had managed to get the dress over her head

and wriggled it down her body. She hadn't had any conversations like that with Abigail and, again, she couldn't help but worry about Emily's influence over her. In many ways, her own daughter was even more naive than she'd been.

Taking a deep breath, she pulled back the curtain. 'I don't think this is me.'

Lucy held out her arms. 'Are you kidding? You look amazing! It takes a decade off you. You must get it.'

Glancing back at herself in the mirror, Ellen tried to see what Lucy could. 'Really?'

'Really. Get it off and buy it and then we can get a drink You'll knock Robert's eyes out in that.'

That decided it.

After a glass of wine with Lucy in a small bar, and with her new risqué purchase swinging in a thick paper bag, Ellen did feel younger and more decadent as they arrived back at the house. She'd almost persuaded herself that Robert had been telling the truth and that all of her suspicions had been the product of an overactive imagination.

But her new-found confidence took a dent when she saw Robert and Charlotte deep in conversation in the same place she'd spoken to Charlotte the night before. It looked serious. But as soon as she pulled back the patio door to join them, Joe appeared from a side room. 'You're back! Successful trip?'

Ellen held up the bag. 'Your wife persuaded me into an expensive purchase.'

He laughed. 'She's good at that. And then she complains when I have to work to earn the money to pay for it.'

Lucy had already disappeared to her bedroom, so Ellen just smiled weakly at his joke. 'I'm just going to show Robert.'

He followed her eyes out to the railing at the end of the property where Charlotte was explaining something which involved lots of arm movements. 'Why don't you save it to show him later? I've got an hour before I need to get back on the phone, I want to give you a proper tour of the house. Lucy always misses out the best features. Shall we?'

The arm he held out to direct her back to the front door obscured the exit to the patio. Was he suggesting this to keep her away from Robert and Charlotte? What were they talking about?

Again, it was impossible to decline without sounding rude. And maybe Joe, with his affable honesty, might let something slip. 'Sure. Lead the way.'

FIFTEEN

There was so much more to the house than she'd already seen. Joe was as proud of the work they'd commissioned as if he'd done it with his own hands. 'Do you see the way they've matched the tiles to the original? You can't can you? It's that seamless.'

When he'd arrived yesterday, Joe had been wearing a well-cut suit. Today, in an open-necked shirt and linen trousers, he had the air of a man about to board his yacht. Talking all the while, he'd led her outside the house so that he could begin his tour with the exterior. Nodding in all the right places, she interspersed his enthusiasm about bricks and mortar with her questions about Charlotte. 'Robert and Charlotte seem to have quite a lot to talk about. Have they been out there all morning?'

Joe was still caressing the wall like a lover. 'Uh, maybe? I've been busy in the office. I'll show you that next. We had a picture window installed that looks up at the Castillo de Gibralfaro. It's like a living work of art. We didn't have time to go inside yesterday. Shall we take a trip up there tomorrow?'

Maybe she was imagining it, but his vague reply seemed purposefully to distract her from her questions. 'Yes. Maybe we

WE BOTH HAVE SECRETS 93

can go tomorrow. I was just surprised to see them so deep in conversation. Robert usually has his head stuck in a book, given half a chance.'

She finished with a little laugh to take the edge from her words. Joe held his hand out for her to go ahead of him back inside the house. 'Well, Charlotte loves a chat. She probably didn't give him a choice. My office is through here.'

To the right of the entrance hall, he opened a heavy wooden door onto a surprisingly wide space. A large mahogany desk with a huge curved computer screen on the left, a dark-green two-seater sofa on the right and – straight in front of her – the window looking up at the castle. It was beautiful. 'Wow. You're so lucky to have this space. I wouldn't ever want to go anywhere else if I lived here.'

He grinned, clearly enjoying her praise. 'I know. It is great. But I'm not here as much as I'd like. Nature of the job.'

She remembered his comment about his and Lucy's relationship. 'Lucy must miss you when you're away?'

He laughed. 'I'm not sure about that. She has a very full life of her own.'

Again, his choice of words seemed to hint at an unorthodox set-up. 'I didn't get the impression that Lucy had a job.'

'No. Not a job as such. But she's involved in quite a lot of women's charities.' He paused. 'You look surprised.'

She hadn't realised her face was so transparent. Of all the people she'd known over the years, Lucy didn't strike her as the fundraising type. 'Sorry, no, not surprised. It's just she hadn't mentioned it.'

He shrugged. 'I guess it just hasn't come up. She says it's particularly important to her because she has daughters.'

This was the perfect way back to the subject of Robert and Charlotte. 'It must be nice to have Charlotte here.'

His face softened. 'It really is. She's a lot of fun to be

94   EMMA ROBINSON

around. I'm very lucky really. Charlotte accepted me from day one.'

That was a strange thing for a father to say. 'What do you mean?'

He looked surprised at the question. 'Charlotte's not my biological daughter. She was about a year old when Lucy and I met.'

A cold trickle moved down Ellen's spine. Why had that not been mentioned until now? 'I didn't realise that.'

Joe was distracted by an email that had popped up on the screen in front of them; he clicked on it with the mouse, typed a few words and sent a reply with a whoosh. 'Sorry, just a quick query. Yes, she was a tiny little thing. When Lucy and I first started dating, she didn't let me meet her. But it was clear that she and Charlotte came as a package. I wasn't sure how it was going to go, to be honest. I'd never really been around children. But the moment I met her, I was smitten. Well, she's a mini-Lucy, isn't she? I couldn't fail to love her!'

It was a beautiful sentiment, but it made Ellen distinctly uncomfortable. She did look like Lucy, but there was something else familiar about her. She swallowed, tried to keep her voice level. 'Does Charlotte have contact with her biological father?'

Joe shook his head. 'No. He's never been on the scene in the whole time I've known Lucy. In fact, I adopted Charlotte when I married Lucy. She contacted him and he was more than happy to relinquish parental responsibility.'

In her head, Ellen was counting the months between when she'd last seen Lucy and when she must have fallen pregnant. Without knowing Charlotte's birthday, it was impossible to be precise. 'Tell me if I'm being nosey but I can't help wondering if it was someone we knew from university?'

Joe looked uncomfortable. 'Look, I probably shouldn't be talking about it at all. It's Lucy's history, not mine. She always tells me off for being so garrulous. Don't mention it to her, will you? Let her tell you about it if she wants to?'

They'd been talking about their children all afternoon while they were shopping and Lucy hadn't mentioned once that she'd already had Charlotte by the time she met Joe. Of course, it wasn't any of Ellen's business, but she couldn't imagine why she might tell her now if she hadn't already.

But if Charlotte was the daughter of someone that Ellen might know, then why wouldn't she want to tell her?

Unless there was a good reason.

With a creeping anxiety that she didn't want to name, she recalled her impression that something about Charlotte was familiar. Of Robert's shocked reaction when she'd arrived last night. Of her age, so close to Grace's. That she'd overheard Lucy apologising to Robert at her arrival. And now, that they'd both stayed home from the shopping trip and were currently locked into a serious-looking conversation.

Joe was talking about something to do with the tiled floor but all Ellen could hear was her heartbeat thumping in her ears. She didn't want to believe it. It couldn't be true, could it? Was she being paranoid or did this all add up?

Was Charlotte actually Robert's daughter?

SIXTEEN

For the next ten minutes, Ellen followed behind Joe in a semi-daze. He was talking about original mouldings and floor finishes and, all the while, her mind was a rolling stream of questions.

Was this why Robert had been so against coming out here in the first place? The reason he didn't want her to get back in touch with Lucy? Had he been hiding a daughter all of these years? Nausea rolled around her stomach, she felt hot, then cold, then hot again. Her whole body was at sea.

'And here we are back at the kitchen.'

She'd barely noticed that they'd returned to the centre of the house. All she wanted now was to get to Robert and find out what was going on. Her throat was so dry that she could barely speak, but – somehow – she forced a smile onto her face. 'Thanks, Joe. That was really interesting.'

His laugh was warm, but her mind was so adrift, it felt as if it was coming from the other end of a tunnel. 'I'm not sure that I believe you, but thanks for indulging me. Now what can I get you to drink?'

She wasn't going to be side-tracked or distracted or misdirected for another moment. 'Actually, I'm fine. I'm just going to check in with Robert.'

'Good idea. I'll see if I can locate Lucy.'

Outside, a breeze rippled across the surface of the pool. Charlotte had disappeared, but Robert was still at the railing, looking out to sea. Even from behind, his body was almost as familiar to her as her own. The way he crossed one leg in front of the other as he leaned forward over the railing, the breadth of his shoulders, the slight wave in the back of his thick dark hair. They'd been married for so long. Surely there was no way he could have hidden a secret daughter all of those years? There had to be an easier explanation.

Barely breathing as she made her way towards him, her shoes silent on the smooth marble tiles, Robert wouldn't have heard her approach. 'Hi. I'm back.'

He jumped a little before he turned. His face serious before he painted on a smile. 'Hey. How was your shopping trip. Did you spend a fortune?'

Their words were stilted and polite. More like the small talk between casual acquaintances than the conversation of a long-married couple. 'I bought a dress that's probably never going to see the outside of the wardrobe. Lucy is very persuasive.'

His laugh was more of a dry cough. 'I can imagine.'

Now, standing in front of him, she couldn't reconcile her fears with the solid, good, reality of him. But she needed to know for sure. 'Look, I was wondering if you wanted to go for a walk. Just the two of us?'

He frowned. 'Now?'

'Yes. I think last night... I said some things and... well, I just want to talk to you about something.'

Was that fear on his face? 'What is it, Ellen?'

She really didn't want to have this conversation here. Had no idea how she was even going to start it. *I just wondered, did*

you father a child twenty-five years ago and forget to mention it?
'I just want some time on our own for a little while.'

She only realised that Lucy was behind her when Robert looked over her shoulder. Then she heard the forced gaiety of her voice. 'Ellen! You survived. Did Joe bore the pants off you? He's very into the building process.'

Gritting her teeth in frustration, Ellen turned towards her. 'No, he was fine. Robert and I were just going to go out for a walk.'

Lucy glanced at Robert, then back at her. 'Don't go. I need you to help me with the lunch. I've bought a crazy amount of vegetables and I need you on chopping duty.'

She hated to say no, but she really needed to get this sorted with Robert. 'We won't be long. I can help when we get back?'

But Robert was quick to find the opportunity to slip out of her grasp. 'It's fine, you go chop and we can walk after lunch. I'm going to ask Joe about the extension you wanted.'

Again, there was no way out without looking difficult. She followed Lucy. If Robert was going to prove elusive, she was determined to get some answers out of her.

Robert disappeared from view as soon as she was in the kitchen with Lucy. She hadn't been lying about the mountain of vegetables. She passed Ellen a chopping board, two fat green courgettes, three ruby red peppers and a knife, setting herself up beside her with a glossy aubergine and a small pile of shallots. 'I want to make ratatouille to go with the fish tonight.'

Watching her knife skills, Ellen was pretty sure that Lucy could've dispatched this lot pretty speedily without her help, but if she was here she was going to make the most of it. 'Joe is absolutely lovely. You make a great couple.'

Holding the end of the knife, Lucy chopped the onion like a pro chef. 'Yes, I'm pretty lucky.'

'I didn't realise until he told me that Charlotte isn't his daughter.'

There was a micro pause in Lucy's chopping rhythm and then she continued. 'She is his daughter. He's the only father she's ever known.'

In her frustration, Ellen had been unbelievably tactless. 'I'm sorry. That's not what I meant at all. It was just a surprise when he told me that he wasn't her biological father.'

Lucy wasn't giving anything away. She sliced the top from the aubergine. The knife loud on the block. 'Was it?'

'Well, we were at university together when I got pregnant and there's only a year between our daughters so I wondered if I might know him. Charlotte's biological father, I mean.'

Lucy swept the cubes of aubergine flesh from the board and took another, bringing the knife down hard. 'Right.'

For someone usually so garrulous, Lucy's reticence was loud and clear. There was a reason she didn't want to talk about this with Ellen and – though it made her sick to her stomach – she had a horrible idea why. 'Do I know him, Lucy?'

Lucy sighed and closed her eyes. 'Yes, you do.'

Ellen's heart thumped in her chest. For all of her suspicions, she hadn't really believed that this was true. Was Robert really Charlotte's father?

Lucy turned and looked at her. Eyes as deep as the pool on the patio. 'It was Ian.'

As soon as she said his name, it was like a tricky jigsaw piece clicking into place. Of course. That's why Charlotte had looked so familiar. It was the eyes. He'd always had piercing blue eyes, though they looked far less cruel on Charlotte. Her face was softened by Lucy's delicate bone structure, her full red lips. 'Ian? I didn't even realise that you two had got back together.'

There'd been a very public break-up between the two of them towards the end of their third year together. Ellen had been relieved for Lucy. Ian was not a nice guy. Even thinking about him turned her stomach.

Lucy sighed. 'You and Robert were in your own "planning for a life with a baby" bubble by that stage. I'm not surprised that you didn't notice.'

Irritating as that was, it wasn't going to derail Ellen from getting to the truth. 'But why did you get back with him? He was...'

She trailed off at the expression on Lucy's face. It was like she was challenging her to be honest. But after the last time she'd attempted to warn her about him, she wasn't about to try again.

'He was fun. And that's what I needed at that point after my best friend had pretty much abandoned me.'

Ellen flushed. 'I didn't abandon you. We were having a baby.'

Lucy shrugged. 'It felt the same. Anyway, now you know.'

Ordinarily, Ellen wouldn't be brazen enough to push further, but the way things had been the last two days, she threw her usual reticence to the wind. 'Joe said that Charlotte doesn't see her biological father. I assume he knows that he has a daughter?'

As if she couldn't trust herself to keep chopping as she spoke, Lucy rested the heel of her hand on the worktop, leaving the knife hovering over the board. 'Of course he knows! Who do you think I am? But his interest in her lasted until just after her first birthday. After that, nothing. Not even a birthday card. He's no loss. Joe has been a wonderful father to her. She doesn't remember anyone else.'

Was that why she was so secretive about it all? Not knowing where in the house Charlotte was currently, Ellen lowered her voice. 'But she does know? That Joe is not her biological father?'

Lucy sighed dramatically. 'Yes. She knows. And she is

WE BOTH HAVE SECRETS   101

sensible enough to understand that any man who can walk out on his one-year-old daughter is not worth knowing.'

She was right there. Robert had absolutely doted on Grace from the moment she was born. The very idea of him removing himself from her life was unthinkable. 'I'm sorry. That must have been tough for you.'

Lucy's eyes were like ice. 'I am tough. Have you not noticed that?'

Not knowing how to answer, Ellen resumed her careful chopping. She was relieved that Lucy's revelations had stopped her anxious speculation that Robert could've been Charlotte's father. But it still didn't answer the question of what was going on between Charlotte and Robert. His shock at her arrival, Lucy's apology that she was there and their intense conversations and engineering of being alone together.

As if she'd conjured her, Charlotte padded into the kitchen in her bare feet. In her cut-off jeans and tight-fitting top that skirted her naval, she could believably have been a film star on vacation. Now she looked at her with fresh knowledge, Ellen could see more of Ian in the shape of her jaw, the arch of her brow. She was definitely his daughter. And, with that thought, another piece of the jigsaw was in her hand and she was frightened to see if it fit.

Charlotte's smile was wide and generous. 'Oh no, have I missed the work again?'

Lucy shook her head. 'Of course you have. Isn't that what you do best? Although there are still mushrooms to chop if you could possibly manage it?'

Charlotte blew her mother a kiss. 'In a minute, dear Mama. I'm just going to show Robert a website I was telling him about. I'll be back in a moment. I promise.'

Heart in her mouth, Ellen watched her go. This beautiful twenty-five-year-old with the body of a model and the brain of an academic. Any man would have to be made of stone not to find her attractive. Even a tired sales executive with a daughter only a year older than her. A man who had been distancing himself from his wife for the last few months in a way that could only – she now realised with pain – signal that he was thinking of leaving her.

Was this possible? Could Robert be having an affair with a girl that young?

She turned to see Lucy looking after her daughter with a mixture of pride and concern. Did she know? Would she condone that? Suddenly, everything was making perfect painful sense. All the time she'd been headed off by Joe or Lucy when Robert was with Charlotte. They knew. They had to know. She felt sick that she was the only one – the only stupid, short-sighted idiot – to not realise what was going on here.

But this was madness. Charlotte was a beautiful, intelligent, young woman. However much Lucy seemed to like Robert, surely she wouldn't want her daughter in a relationship with a married man in his late forties?

And then it hit her. What had Lucy said about Abigail two nights ago? 'You've got to let them live their own life.' She didn't want to be the mother who demanded that her daughter give up her boyfriend. No, she was way too cool for that.

She wanted Ellen to do it.

SEVENTEEN

The time to be polite was well past. Ellen grabbed a kitchen towel to wipe her hands. 'I'm going to speak to Robert.'

Lucy jolted her attention away from watching at her daughter. 'He's fine with Charlotte. Let's get this in the oven and then maybe we can sneak in a glass of something before we join the others.'

That's what all this had been about, hadn't it? Lucy had been making sure that Ellen saw – and heard – just enough to make her suspicious. The whole reason they were here was for her to catch Robert and Charlotte. Hurt and angry, Ellen wanted to hear her admit it. 'Why did you invite us this week?'

Lucy's eyes widened at her tone. 'Because I imagined it would be nice to catch up. We haven't seen each other in close to thirty years.'

She thought she was so clever. Just as she had all those years ago when she'd tried to pull Ellen away from Robert. 'We could have met for a coffee. Chatted over the phone. But you invited us, both of us, to join you here and then Charlotte just happens to show up unannounced.'

Lucy frowned. 'I live here. This is where I am and I thought you'd like to come out. When I spoke to you, you said you needed a holiday. Judging by the way you've been behaving, I think you were right.'

Ellen almost laughed. The way *she* had been behaving? 'I don't have time for this. I'm going to speak to Robert.'

But, again, she was beaten. In those few moments between Charlotte stepping outside and her argument with Lucy, Robert had disappeared. Now Charlotte stood alone at the barrier, looking at her phone rather than the beautiful view in front of her.

As she approached, Charlotte looked up and smiled. 'Robert has gone for a walk.'

Another one? And why would he leave without telling her? 'Sorry? He's gone?'

'He said he had a headache and wanted to walk to clear it.'

This was getting ridiculous. 'Which way did he go?'

She at least had the decency to look a little guilty. 'I'm not sure. Maybe the beach? He'll probably be back shortly. He knows that you're preparing dinner.'

Ellen couldn't give two hoots what this girl did or didn't know about her husband. 'I'm going to find him.'

As she turned to leave, her sandals squeaked on the polished floor and the left one slipped from her foot. The was no way she could catch up with Robert in these. Without bothering to speak to Lucy as she passed, she hurried to change them.

In the bedroom, Ellen pulled off her sandals and dropped heavily onto the bed. Bending over her knees, she tried to jam her feet into her tennis shoes without bothering to untie the laces. She felt sick. With fear, with shock, with disgust. She wanted anything to be true but this. But there was no other explanation that made sense.

But this didn't make sense either. This was *Robert*. Her Robert. Their marriage wasn't perfect – who's is? – and maybe they had taken each other for granted, got stuck in a rut, but an *affair*? Never in a million years would she have seen this coming. How could he do this to her? To their family?

Beside her on the bed, her phone buzzed and she snatched it up in the hope it was Robert. Her heart sank as she saw it was Grace. 'Hi, love. I'm just getting my shoes on to catch up with your dad. Is this urgent or can I call you back?'

'It's not urgent. It's just about Max. And his kids.'

Ellen had to put her fist in her mouth to stop the groan she felt about to come. This was quite possibly the worst moment in the whole history of time for her daughter to be asking her about her waste-of-space boyfriend and his children. 'Sweetheart, I need to catch your dad up. Can I call you back in an hour or so?'

'Can't you talk to me while you walk?'

There was no getting away with it. 'Yes, I can. Hold on, I'll put you on speaker while I sort out my shoes.'

Grace barely took a breath. 'Okay. Well, the thing is, Max and I have been together for over a year now so it's weird that I still haven't met his kids. Do you think it's weird?'

Ellen's feet must've swelled in the heat because she couldn't ram her right foot into its shoe, she'd have to undo the laces. 'Well, do you want to meet his children?'

This time, Grace sounded less certain. 'It's not that I particularly want to meet them. To be honest, it would be a little weird seeing him in Dad-Mode. But it makes me question how serious he is about us. I mean, shouldn't he be keen for me to meet his kids?'

The laces in Ellen's trainers were as tight as her chest. Trying to loosen them, she bent back her fingernail. Dammit. 'Have you asked him?'

Much as she wanted to have this conversation and was pleased that Grace wanted to talk to her about it all, Ellen was desperate to go after Robert. The longer this went on, the more likely he'd be difficult to find. From her shopping trip with Lucy, she knew that there were so many side streets in the sprawling Malaga town that she'd never find him if he got too far.

'No, he never wants to talk about his family.'

She couldn't do this. The pain in her fingernail, the stupid damn laces, the desperation to confront Robert, the fear that her marriage was over... she erupted with the force of a long-dormant volcano. 'Grace, for goodness' sake, think about it! He changes plans at the last minute. He doesn't want you to meet his children. He says his wife is making the divorce difficult. Why can't you see what's going on?'

Grace's voice was cold. 'What are you saying?'

Finally, the laces were loose enough for her to pull the shoe onto her foot. She snatched up the phone from the bed and turned off the speaker. 'He's obviously still married, Grace. He's telling you he's getting divorced to keep you interested but he isn't bringing you into his life at all. He's lying to you.'

Grace huffed like a petulant child. 'You don't even know him. He wouldn't lie.'

Ellen wanted to scream. 'Exactly! We don't know him because the two times you arranged for us to go out for dinner he had to mysteriously cancel. Isn't that convenient?'

The anger was bubbling out of her like molten lava. Somewhere in the back of her rational mind she knew that this wasn't all to do with Grace and Max. It was about Charlotte and Robert. How could her husband be the Max in this situation? How could her daughter – however unwittingly – be doing to someone else's family what Charlotte was doing to theirs?

'The first time he had to cancel because of a work trip and the second time because his kids were sick. You can't hold that against him. Dad would've done that if it was us and you were dealing with me and Abbie throwing up everywhere.'

Ellen closed her eyes. She was right, Robert would've cancelled to be at home and help out. Had done on more than one occasion when she'd called him to say he was needed. But she wasn't sure that Robert was the best comparison for Grace to be using right now. And with that thought, another surge of anger carried the words from her mouth. 'Wake up, Grace! You're dating a married man. You're his... mistress.'

Though the word was archaic and conjured images of a mini-series from the eighties with women in thick make-up and shoulder pads, she knew the impact it would have on her kind and well-meaning, if naive, daughter. She wanted the weight of it to shock her, make her see sense.

That daughter was now as angry as she was. 'I can't believe you're being so horrible about him. This is why I don't call you for advice!'

And she hung up.

Ordinarily, Ellen would take a deep breath, give it ten minutes and call her back. But – for once – Grace was going to have to figure this out for herself. Ellen had other things on her mind right now than her daughter's love life. She needed to go.

Back in the kitchen, Lucy was still preparing food as if the whole world wasn't falling around their ears. Charlotte was helping her and the sight of this domestic harmony brought a violence to Ellen's body that she'd never experienced. But she wasn't about to get into anything with the two of them until she'd spoken to her husband. She fought to keep her voice calm and cold. 'I'm going to see if I can catch up with Robert.'

Lucy glanced at Charlotte as if to prevent her from speaking. 'Of course. I'll call you if he gets back here before you do.'

That was the very least they could do. Wasn't this all their fault? Ellen's phone beeped in her hand. Damn. The battery was low. There was a battery pack in the bedroom. This was starting to feel like a nightmare where everything conspired to keep her in this house. Keep her from her husband. Without saying goodbye, she returned to their room to get it.

She wanted to scream with frustration when she found that the battery pack was no longer charging beside the dressing table. Had Robert taken it? *Where was it?*

Knocking her shin on the corner of the wooden bed as she almost flew to the other side of the room, she swore aloud. Either side of the bed, each of the heavy cherrywood tables had a deep drawer and she yanked Robert's open. A faint draught of his aftershave spilled from his belongings and took her breath. Underneath the book he had barely touched since the flight, she could see the corner of the rectangular black portable battery.

As she snatched it up, it revealed something else. A spiral bound notebook that she hadn't seen before. With its cover folded back, she could see at a glance what looked like a letter in Robert's handwriting. It was unfinished. And it began *Dear Ellen.*

EIGHTEEN
1999

Ellen had never felt so awful in her life.

She forced herself under a scalding shower, hoping to wash away her shame along with the alcohol coming out of her pores. Her mind replayed the night before like a show reel, the argument with Robert, the look on his face, her search of the campus which confirmed that he had disappeared and didn't want to speak to her. What had she done?

Without even bothering to dry her hair, she pulled on jeans and a shirt and gathered up the notebook and pens she needed for her lecture. She hadn't been able to find Lucy last night, either. No one in her accommodation had seen her. If she could find Lucy, she'd know what to do. She had so much more experience in relationships than Ellen.

By 9 a.m., she was sitting in a stuffy lecture theatre listening to the most boring professor on campus droning on about endosymbiotic theory. She wrote down notes – organelle function, the evolution of eukaryotic cells, prokaryotic ancestors – but none of it made it anywhere near her brain. All she could think about was what a fool she'd been the night before. She could only see the look of disappointment on Robert's face at the way she'd spoken about that poor girl. 'You are being cruel and unpleasant and I don't know why. You sound more like Lucy than yourself.'

She was heartbroken. She'd made the biggest mistake of her life.

Straight after the lecture, she was on her way home when she spied Lucy across the quad. She waved to get her attention. When that didn't work, she called out. 'Hey!'

Had Lucy glanced in her direction before turning the other way? Surely, she must be mistaken? Though her stomach still felt precarious, Ellen picked up the pace to catch up with her friend. 'Lucy!'

This time she turned; her face so pale it was like looking in a mirror. Her books clutched to her chest like a protective shield. 'Hi, Ellen.'

'I tried to find you last night. Where were you?'

She shrugged. 'I told you, yesterday. I had a paper to finish. I was in the library.'

That was strange. Last night, she'd looked there and not found her. Still, that didn't matter right now. 'I wanted to talk to you. I had a fight with Robert.'

This should get a reaction. Unlike Lucy and Ian, she and Robert weren't known for any drama. On the contrary, she'd always felt lucky that they just got along.

But Lucy didn't look surprised. 'Oh.'

She had hoped for a bit more support. How many times had she listened to Lucy's relationship woes? 'I was an idiot. Jealous. I really might've ruined everything.'

Lucy's face was unreadable. 'Well, maybe it's for the best.'

Ellen's heart plummeted to her feet. What did Lucy know that she didn't? 'For the best? I don't understand. What does that mean?'

There wasn't a drop of sympathy in Lucy's tone. 'Well, if

WE BOTH HAVE SECRETS   111

you're going to split up. It's better that it happens now rather than on top of our final exams at the end of the year.'

Ellen had to cover her mouth to stop her lips from trembling. Split up? This wasn't what she'd wanted to hear. She'd hoped that Lucy would tell her that everything would work out. That she and Robert were meant for each other. Maybe even that Lucy would tell her what to do to make this all okay again. 'I don't want to lose him.'

For the briefest moment, Lucy's face softened, then she shook her head. 'Look, I've got to get to a class. I'll speak to you later.'

Feeling even worse than she had this morning, Ellen wandered back to her house. She had classes, too, but all she wanted to do was to get back in bed and pull the quilt over her head.

When she saw the bright-yellow sticky notes on her bedroom door, she could have wept.

I'm sorry.

I love you.

Find me in the library.

She touched each of them in turn as if they were precious artefacts, running her fingers over the raised scratch made by his pen. He must've come to speak to her while she was in her lecture. A rush of relief and hope flooded through her body. Had he forgiven her?

One glance in the mirror inside her room confirmed that she looked as dreadful as she felt. As quickly as she could, she brushed her hair into a ponytail, rubbed some foundation onto her face, pulled on a fresh pair of jeans and a fitted shirt and made off for the library.

The Biology and Chemistry sections were on the same floor, so she and Robert often studied together in the same place. It made it easy to find him among the rows of desks. As soon as he saw her coming, Robert strode down the aisle towards her and took her into his arms, whispering 'I'm sorry I left you' into her hair.

Tears fell from her eyes onto his shoulder, she breathed in the scent of him like a drug. Her voice muffled by the thick cotton of his shirt. 'No. I'm sorry. I was so horrible. I deserved it.'

They weren't talking loudly, but the librarian at the far desk frowned at them. Robert pushed Ellen gently away from him and, holding the tops of her arms, tilted his head to smile at her. 'I'll get my things and we can sit outside and talk.'

On the bench outside, they couldn't keep their hands off each other. She didn't care a thing for the frosty January air as long as she had Robert's arms around her. He kept kissing her cold face. 'Where did you go after I left? Did you stay there?'

She shook her head. 'No. I looked everywhere for you. Where had you gone?'

She wanted to ask if he'd gone somewhere with that girl but didn't want to start them off again. 'I went back to the house. But I had a long walk first. I was so wound up. It just wasn't you, acting like that. You worried me.'

A hot blush bloomed on her cheeks. 'I know. I'm sorry. I don't really know where that came from. I was worrying about stuff and, I don't know, I was stupid.'

'I'm sorry, too. I should have stayed and worked out what was wrong. Let's never do this again.'

She slipped her hands inside his coat where it was warm and welcoming and laid her head on his shoulder. She never wanted to be anywhere else again. 'Lucy said that it was for the best. That if we were going to split up it was better now than later.'

She felt him stiffen. 'Lucy? When did she say that?'

'This morning. I saw her on my way back. I don't think she meant it like that. She was being a bit weird.'

He didn't answer immediately but, when he did, it sounded considered and serious. 'I'm not sure you should be listening to Lucy. This has got nothing to do with her. It's between you and me, Ellen. Our relationship has nothing to do with anyone else.'

She held onto him tightly, pushing away the dark thoughts that threatened to ruin this moment. Yesterday was yesterday and today was today. 'I liked the sticky notes. I'm going to keep them. They feel like little love letters.'

He kissed the top of her head. 'Then I'll make sure I leave you plenty more little love letters in future.'

NINETEEN

Ellen sank down onto Robert's side of the bed, the notebook trembling in her hand. *Dear Ellen.*

Robert's handwriting was almost as familiar as her own. The oversized capital letters, the slight lean to the left. Even though this letter was clearly meant for her, it felt invasive to be reading it. It had been hidden, after all. Not ready for her eyes to see the contents. But the time for reticence was over. She took a deep breath and started to read.

Dear Ellen

This is the third time I've started writing this. I have something to tell you and I'm not sure how to put it into words. I'm going to get it wrong. Writing it down seems the best option. Didn't you always say you used to like it when I wrote you little notes? But this one isn't very romantic. I'm afraid.

As she read, the hairs on the back of her neck rose. Robert's voice came through so clearly in the way that he wrote that he could almost be beside her. So, why wasn't he beside her? Why had he written this down rather than just telling her to her face? Yes, there'd been a distance between them lately, but surely not enough that he couldn't just speak to her?

Before I begin, you have to understand how much I love you. You might question that once you find out what I've kept from you, but it's true. I couldn't have asked for any more from you. You've been a wonderful wife to me and an even better mother to our girls.

Though she tried to swallow, Ellen's throat was too tight, too dry, to comply. There actually was a secret. A reason that he had been behaving so strangely. Was she right? Was it Charlotte? Her whole body began to tremble, her heart knocking at her ribs. Was Robert really having an affair? How long had it been going on? Like a torch in a dark room, her eyes swept across the page, racing to get to the 'terrible secret'. Why was he dragging this out so slowly, so painfully? *Just tell me.*

I also want to say that I am sorry. Deeply sorry. What I'm about to say is going to blow our lives apart, but there's nothing else for it. I've tried so hard to keep it from you, not wanting to cause you pain. But I can't hide it any longer. I wasn't made for a double life. I would have made a terrible spy. And you know as well as I do how bad I am at keeping secrets.

It was becoming difficult to breathe, the air in the room so thick with her own fear. Robert *was* terrible at secrets. There hadn't been a birthday gift in nearly thirty years that she hadn't guessed. If she wanted to keep something from the children, she'd have to keep it from him, too. Memories of family celebrations flashed across her mind and these fleeting portraits of Robert – her Robert – made her heart ache. Palm pressed to her mouth, in an attempt to stop the pain from escaping, she forced herself to take each sentence slowly, preparing herself for the decimating blow.

> *For days now, I've been planning to tell you. Ever since we dropped Abigail at university. Once it was just us, I thought I could do it. Each morning I would wake up and decide 'Today is the day. I'm going to be honest.' But then you'd open your eyes and smile and the day would begin and I just couldn't do it. Couldn't tear a hole in our lives and destroy everything we'd built together.*
>
> *You deserve the truth. But I don't know if there's any coming back from this, Ellen. And I'm terrified that you won't ever forgive me. Charlotte says that*

And that's where it ended. With icy fingers she flipped through the pages of the notebook to find more, but there was nothing. Where was the rest? Why had he stopped? And when had he written this? Today? Yesterday? On the plane on the way out here with her sitting next to him oblivious to the guillotine above her neck?

Wrapping her free arm around her own waist, she clutched the notebook in the other hand and tried to hold herself together as she reread each line, looking for something she'd missed, the panic rising higher and higher in her chest. Despite everything she'd suspected, she hadn't really believed that Robert would do this to her. That she wasn't imagining the whispers and the glances and the obstructions she'd faced since the moment they'd arrived. There really was something going on. Robert had been keeping secrets from her that he wasn't brave enough to say to her face and she pretty much knew that one of those secrets was outside in the kitchen speaking to her mother. Enough was enough.

Tearing the letter from the notebook, she threw open the door to the bedroom and strode through to the kitchen. Behind the counter, Lucy pulled dry leaves and dead petals from a vase of red blooms. Charlotte watched from a bar stool, legs swinging like a young child's. They looked so effortlessly wholesome and innocent. Ellen couldn't bear it.

'What the hell is going on?'

Charlotte's face paled in front of her. 'Sorry?'

Did this girl think she was stupid? As naive as her own daughter? She waved the letter in the air. 'This is from Robert. I know he's been keeping a secret. And I know you know what it is.' She glared at Lucy who had stopped pruning and was holding onto the side of the work top.

Lucy's voice was aggravatingly calm. 'Let's slow down here. What has Robert said?'

Ellen looked at the letter in her hand, prepared to read from it. But there weren't any details to share. 'He says he has a secret and he's sorry and he mentions Charlotte. So you clearly know what's going on here.'

She stared at Charlotte, challenging her to tell the truth before she had to ask outright. Would she just lie again and say she knew nothing?

Charlotte's hands fluttered to her mouth, then dropped to her sides where she formed them into determined fists. 'I can't tell you. It's not my place. Robert has to—'

'Are you having an affair with my husband?' The words came out in a roar and it was all she could do not to lunge across the counter and grab Charlotte by the arms, shake her until she told the truth.

As if she sensed this, Lucy stepped closer to her daughter. 'That's enough, Ellen. This is between you and Robert.'

Charlotte's shoulders slumped as she started to cry softly and – in that moment – she looked like a frightened little girl. What was Robert thinking getting involved with someone so young? Still, Ellen couldn't muster any sympathy for the woman who was tearing apart her marriage. Her voice was pure steel. 'Tell me the truth. Are you having an affair with my husband?'

'No. No. I'm not.' She glanced at her mother, who put an arm around her. 'But I cannot tell you any more than that. You have to speak to Robert.'

She wasn't going to get anything out of the two of them while they presented this united front. She didn't believe for a second that one or the other of them didn't have something to do with this. 'Don't worry, I'm going to speak to Robert and then we'll all know the truth.'

With every ounce of strength she could muster, she turned on her heel and made for the front door. Slamming it closed behind her, she managed two steps forward before her legs threatened to give way beneath her and she was forced to bend her knees until she crouched close to the ground.

All alone in the centre of the sweeping driveway, heart racing, hands shaking, her whole body wound as a tight as a vice, she bent her head forward onto her knees and sobbed. Whatever Robert said when she found him, whatever his reasons for what he'd done, their lives – their family – had been ripped into a million tiny pieces.

TWENTY

A punishing sun burned Ellen's shoulders as she raised herself to standing. Either side of the gateposts, ornate planters stood sentry, full of blooms that choked her with their dry dusty fragrance. Even if Ellen had had any knowledge of the landscape around here, Robert had been gone so long now that her chances of finding him were near to impossible. His morning walks meant he'd know far better than her the best places to walk, to think, to hide. But she had to try. If nothing else, it got her out of that house, away from Lucy and Charlotte and the deceit they'd spun around her in the last couple of days.

Turning left out of the front gate gave a view of the harbour all the way down to the lighthouse. Cruise ships dropping off tourists to browse the stalls of clothes and jewellery and confectionery and wine. If Robert wanted to think and clear his head, he wouldn't be among all that noise.

Walking downhill had got her to the beach much faster than she'd anticipated. Everywhere she looked, family groups sprawled out on the sand. Happy holidaying parents and children, spending time with one another. Dads holding their toddlers so that their feet dipped into the clear blue water,

Mums collecting shells to decorate sandcastles, children running into the sea and out again, screaming about the cold water. It felt like a blink ago that this was them. Robert, Grace, Abigail and Ellen. How had she got to here? Searching for her husband to beg him to tell the truth.

Charlotte said that they weren't having an affair, but why should she believe her? The kind of woman who had an affair with a married man nearly thirty years her senior wasn't necessarily going to be the most truthful of people, was she?

Then she thought of Grace – only a year older than Charlotte – and how naive she was. Was it possible that Charlotte hadn't known that Robert was married? Had he told her – like Max was telling Grace – that his marriage was unhappy, near the end, or worse, that they were separated?

But that didn't make sense. Because of Lucy. Lucy would've known that they weren't separated because she had invited them both here. And whatever was going on between them, Lucy knew about it. Otherwise, why would she have apologised to Robert for Charlotte's sudden appearance last night?

Lucy had been surprised to see Charlotte arrive. Robert had looked shocked. But maybe Charlotte had known all along that they would be there. Maybe she, like Grace, was trying to force Robert's arm. Push him into making a decision once and for all. She could almost imagine her telling him this last night. 'Tell her or I will.'

Was that why she'd been so friendly? Perhaps all the time she'd been chatting to Ellen, she'd side-eyed Robert. *Look how easily I can tell your wife. Look how quickly I can ruin your life.*

Or maybe she wouldn't be ruining his life. Maybe he'd feel liberated to have the secret out in the open. To be able to leave her. Maybe it would only be her life that was ruined.

And their girls. She felt a stab of pain in her stomach at the thought of having to tell them that their parents' marriage was over. All she'd ever wanted for them was a stable home life, parents who were always there for them. Hadn't she even sacrificed her own career because it would have taken her away from home?

The timing of this wasn't a coincidence. Abigail leaving for university was the beginning of the end for their family living all together. She had hoped that this might be the start of a new adventure for her and Robert. He had clearly been thinking the opposite.

And Lucy. How had she been brought back into their lives? Surely it was too big a coincidence for her daughter to be having an affair with her old friend from university. Had she had it right the first time? Was it Lucy who was having the affair?

Glancing this way and that at every dark-haired man on the beach, she was beginning to lose hope of ever finding Robert. Maybe he'd returned to the house by now? She pulled out her phone and called Lucy. It rang three times before she answered.

'Has Robert arrived back there?'

'No. He's not here. Why don't you come back, Ellen? He's just gone for a walk. He'll be back soon. He obviously needs some time to himself.'

What made her think she knew what Robert needed? Ellen wanted to scream at her. 'What does he need time for, Lucy? What do you know?'

Lucy was quiet for about three beats. 'I can't tell you.'

Now she really did want to scream. How dare she keep secrets with her husband?

She ended the call and picked up the pace. For all her confidence, Lucy didn't know her husband like Ellen did. He didn't do things like this. Why was he pulling away from her and keeping secrets from her? Although hadn't she kept secrets from him, too? Was this a punishment? Was there any way he could know?

And then she saw him. Almost out of eyeshot, further along the coastline. But she'd recognise that walk anywhere. 'Robert!'

The breeze took her words. A couple walking in front of her, hand in hand, turned to look at her, but Robert kept on walking.

She quickened her pace, her lungs burning with the effort. She tried again. 'Robert, wait!'

This time he turned and his face made her stop dead in her tracks. This wasn't a man out for a walk to clear his head. His haunted eyes, the set of his mouth: this was a man in deep emotional pain.

At the sight of him like this, her legs almost gave out beneath her. Robert never looked flustered, never looked upset. He was as calm as a deep pool. But maybe it was true that still waters ran deep. What was beneath the surface?

Though he'd turned at the sight of her and stopped in his tracks, he made no move to come towards her. Instead, he waited for her to draw level before speaking. 'How did you find me?'

Her heart plummeted at the tone of his voice. 'Luck, I suppose. I just kept walking.'

He nodded. 'I'm sorry that I just left without telling you where I was going. I needed some time to work out what I was going to say.'

What he was going to say? Since when did he have to weigh his words before speaking to her? This had to be bad. It had to be really bad. 'I found your letter.'

He looked confused for a moment and then light dawned in his eyes. 'Oh, yes. That was Charlotte's idea. I was worried about how to tell you everything in the right order and she suggested the letter. I couldn't do it, though. It didn't work for me.'

Charlotte's idea? So this was to do with her. Damn her and her lies. And Lucy. 'I know what you're going to tell me, Robert.'

He looked surprised. 'You do?'

'It's Charlotte, isn't it? Something's going on between you and her? I can't believe it, but it's the only explanation for your secretive conversations.'

Robert looked so sad at her words that, had she not been hating his infidelity, she might have felt sorry for him. But he shook his head. 'Nothing is going on between us. Well, not in the way you think.'

Ellen's head was a whirl, firing in one direction to another. Now she was back to thinking that Charlotte might be his daughter after all. Was it Lucy he was having an affair with? 'Just tell me what's going on, Robert. Who is Charlotte to you?'

He reached over and took her hand. 'Charlotte is part of a specialist medical team for heart conditions. She works with my consultant.'

TWENTY-ONE

Medical team. Specialist. Consultant. Where had this come from? Ellen had been certain that Robert's secret was to do with matters of the heart but not for a second that it was his actual physical one. She reached out and clutched his arm. 'What do you mean? I don't understand.'

'Let's sit down.'

Taking her hand, Robert led her towards the back of the beach. Stumbling after him, her mind fired off in a million directions, terrified about what she was about to hear. At the edge of the beach, where it met the pavement, Robert swept sand from a low wall and they sat down together.

'Do you remember that I had to go to London a few months ago for a medical?'

She did remember. It was about a week after Abigail's final exam and they'd had a family dinner planned that night. Grace was supposed to be bringing Max but he'd – surprise, surprise – not been able to make it at the last minute. 'I do remember. It was for your health insurance.'

He nodded. 'Well, they found some irregularities. With my heart.'

WE BOTH HAVE SECRETS 125

The way he was looking at her intently, enunciating every word as if he was speaking to her on a long-distance phone call, still didn't make it any easier to understand. 'Your heart?'

He paused again. 'Yes. I have a descending thoracic aneurysm. It's a chronic heart condition that can be fatal. There is surgery, but that has its own risks.'

Shock made her brain slow to comprehend. Maybe she could've taken this in if he hadn't kept it from her for so long. 'Why didn't you tell me? That night, when you got back, I was angry with you.'

She had a vivid memory of being cross because he was late home and they'd had to rush to get to the restaurant. Once they were there, supposedly celebrating their daughter's end to her school days, he'd been quiet and hadn't entered into the spirit of it. When the girls had suggested continuing on somewhere else for another drink before they went home, he'd told the three of them to go ahead without him. He was tired, he said. She'd accused him later of putting work before his family.

He shrugged. 'I just didn't know how to tell you.'

There were a million questions about the condition, but she was still confused as to where Charlotte entered the story. And Lucy. 'Does everyone back at the house already know about this?'

It wasn't important in the light of what he'd just told her, but she couldn't help but feel hurt that he hadn't been able to confide in her. What did that say about their marriage?

Robert rubbed his eyebrows with his finger and thumb. 'That's where it gets a little complicated. I tracked Charlotte down. Well, not her exactly. I researched who were the leading doctors in their field dealing with my kind of condition. You know how I love a bit of research.'

His smile was weak, but she did her best to return it. It was a long-standing family joke that Ellen would buy a new car or book a holiday in the same amount of time it took Robert to meticulously research the best brand of dishwasher tablet. 'Charlotte can't be old enough to be the leading doctor for anything.'

'No, she's not. But she works with a guy who is. I tried to get an appointment with him, but he's all booked out with private patients. I happened to be in the area of his office on Harley Street and so I decided to just turn up there, see if there was any way I could charm his receptionist into getting me in for a consultation.'

She shook her head at him in amazement. His confidence never ceased to amaze her. 'And did she?'

He shook his head ruefully. 'No. But when I was on my way out, I bumped into Lucy. She was there to meet Charlotte for lunch.'

It was amazing that he'd recognised Lucy among a sea of faces on the street. Ellen had struggled to recognise her at the airport and she'd been looking out for her. 'How did you know it was Lucy?'

'I didn't. She recognised me. Said I hadn't changed. When she told me she was there to visit her daughter, she was so proud that she told me who she was working for and—' he held out his hands '—it was like a gift.'

'Lucy got you in to see the doctor?'

'Kind of. She invited me out to lunch with her and Charlotte and I explained my position. Charlotte said she'd speak to the consultant, see what she could do.' He looked a little embarrassed. 'Apparently, he'd been to the same school as I had. A few years before.'

There it was. The old school tie doing its thing. This time, though, she was grateful for it. 'And he saw you? He's going to make it all okay?'

He held up his hands. 'It's not as straightforward as that. He did see me and he sent me for another raft of tests. It's a complicated condition and procedure. He needed to know it can be done.'

'And can it?'

Breaking eye contact, Robert looked down at the sand and then out to sea. If she hadn't known him as well as she did, she might have imagined that he was struggling not to cry. Taking a deep breath, he turned back to her with eyes full of uncertainty and pain. 'I don't know. I have some decisions to make. Charlotte was able to access my test results earlier. That's what we'd been talking about when you got back. She hadn't wanted to but I persuaded her into it. The condition has progressed faster than I'd expected. I need to make a decision soon. About whether to have the surgery.'

Trying to keep herself upright, Ellen pushed her palms downwards onto the rough cement of the wall. Every muscle in her body tightened with fear. 'And if you don't have it?'

Her heart beat once, twice, three times in her ears before he answered. 'Let's go back to the house. Charlotte can explain it all a lot better than I can.'

He stood up and held out his hand to pull her up to standing. Terrified to push him for an answer, she followed without speaking.

It wasn't until they'd passed the main crowds of tourists and were on their way – slowly, carefully – back up the hill towards Lucy's house that she trusted her voice. 'How have you been able to keep this to yourself? You must've been visiting the doctor, going for all of these tests.'

Robert swallowed. 'I'm not proud of myself, but I've been stretching the truth a little. When I've been telling you that I'm working away, I've actually had hospital visits.'

More subterfuge. 'And Lucy?'

'I did stay over at Lucy's one night because I had to be at the surgery really early. She and Joe have an apartment in London, which is only a short cab ride from there, and she was insistent that I didn't stay in a hotel.'

'And that's where you met Joe?'

He looked surprised. 'Yes. How did you know that?'

'He's not as good as you at keeping secrets.'

His smile turned down at the edges. 'I'm sorry, Ellen. I just didn't know what to do for the best.'

All of this was immaterial. Robert was ill. Really ill. 'What's going to happen next? Can they fix it? What's the treatment?'

'To be honest, I couldn't really take it all in when Charlotte was explaining the test results. It all got too much. That's why I came for a walk. When we get back there, I'll ask her to go through it all with me again. Listen properly this time.'

She squeezed his hand. 'Go through it with *both of us*.'

In more ways than one, the walk up the hill was harder than the walk down had been. In places, it was so steep that she wanted to stop and catch her breath. Calm and supportive as ever, Robert was clearly trying to protect her by not going into too much detail. Hadn't he always been like that? Her safe place, her support, her foundation.

Now she had to be all those things for him. But what – oh, God – what if it was too late for that? What if she was going to lose him forever?

TWENTY-TWO

Lucy opened the door before they'd even got close enough to knock. She glanced from Robert to Ellen. 'Everything okay?'

Ellen still wasn't sure that she could forgive her. 'If you mean, has Robert told me the big secret, then yes, he has.'

Lucy looked relieved. 'Good. Come in.'

In the sitting room, Charlotte was pacing up and down, her face pale and tight. Relief came off her in waves. 'Oh, thank God. You found him. I was worried that... it doesn't matter what I was worried about.'

Robert held out his arms and gave her a hug. 'Did you think I was going to do something stupid?'

Ellen watched the two of them. Was the news that bad? 'Robert has told me about his heart condition, but I don't really understand.'

Charlotte's face was sympathetic. 'It's a lot to take in at once. Shall we sit down?'

Lucy was tactful enough to make herself scarce, although she probably knew all of this already. Now that Ellen knew the truth, Lucy's behaviour towards Robert – the attentiveness, the whispered conversations, the kindness – all made a lot more sense.

Due to the lovely weather, they hadn't spent any time in the living room. With the same marble floor as the kitchen and a thick glass coffee table, it might've felt clinical, but the couches of soft white leather provided a welcome respite after their climb.

Charlotte leaned forward, her forearms on her knees, her eyes fixed on Ellen. 'I know that you're a biologist, so you already know that the aorta is a blood vessel that carries blood from your heart to all parts of your body.'

Right now, Ellen felt as if her brain were empty of all knowledge. 'It's been a long time since I studied this kind of biology. Please explain it to me as you would to anyone else.'

Charlotte nodded. 'Okay. Well, an aortic aneurysm is a swelling or bulging at any point along the aorta. It usually happens because the wall of the aorta has become weak and has lost its elasticity, so it doesn't return to its normal shape after the blood has passed through.'

With her brain still in shock, it was so difficult to take this in. 'And this is obviously very serious.'

'Yes. A thoracic aortic aneurysm can be extremely dangerous if there is an aortic dissection. That's a tear between the layers of the aorta's wall. If it's not treated immediately, it's life-threatening.'

Ellen turned to Robert. 'How did we not know this? Why were there no symptoms?'

Charlotte continued, her voice gentle but clear. 'Thoracic aortic aneurysms are often small and they can grow slowly. Most of the time there are no symptoms. Which is why Robert was so lucky that his was picked up in a routine health check.'

Lucky was not something she felt at the moment. 'And what treatment can he have? Your boss, is he good? What does he recommend?'

'Mr Grayson is a leader in this field. Even once an aneurysm has been found, it can be difficult for doctors to know how quickly it might grow. We've been checking Robert regularly with echocardiograms and CT scans, and the latest scans show a marked increase in the growth rate. Mr Grayson is recommending surgery as soon as possible.'

Surgery. On his heart. Ellen swallowed down her fear. 'And what is the surgery?'

'We would have to remove the section of the aorta where the aneurysm is and replace it with a new aorta made of synthetic material. A graft.'

Now came the most frightening question of all. 'If he has the surgery, will he be okay?'

She paused longer than Ellen liked. 'Most people recover well and return to their normal life.'

Most people? 'Not everyone?'

Charlotte looked from Robert to Ellen. 'All surgery carries risks.'

Ellen tightened her grip on Robert's hand. 'That's the choice. Live with it not knowing when it could cause a fatal heart attack or have the operation with the risk that he might not make it through.'

Charlotte swallowed. 'I'm afraid so. I'm sorry.'

In this capacity, detailing Robert's prognosis, Charlotte seemed so much older and wiser than her twenty-five years. How had Ellen regarded her as silly and shallow enough to have an affair with a married man? Her face burned at the thought.

Beside her, Robert had been as silent as a rock, looking down at his hands. She turned to him. 'And you've been carrying this information all on your own?'

Before he could answer, Charlotte stood. 'I'm going to go and see if Mum wants to take a walk to the cheese place. Dad's holed up in his office, so you'll have the place to yourselves.'

Ellen managed a smile for her, this clever, sensitive girl. 'Thank you. And I'm really sorry for before.'

Charlotte shook her head. 'There's no need to apologise. Really.'

After waiting for Charlotte to leave and close the door behind her with a gentle click, Ellen spoke to Robert again. 'This must have been so hard for you.'

He nodded, still staring at his fingers as if it were all he could do to stave off tears. 'It has been a lot. The not knowing has been hard. You can deal with problems if you know what they are, but the tests took a while.'

The lump in her throat was so sharp that it was painful to swallow. 'And now? How are you feeling about what Charlotte just said?'

It was a stupid question, but they had to start the dialogue somewhere. She rested a hand on his shoulder and he turned his head towards her, eyes suspiciously bright with unshed tears. 'To be honest, I'm pretty terrified.'

She was terrified, too. Unable to even contemplate the idea of losing him. 'We will get you through this. We have to. For the girls. For us. We have to face this head on. The operation Charlotte mentioned?'

He wiped at his eyes with the back of his hand and sat up straighter in his seat. 'You heard what she said. The problem with the operation is the risk that I might not come through it. I'm not ready to face that. I'm not ready to leave you, Ellen. To say goodbye to the girls.'

A sob escaped before she could cover her mouth with her hand. She wasn't ready for that either. Would never be ready for that. 'But if you don't have the operation yet, then how long can you leave it?'

He held out his hands. 'How long is a piece of string? No one knows. I could have an event at any time.'

WE BOTH HAVE SECRETS 133

It must've been like living with a hammer waiting to fall. 'Why didn't you tell me? I still don't understand.'

'I couldn't bear the idea of hurting you. Of making you feel as scared as I did. Once I told you, it would be real. I would see it in your eyes.'

It was as if time had stopped in that room. Before this moment and after it were two different countries. Yesterday she was worried he was going to leave her for another woman; today he might leave her for reasons she couldn't even fight.

He reached over and placed his warm hand over her two clasped ones. 'I'm sorry, Ellen. I'm sorry to do this to you.'

'You don't need to be sorry. I'm the one who is sorry. For jumping to the insane conclusion that you were thinking about another woman when you were carrying all of this.'

His face, so familiar to her, was cast in a shadow that she couldn't smooth away with a cool palm or a kind word. Age had softened his jaw and lined his brow, but his eyes were the same clear, kind, beautiful blue she had fallen in love with over two decades ago.

'I haven't handled it well. I know that I've been pulling away from you. I've just never kept anything from you and I knew that I would confess everything if I was too close. I know this is going to sound ridiculous, but I even considered trying to make you want to leave me. I thought that might be easier for you.'

'How could that have been easier? I never want you to leave me. And I had noticed you being distant but I was scared, too. I worried that you didn't love me any more.'

It sounded weak, childish, needy to put those feelings into words. How envious she'd been of other couples on romantic nights out or husband's surprising their wives with thoughtful gifts or trips to Paris. Nights when Robert had been – she'd believed – away with work, when she'd laid in bed in a quiet house and wondered if this was what her future held.

'I wish I had known that you were feeling like that. I'm so sorry. I've never kept a secret from you before, I swear. And I never will again. Let's promise to be totally honest with each other, whatever happens.'

What was more painful? The 'whatever happens' or the promise to be honest when she knew that that was something she couldn't – wouldn't – ever be able to say back to him.

A gentle knock on the door preceded it opening to reveal Joe's tentative smile. 'I'm so sorry to interrupt, but I need to grab my phone. I left it on the table and I'm expecting a really important call or I would've left it.'

Robert was straight back into polite mode. 'Of course. Don't apologise, this is your house.'

Joe did an exaggerated tiptoe across the rug. 'Please don't tell Lucy or Charlotte. I was under strict instructions not to leave my office.'

His comedic grimace brought a much-needed momentary relief. Robert mimed zipping up his lips. 'I promise to keep your secret.'

Secrets. From innocuous to life changing. Perhaps it was always going to come to this for her and Robert. A secret being their undoing. But if she deserved it, he most definitely did not.

Joe plucked his phone from the arm of the couch and made for the door. 'You won't hear another peep from me, I promise.'

As soon as the door clicked behind Joe, Robert reached out for Ellen's hand again. 'I'll go and see my consultant as soon as I get home and find out more about the operation. Maybe you could come with me this time?'

She returned his squeeze of her hand. 'Of course.'

He smiled. And then he clutched his heart and grimaced.

For a slice of second she thought he might be playing around, but his face turned grey. 'Robert. What's happening? Are you in pain?'

He slid down the sofa as he whispered. 'Get Charlotte.'

TWENTY-THREE

'Joe! Joe!'

Ellen screamed at the top of her lungs as she hunched over her husband, checking that he was breathing.

Joe was there in seconds. 'What is it... oh no, I'll call Charlotte.'

He was on the phone in seconds. 'Charlotte. Where are you? It's Robert. He's collapsed.'

Jagged terror ripped through Ellen. 'Can you hear me, Robert? Can you hear me? Charlotte is coming.'

His voice was weak and uncertain. 'I'm okay, I just felt lightheaded. I'll be okay.'

And then his eyes rolled back in his head and he passed out.

Charlotte must've run from wherever she'd been because she was out of breath as she crashed into the sitting room. 'What happened?'

'I don't know. He was talking one minute and the next he clutched his chest and looked as if he was in pain. He was talking and then he just passed out.'

How could this be happening? He'd only just told her about

it. It had sounded like he had time to make a decision. Was it too late?

'Robert? Can you hear me?' Her voice was strident, echoing from the walls and the marble floor. 'It's Charlotte. Can you hear me?'

As if she'd slipped into water, everything around Ellen slowed and muffled as she waited, suspended in time, for Robert to reply. Charlotte's voice – calling his name over and over – was almost drowned out by the sound of her own heart thudding in her chest. She willed Robert to come back to her. He couldn't leave her. He wouldn't leave her, would he? *Wake up. Please, wake up.*

At last, his eyelids fluttered and opened and relief coursed through her like a river bursting its banks. 'Is he okay?'

Charlotte didn't answer. Her full attention was focused on Robert. 'Slowly now. Deep breaths. Don't try and move.'

Later, Charlotte said it had been a few minutes before Robert was sitting up and drinking a glass of water, but it'd felt like hours. Robert had always been strong, confident, in control of any situation. Now he looked weak, defenceless and vulnerable. She'd worried over the last few weeks – and even more over the last three days – that she was in danger of losing her husband. But not for one minute had she anticipated it might be like this. Sudden. Shocking. Irrevocable.

Charlotte breathed out and sat back on the sofa. 'You scared us all for a moment, Robert.'

Robert smiled weakly over the top of the glass of water he was sipping under Charlotte's watchful eye. 'Sorry about that.'

A sob broke free from Ellen's chest and out of her mouth. 'I was so scared. You were... Oh Robert, I was so scared.'

'Hey...' He held up his arm and she leaned in to him, trying her best not to put any weight onto his chest '... I'm okay. I'm still here.'

But for how long? The surgery might be terrifying to

WE BOTH HAVE SECRETS 137

contemplate, but there was no choice. Without it, this could happen any time and next time he might not be so lucky. She looked at Charlotte who was taking Robert's pulse with her fingers, timing it on her watch. 'He has to have the surgery, doesn't he?'

Charlotte moved her lips as she counted the last few beats, finishing with a smile and a nod at Robert before she turned to Ellen. 'As his doctor, all I can do is tell him the risks and benefits of either option.'

'And as his friend?'

'Ellen, I can't answer that.'

'What would you do if it was your dad?'

They both looked up at a white faced Joe who was patting Robert on the shoulder. Charlotte frowned. 'If it was my dad, I'd want him to have the surgery.'

Ellen shuffled closer to Robert. 'You need to have the operation. You can't risk this happening again. What if you'd been driving or you were alone?'

She shuddered at the images crowding into her head. Robert sighed. 'I know. But we have to talk through some things first. With the girls. I need to sort out finances and—'

'No!' She pulled away from him, desperate to stop him from finishing that sentence. 'You are not going to have to talk about finances or anything else because you're going to come through this and everything is going to be good again.'

'Ellen, we have to be practical about this.'

'I don't want to be practical. I want to go home and get you seen to urgently. I want you to be well.'

Charlotte's voice was gentle. 'Ellen is right, Robert. Getting home to the UK is urgent. This could happen again at any point. We need to get you back to the hospital and run some tests. See what's going on in there.'

In her bag, Ellen's phone rang and – with the habit of a lifetime – she reached to pick it up and scanned the screen. 'It's Abigail.'

'Don't tell her anything.' Robert's face was a warning.

It took every ounce of control Ellen possessed to keep her voice clear of her fear. 'Hi, sweetheart. What can I do for you?'

'I was trying to call Dad but he's not answering his phone '

'You were trying to call Dad?' she repeated in order that Robert could decide whether he was well enough to speak to her. He shook his head. 'I think Dad's in the shower. What do you need? Can I help?'

'I don't think so. My toaster won't work. I knew Dad would be able to tell me what to do.'

It was such a mundane request, but it brought fresh tears to Ellen's eyes. That's what they did. When things didn't work or broke or were too difficult to understand, they asked Robert. All three of them. 'Can you borrow someone else's toaster for now? Then maybe Dad can call you later?'

'I suppose I could. But can you get Dad to call me? He'll know what to do.'

'Of course I will.'

'Thanks, Mum. Love you.'

'I love you, too.'

Robert raised an eyebrow. 'Her toaster?'

She nodded. 'We're going to have to tell the girls what's going on.'

He shook his head. 'Not yet. Not until I know what I'm going to do.'

'But you have to have this operation.'

The door opened and Lucy came in. 'Can I get anyone anything?' She squinted at Ellen. 'You look like you could do with a stiff drink.'

Robert moved slowly into standing. 'I'm going to have a nap, I think. I'm exhausted.'

She stood next to him. 'I'll join you.'

WE BOTH HAVE SECRETS 139

He waved her away. 'No, you have a drink with Lucy. I won't be able to sleep if you're hovering over me.'

She was terrified at leaving him alone. 'What if something happens?'

'You can check on me once I'm asleep. How about that?'

As a compromise, Ellen sat on a stool in the kitchen, which was closer to the bedrooms. From a squat glass bottle with a long neck, Lucy poured an inch of dark-brown liquid into two lead crystal tumblers. 'It's Spanish brandy. It'll take the edge off the shock.'

Ellen was about to refuse – she wanted all her wits about her to listen out for Robert – but she could do with something to stop her hands from trembling. The sweet smoky brandy hit the back of her throat and the strength of it made her cough. 'Thank you. I think.'

Lucy raised her own glass before taking a smaller sip. 'It helps if you don't inhale it.'

The first time she'd ever drunk proper spirits had been with Lucy. When Ellen was at sixth form, they all drank sickly sweet alcopops and cheap fortified wine. It wasn't until she got to university that Lucy introduced her to vodka that she kept in the fridge and whisky that she insisted they drink at the end of the night.

She took another, smaller, sip. 'How long have you known?'

Swirling the amber brandy around in its tumbler, Lucy cleared her throat before she spoke. 'About Robert's illness? Two months.'

Two months? That was back in the summer. Before Abigail's exam results. Weeks and weeks ago. 'And, in all that time, you didn't think to call me. Tell me what was going on?'

As she cast her hands outwards, Lucy's brandy threatened to slip over the edge of the glass. 'It wasn't my place, Ellen. Plus,

Charlotte is part of his medical team. It could've got her in all kinds of trouble if I was calling Robert's wife.'

These were excuses. 'But you were supposed to be my friend.'

Lucy's laugh wasn't particularly kind. 'We hadn't seen each other in over twenty years, Ellen. I'm not sure you can pull that card on me.'

The reasons for that were a whole other conversation, but this wasn't the time for digging over the past. 'I can't believe he didn't tell me. We've been married for so long. How could he keep this from me?'

Lucy took a deep breath. 'People keep secrets. Sometimes it's to protect other people. Sometimes it's to protect themselves.'

Was Ellen imagining it, or was Lucy looking at her as if she was trying to project a message into her mind? 'How was Robert protecting himself by keeping this a secret?'

Lucy took another sip of the brandy. 'I wasn't talking about Robert.'

Ellen turned as the door opened and Joe strode in. 'Do you have one of those for me?'

Reaching up to the cupboard behind her, Lucy had to stretch up on her toes for another glass. 'Did you get the flights sorted?'

'Yes.' He picked up the bottle of brandy and poured himself a generous measure into the tumbler Lucy had slid in front of him. Then he took a large gulp before smiling at Ellen. 'I know you have return flights booked, but I assumed you wouldn't want to wait, so I've booked three seats for you, Robert and Charlotte to fly home in the morning. She needs to get back and we thought you'd feel more confident if she was with you.'

It was like being treated as a child, but she was grateful for it. 'Yes. Thank you. You'll have to tell me what we owe you.'

He waved away her offer of payment in the way of someone

who has never had to worry about money. 'Charlotte says that you mustn't mention that Robert has been feeling unwell or they may not want to risk him getting on. But it's imperative that he gets back home so they can do a scan or whatever it is they need to do.'

She wasn't comfortable with that, but she was also desperate to get Robert home. And, right now, she'd do whatever Charlotte told her. 'Okay.'

TWENTY-FOUR

The flight home was very early in the morning, but Joe had generously booked them into Business Class and – with the combination of the early start and the comfortable seat – Robert fell asleep almost immediately after take-off.

Ellen was expecting Charlotte to slide in ear buds and lose herself on Spotify or Netflix for the journey, much as Grace or Abigail would've done. But she smiled at Ellen. 'How are you feeling?'

Guilt. Terror. Shame. There were so many different emotions that it was difficult to select one. 'Well, like I said yesterday, I'm mortified that I accused you of having an affair with my husband.'

She'd spent a lot of the evening before apologising to Charlotte, and to Lucy, for her behaviour. They'd been more generous with their forgiveness than she deserved.

'Please, you really need to stop thinking about that. I can understand how weird we must've seemed to you. But what about Robert's condition? Do you want to talk about that?'

It was so kind of her and, actually, she did want to talk about it. Maybe she could ask Charlotte the questions she was afraid to ask Robert. 'It's been a real shock. And I'm scared about what is going to happen. Be honest with me. How likely is it that I'm going to lose my husband?'

Clearly, Charlotte had been expecting this question. 'It's difficult to say. But, from his last tests, he would likely only have one to two years without the operation.'

One to two years. That was unthinkable. 'I'm going to persuade him to have the operation if I can. I know there's risks, but if it goes well, he should have a normal life after that, shouldn't he?'

Against Charlotte's advice, she'd been researching the condition online late into last night. In the end, the medical jargon had swum in front of her eyes and she'd fallen asleep with her reading glasses on and her mobile in her hand.

'Yes. If all goes well with his surgery, his prognosis should be very good.'

It was the 'if all goes well' that terrified her. Before going to sleep last night, Robert had repeated his desire to get all his affairs in order before 'going under the knife', as he'd so elegantly put it. For her, this seemed like tempting fate.

Also, they had more than themselves to consider in all of this. 'I'm dreading telling the girls.'

'I can imagine. I know how I'd feel if it was my dad.'

Looking at her now, Ellen could see the likeness to Ian. No wonder she'd felt Charlotte looked familiar.

She was also astute. 'I know you want to ask me about it.'

'What?' Ellen tried to look innocent.

'My dad not being my biological father. I know that Mum told you.'

Of course she had questions, but it would be rude to ask. 'It's none of my business. I can see how close you are to your dad.'

'I am. We always have been. Weirdly, my personality is

much more like his than my mum's. Of course, I have no idea if I'm like my biological father.'

She had said that Ellen could ask questions so she ventured one. 'You've never seen him at all?'

'Not that I can remember. Mum says that he was around for the first year after I was born. That he was actually quite taken with me when I was a baby. Then the second year he was in and out of our lives. I think there was some infidelity, which she hasn't gone into. And then he was gone. I do have a few pictures that she's given me, but I don't have any actual memories of my own.'

'And you've never been curious about meeting him?'

Charlotte considered the question. 'There was a time at medical college when we were looking at genes and gene therapy when I did wonder. Mum has never stood in my way, nor Dad. They both said they'd help me if I wanted to look for him. Not that it would be difficult to track him down, I'm sure. But there's something... I don't know. I get the feeling that he did something really bad to Mum. Worse than cheating. I think he really hurt her. And I don't think I want to go down that path. I wouldn't want to meet someone like that.'

Charlotte clearly had a strong moral compass. She wished Grace had one of those. 'I can understand how you feel.'

Flicking the ring pull on her mini can of diet coke, Charlotte looked too young to be so wise. 'Actually, other than Mum, and Robert, you're the only person I've met who has known my biological father.'

'Has your mum not told you anything about him?'

'I know he came from a wealthy family.'

She was right about that. Of everyone in that privileged group, Ian always had the most cash. He'd boast about the fact that, because his parents were divorced and he lived with his mother, his father's vast fortune hadn't been taken into account and he'd received a full maintenance grant – back in the day when those were a thing. While she was counting the pennies of her own grant to make sure she had enough for groceries before she went out for the night, he spent his entire term's money from the government on two Versace shirts.

She wasn't about to tell Charlotte any of this. Or about how arrogant he was, how gleeful in parading his wealth. 'Yes. I believe his family were well off. He went to a top school, I think.'

That was something else she wouldn't tell her. How he'd boasted about the fact he'd flunked his exams – *I was too busy partying* – but his father had paid for him to attend a 'crammer' on his year out. A college that basically spoon-fed facts into your short term-memory just before retaking the tests. 'That's why I ended up in this crap hole,' he used to say. His rich friends would laugh and nod their heads in understanding. Robert would frown and say nothing. Lucy would tell him he was a prick. Ellen would boil in her skin at his dismissiveness of the place she'd worked her backside off to attend.

Charlotte must know about his school because she nodded. 'What was he like? I mean, I think he must've been a bad person, but then I don't understand why my mum was with him.'

She had to tread carefully now. Having no idea what kind of history Lucy had woven for her daughter, she didn't want to be unravelling any stitches. 'Well, he could be a lot of fun. He was adventurous. Clever. Witty. I can imagine that was quite attractive.'

She didn't add that he and Lucy had been on and off more times than a light switch. She hadn't known why Lucy bothered with him. Coming from a wealthy family and a good school herself, she surely hadn't been dazzled by his easy life and spending habits. He was good looking, yes. But that wasn't enough to put up with the way he treated her sometimes.

'Do I look like him, do you think?'

146   EMMA ROBINSON

With her head tilted to the side, eyebrow raised, she could've been his double. But from what she'd seen of Charlotte so far – kind, attentive, caring – the resemblance was only skin deep. He didn't deserve any credit for this beautiful clever girl. 'You have his colouring. But your features are all your mum.'

Charlotte seemed to like that answer. 'Are your girls like you or Robert?'

'I'll show you.' Ellen never needed any persuading to show off her girls. Scrolling through her phone, she knew immediately which photo she wanted to show Charlotte. A picture of the four of them at dinner a few months ago.

Charlotte leaned in to look. 'Wow. They're both beautiful. I think your older daughter – Grace, is it? – looks like you. And the younger one is like Robert.'

'Abigail? Yes, she's his mini-me. She's the one at university with your sister.'

Charlotte rolled her eyes. 'Good luck to her. Emily is... well, she's a one-off. What does Grace do?'

'She works in the City. She's renting a house in London now, so we don't see as much of her as we'd like. I'm planning on calling her as soon as we get home.'

Robert was still adamant that he didn't want her to tell the girls anything yet and, while she agreed that it wasn't a conversation to be had over the phone, she wanted to get them both home as soon as they got back.

He'd been against that, too. 'Abigail can't come home; she's only been at university for a few days. This is an important time for her.'

Of course he was right. These first few days she'd be making the friendships that, even if they weren't the lifelong ones yet, would be the people to get her through those tricky first few weeks of being at university.

However, Grace would definitely have to be told straight away. But Ellen had called her twice last night and three times that morning before and after they'd arrived at Malaga airport. Grace wasn't picking up. 'I think she's still angry with me for what I said about Max.'

'What did you say?'

She'd given him a brief summary of their conversation. 'He's still married, Robert. I'm sure of it.'

'Less than twenty-four hours ago you thought I was having an affair with someone the same age as our daughter. Do you think you might have it wrong?'

He'd been teasing her, but this wasn't the same thing. 'Aren't you worried that she might be having a relationship with a married man? That she might break up a family?'

'Right now I'm more concerned about our family. Grace isn't silly. We have to trust that she knows what she's doing.'

Though his faith in their daughter was admirable, she worried that it was misplaced. There was a side to Grace that was... well, she wasn't as sensible as Charlotte, who was regarding her with a maturity and empathy in excess of her youth.

'I can imagine how you feel. It will be really scary for them. But they'll need to be told because they'll have to be tested.'

This was new information. 'What do you mean? Tested for the same thing that Robert has?'

Charlotte screwed up her nose as she nodded. 'I'm afraid so. Robert's condition can be hereditary.'

Ellen's heart flipped over in fear. Hereditary? The girls would have to be tested? Up until that moment, she hadn't known it was possible to be more terrified than she already was. But this was even worse.

TWENTY-FIVE

1999

Considering that she was a biology student, it had taken Ellen a surprisingly long time to realise that she was pregnant.

Stress, erratic eating and late-night study had sent her cycle all over the place, so she was barely aware that her period was late. Even the nausea didn't raise any concerns to begin with. It was her final year, she was studying every moment she could and she put it down to exhaustion and living off of freeze-dried noodles.

In fact, it wasn't until she was actually sick one morning, that she began to put two and two together until the possibility of a baby actually made three.

She was terrified about telling Robert. As a chemist, he'd already been offered a really great opportunity with a pharmaceutical company. Bored of the actual science, he was going into the business side of things and they were willing to fund an MBA while he was working for them. Of course, it didn't hurt that his father played golf with the CEO.

Ellen didn't have a job lined up. She'd thrown all of her energy into studying and was trying to juggle that with applying

WE BOTH HAVE SECRETS 149

for jobs. There was a careers fair coming up and she'd had all her hopes pinned on impressing someone there.

Not that she'd be impressing anyone with a green face and a faint aroma of vomit.

Lucy had been the one she'd told. The one who'd bought the pregnancy test on her behalf and had held her hand as they'd waited for the result. When that thin blue line appeared, she'd wept.

Lucy had told her that she didn't need to have a baby – *'This isn't 1950, Ellen. You get to choose'* – but Ellen hadn't known what she wanted. She'd known, though, that she had to tell Robert.

For him, it would've been a regular evening. He'd met her from the library, planning to catch the bus back together to where he was still living off campus. All the way back, with every jolt and hiss of the full bus, she felt the tension increasing. At the stop before theirs, a heavily pregnant lady got on and Robert stood to give her his seat. Wedged next to her, it was impossible not to consider whether this would be her future. Would Robert be as gentlemanly then?

As soon as they got off, Robert took her hand again. 'Straight to mine or do you fancy a pint at the pub on the corner?'

There would be other people at his house and she was still unable to tolerate the smell of beer. 'Actually, can we go for a walk in the park?'

He'd looked surprised but shrugged. 'Okay.'

There was no easy way to say the words that might change his life forever. No way to soften their impact. 'I'm pregnant.'

He stopped dead still and paled in front of her eyes. 'Pregnant?'

She nodded, then pointed at a bench a few steps away. 'Shall we sit down?'

He dropped heavily onto the seat of the bench and she perched beside him, waited for him to speak first. 'Are you absolutely sure?'

She nodded. 'I've done two tests.'

Lucy had waited in her room for her while she took both tests at once into the bathroom and did what she needed to do. Then they'd sat and watched them until the traitorous second line appeared.

A little colour came back into Robert's cheeks. He reached out and placed his hands over hers, which had been nervously shredding a tissue. 'How are you feeling about it? What do you want to do?'

That was the million-dollar question. 'I don't know. I keep going back and forth. Lucy thinks...'

She trailed off at the expression on his face. 'This is probably a situation where we can live without Lucy's opinion. What do *you* want to do? I'll support whatever you want.'

He still wasn't giving an opinion. 'Really? I mean, if I have a baby, what's that going to look like? For us?'

She'd tossed and turned all night thinking about it, careening from idealised set-ups with the two of them pushing a pram to nightmares of her alone with a screaming baby.

His eyes shone with an honesty that she desperately wanted to trust. 'We would be together. We'd make it work.'

But she wasn't sure that he'd actually thought this through. 'We're barely twenty, Robert. We were children ourselves not long ago.'

He shifted in his seat to face her. 'I know. But I also know that I love you and – for me at least – this was always on the cards at some point.'

She was amazed. 'You'd thought about that?'

He laughed. That deep rich laugh she loved so much. 'Of course. I've considered how I would propose to you, where we might live, how many kids we'd have. Haven't you?'

WE BOTH HAVE SECRETS

She smiled for the first time since she'd taken that test. 'Yes. I have, too. I've even imagined what kind of wedding we might have.'

His smile broadened. 'Yeah, that part I'm happy to leave to you. Unless you want to run away and get married on a beach somewhere. Then I'll have very positive thoughts.'

Though they'd talked about their ideal lives during lazy weekend mornings in bed, they'd never talked so openly about their joint future before. It was exciting. 'What about all our other plans. Careers? Travel?'

'We can still have careers. I already have a job lined up so money will be okay. With regards to travel, I covered a lot of countries during my gap year, so that one would be more of a sacrifice for you than me. Although we could also just strap the baby to our backs and take it with us.'

The baby. She hadn't dared to think about the actual baby that was growing inside of her. 'Do you really think we can do this? What about our parents?'

Her own mum and dad had sacrificed so much for her to be able to come to university. They'd been so proud of her. Would this ruin all their hopes and dreams?

But Robert had an answer for that, too. 'They're all going to be shocked, possibly disappointed. But then they will be grandparents and they'll love it. Just like we will. And we can show them that it won't change anything. It's just a bit quicker than we might have planned. We'll show everyone it can be done.' He nudged her. 'Even Lucy.'

Tears filled her eyes as she looked up into his. 'So, we're doing this? We're having a baby.'

He leaned in and punctuated every word with a kiss. 'We. Are. Having. A. Baby.'

She giggled beneath his lips. They were having a baby.

TWENTY-SIX

In the quiet waiting room, Ellen marvelled at the fact that Robert could get an appointment with his consultant the very next day after they'd flown home. The power of private healthcare. It had been a very different story for her own father fifteen years ago when he'd had to wait months between appointments for the respiratory problems that had eventually claimed him.

Around the pale-green walls, an assortment of mismatched armchairs gave the feel of an elderly person's living room. Aside from the receptionist, they were the only ones in the room. On the facing wall, above an ancient radiator, hung a large gilt-edged canvas of an old oak tree stretching out three branches from its thick strong trunk.

Although it had been good to get home yesterday, she'd barely slept a wink, thinking about this appointment today. She could only imagine how Robert must feel. She squeezed his hand. 'Are you okay? What's going through your mind?'

He returned the squeeze. 'Just thinking about the car insurance.'

She hadn't been expecting that. 'Why on earth are you thinking about that?'

He looked surprised at the question. 'I'm making a list. Of all the little things that you might not know need doing. The cars are on a multi-car policy. You need to call them in March. I need to put it on the list.'

Even though she shook her head at him in exasperation, her heart ached for all the little things that he did for their family that she never even considered. And also because he was thinking about a time when he wouldn't be able to do them. 'Please stop doing that.'

He shrugged. 'It helps me. To keep my mind busy.'

She could understand that, even if it was impossible for her to think about anything else right now. When she'd woken this morning, there'd been about five blissful seconds of being back in their own bed before she remembered where they were going today. Rolling onto her side, she'd watched the rise and fall of Robert's chest as if it were the most beautiful thing she'd ever seen.

To the left of the old oak tree, a door clicked open and swept across the deep pile beige carpet. A man strode towards them with his right hand ready to shake theirs. 'Robert. How are you doing? Charlotte tells me you had a bit of a fright?'

They were like this, men like Robert. Talking about the most terrifying moments as if they were trivial.

Robert shook his hand. 'You could say that. This is my wife, Ellen. Ellen, this is Mr Grayson.'

She'd forgotten that consultants were always 'Mister' rather than 'Doctor'. 'Hello. Pleased to meet you.'

Mr Grayson – the man holding their entire future in his hands – looked to be in his mid-fifties. Square-shouldered and ramrod straight, he wore an expensive suit with style. Though not conventionally handsome, his kind eyes and obvious charisma gave him a charm that made him attractive. His handshake was firm, confident. 'I'm very pleased to meet you, too. Come through.'

154   EMMA ROBINSON

The room they entered was exactly as she'd pictured a Harley Street doctor's office to look. A heavy mahogany desk, bookshelves with medical journals, a surgical bed in one corner with a curtain rail around it. He held out his hands for them to take the two seats on this side of the desk before sliding into his own. 'I know that Charlotte has already talked you through the test results. Would you like me to go through them again?'

After glancing briefly at Ellen, Robert shook his head. 'No, I think we both understand everything. I guess my only question is how soon you would recommend me having the surgery.'

Steepling his fingers, Mr Grayson leaned towards them, his face serious but gentle. 'If you are planning on going ahead with the surgery, my recommendation is that we get it done as soon as possible. We don't want to run the risk of another episode before we have a chance to resolve the problem.'

His use of euphemisms didn't make this any easier to hear. Robert's 'episode' in Lucy's living room had been terrifying to watch. Ellen swallowed the acid in her throat. 'How soon would that be?'

He picked up a pair or reading glasses and clicked the mouse in front of a computer screen. 'I've actually got a theatre booked for Monday which is no longer needed. We could slot you in there?'

It was surreal. He made it sound as if this was as easy as booking a show, although Ellen wouldn't let the reason for the theatre no longer being needed play on her mind.

Robert rubbed at his temples. 'That's pretty soon. Do you have anything later?'

She looked at him in exasperation. They weren't reserving a train ticket. 'The doctor has said you need to get this done as soon as possible, Robert.'

'I know. I know. It's just...'

Mr Grayson removed his glasses and tapped at his lips with one of their arms. 'I do understand. It's moving very fast. Your condition is an unpredictable one, Robert, and I would like to perform the surgery before there has been any further deterioration. But if you need some time to think about this, we can leave it for another week? I could book you in to come back to discuss it then?'

Robert turned to look at Ellen. Whatever he saw in her face must have decided him, because he turned back to Mr Grayson with a determined nod. 'No. Let's go with Monday.'

'Good. I'm going to ask my PA to email you the consent form to read through and then you'll sign it when you arrive for the surgery. If you have any other questions that arise over the weekend, please use the number I gave you.'

Ellen sent a silent prayer of thanks for the medical insurance supplied by Robert's company. He may have grown to hate that job, but this perk was definitely worth having. 'Charlotte mentioned that the condition was hereditary? We have two daughters.'

'Ah, yes.' The reading glasses were back on and he clicked away at the computer. 'They are twenty-six and eighteen?'

Ellen nodded. 'Yes. Our youngest has just started university.'

'At their age, there's not a huge rush to get them tested, but if you want, we could do it on the same day? On Monday?'

Monday? That was too soon. 'Not Monday. I think that would be a lot to cope with on the same day that Robert's in surgery.'

A clock on the wall behind them ticked loudly into the silence. Robert looked surprised. 'You said you wanted all of this dealt with as quickly as possible?'

How could she explain this in a way that wouldn't make him suspicious? 'I just need to focus on getting you better. Then we can get the tests done. It's too much all at once.'

Mr Grayson smiled kindly. 'Well, you can talk to your

156   EMMA ROBINSON

daughters about it and see how they feel. They are both adults so it will be their decision whether to get the test at all.'

Ellen hadn't even considered that. In her head, they were both still her babies. Though it made her anxious to think about it, Mr Grayson was right. Decisions like this were no longer hers to make.

Back outside in the late October sunshine, the hum of the traffic and chatter of pedestrians was jarring after the hushed tone of Mr Grayson's office. Everyone in the world was continuing their lives while, for them, the button had been paused on everything. Robert took a deep breath. 'So, that's it, then. Monday.'

Three days. Seventy-two hours to get themselves prepared for Robert's surgery. Had she done the wrong thing in pushing him to do it straight away? 'You're okay with that? You didn't want to put it off another week? I just thought—'

He held up a hand to stop her. 'You were right. I need to get it done. Then I'll be all fixed up and we won't have to worry any longer.'

From your lips to the ears of God. Wasn't that what her mum used to say? Ellen sent her own silent prayers with it. 'Good. And I'll book time off work so that I can wait on you hand and foot until you're fighting fit.'

His smile didn't quite reach his eyes. 'Sounds good to me.'

She knew how hard he was trying to be strong for her. 'Shall we go home? We have to call the girls. They need to come. I can collect Abigail in the morning.'

Finally, he gave in. Halfway. 'I know we need to tell them, but I don't want to drag Abigail back here so soon. Let's speak to Grace tomorrow and then we can go and see Abbie on Sunday. If she wants to come, we can bring her home with us on Sunday afternoon and then you can drop her back to Canterbury on Monday or Tuesday.'

WE BOTH HAVE SECRETS 157

The seamless transition from 'we' to 'you' wasn't lost on Ellen. Concerns about the operation prickled in her stomach. She wasn't going to argue with him now. Telling Grace first was a good idea. 'I'm going to call her now. She might be making weekend plans.'

Grace was still not answering calls from Ellen's mobile, so she left a voicemail. She tried to keep her voice free from anything that might worry her. 'Hi, Grace. It's Mum. Can you call me? I know you're still cross but something important has cropped up and we need you to come over.'

They were just about to leave when they heard their names called from behind and saw Charlotte hurrying towards them. In a suit and black court shoes, her hair in a sleek ponytail, she looked every inch the professional. 'Sorry, I was hoping to catch you on the way out. I've just seen the schedule. You're having the operation on Monday?'

'Yes. Mr Grayson thinks sooner rather than later.'

'Well, he would know. He's really good, Robert. The best. You're in very capable hands.'

That was good to hear. Ellen reached out and squeezed Charlotte's arm. 'Thank you for everything you've done. Much as I've complained about the old school network over the years, I am selfishly grateful that you were able to get Robert seen by Mr Grayson.'

Charlotte smiled. 'Me, too. It was really fortunate that you saw me with Mum that day. It must've been fate.'

Maybe it was fate that they'd met Lucy all of those years ago. 'And fortunate that your mum went to the same posh school as Mr Grayson.'

She'd meant it as a joke, to lighten the sombre mood, but Charlotte frowned. 'It was Robert who went to school with Mr Grayson, wasn't it?'

She looked at Robert for confirmation and he nodded. 'Yes. Not at the same time as I was there, though.'

Charlotte smiled at Ellen. 'Mum didn't go to a school like that. She went to a regular state school.'

Surely she must have that wrong? It was Ellen's turn to frown. 'Are you sure about that? When were at university, she definitely said she went to a private school?'

Charlotte laughed. 'Definitely sure. She used it as a way to chastise me whenever I didn't work hard enough at school. Reminded me how fortunate I was. You must be confusing her with someone else.'

Ellen definitely wasn't confusing her with someone else, but she didn't want to say anything critical about Lucy. It was strange, though. Why would she lie?

Before she could ask anything else, her phone rang in her hand. It was Grace, calling her back. She took a deep breath and answered.

TWENTY-SEVEN

Grace lived in a house share in Walthamstow with two other girls who also worked in the City. One of them was a self-confessed Mrs Hinch fan with a cleaning obsession, so Ellen was expecting the sparkling surfaces and the wave of Zoflora when Grace opened the door. She looked immaculate too, as if she'd just dressed up for a night out. Robert reached out and gave her a huge hug. 'You look lovely, Gracie.'

'Thanks, Dad. Although in the interests of full disclosure, Max is coming to take me out in a couple of hours so I've been getting ready for that.'

Her greeting of Ellen was less warm. 'Hi, Mum.'

Grace was a sulker. She always had been. Maybe she got it from Ellen who, although she wouldn't exactly call it sulking, did find it difficult to let things go when someone hurt her. Abigail and Robert were the opposite. They'd moved on from an argument almost before you'd finished having it.

Today, though, Ellen couldn't bite her lip and let it pass. 'Can I have a hug, too?'

Surprise on her face, Grace opened her arms and took her in. Though she'd been taller than Ellen for years, it still felt odd that this fully grown woman was her baby. Robert was right, she shouldn't meddle in her affairs, however much she believed she knew better. 'Where's Max taking you? Somewhere nice?'

Either the power of the hug or excitement about her forthcoming evening trumped the desire to punish her mother for speaking out of turn. 'I don't know yet. He said it's a surprise. I'm really excited about it. Come into the kitchen, I'll make coffee.'

Also pristine, the kitchen had all the hallmarks of a trio of twenty-something girls with an Instagram fixation. A glittery kettle, matching toaster and six mugs lined up in order of how dark a shade of pink they were. From one angle, it would look like the kitchen of a wealthy woman; pan out and it was the size of a broom cupboard.

'It's nice to have you over, but you don't often come this way. Why couldn't you just tell me the news over the phone yesterday?'

Before replying, Robert glanced at Ellen as if to warn her. They'd talked about this last night, how much to tell the girls. He didn't want to worry them more than was necessary, while she knew that they'd want the whole truth.

He kept his voice light and smooth. The same tone he'd used when he'd told a four-year-old Grace that there were no such things as monsters. 'Let's wait until we're sitting down with our drinks. Shall we?'

Grace's head turned quickly in their direction, the spoon of coffee hovering over the mug. 'Is it something serious? Should I be worried?'

This was a phrase Ellen used to use all the time. She recognised Grace's request to be prepared for any emotional upheaval, her need to know what was coming. They were so alike. It's why they were so close and also why they fell out. She wished again she could protect her from the worry about

WE BOTH HAVE SECRETS 161

Robert. 'Make the coffee, sweetheart and then we can tell you everything.'

Grace opened her mouth to push them for an explanation – another reason they often fell out – but must've seen something in their expressions to make her wait.

In the sitting room, she perched on the edge of her seat. Coffee untouched on the long low table that ran parallel with the sofa. 'What is it?'

Robert took a deep breath. 'They've discovered an anomaly in my heart. I need to have surgery.'

This is the conclusion he'd come to last night. Make the description brief and try to keep the emotion out of it.

Even so, Grace's eyes widened. 'Your heart. That sounds serious, Dad. What kind of operation? Is it dangerous? When will you have it?'

Torn between wanting to let Robert finish and moving onto the other sofa to console her daughter, Ellen sat on her hands and did as she'd promised and let Robert explain.

'It's a heart condition that I've probably always had, but now they know it's there, they want to get it fixed as soon as possible. I'm going to have the surgery on Monday.'

Grace's mouth fell open. 'Monday? This Monday? Two days' time? It must be really serious if they're rushing you in that fast.'

It amazed Ellen to see how calm Robert could be, how far down he could push his own concerns to ensure that he protected his daughter from her own. 'It's the private healthcare that I get through work. They do everything fast. You should see how quickly they made me a coffee when I got there.'

Robert's attempt at humouring her out of her concern wasn't going to cut it. 'Dad. I'm not a child. What's going on? Is this serious? Mum?'

The fear in her eyes as she turned her attention to Ellen forced her out of her seat and next to her daughter in moments.

It was all very well Robert saying that she needed to make it seem as if this was all okay, that rushing to comfort Grace would make her feel as if there really was something to be scared of. But there *was* something to be scared of and she couldn't see her daughter anxious and not try to soothe her. With her arm around her, she ignored Robert's frown and spoke softly. 'It is a big operation, sweetheart, but your dad is very fit and healthy and strong. He's going to be okay. We need to get the operation over and done with on Monday and then we can all help to get him better.'

Grace chewed on her lip. Knowing that tears were about to come, Ellen reached for her handbag and pulled out a packet of tissues. When she took it, Grace held it under her eyes to save her mascara. 'Does Abbie know yet?'

Robert shook his head. 'No. I'm still undecided whether to tell her. She's only just got to uni.'

Grace's fear flipped quickly to outrage. 'You have to tell her.' She turned to Ellen. 'Tell him, Mum.'

It had always been this way. It was always fun and games between the girls and Robert. He was the jokey one. The easy one. Until he imposed a rule they didn't like and then they were straight back to Ellen to fight their corner. Which she always did. 'We are going to tell her. Robert, you agreed.'

He ran his hands through his hair. 'I know. I just don't want to. We'll go and see her tomorrow. You can come if you like?'

Now it was Grace's turn to look torn. 'I would, but I'm just not sure what's happening with Max. This surprise tonight might be an overnight thing. I'll come to yours tomorrow night though? Stay over the night before your operation. Be with you both? And Abbie if she wants to come home?'

Robert started to tell her there was no need, but Ellen rubbed her back. 'That would be lovely. I'll make a lasagne.'

Now the worst of the news was over, they drank their coffee and told Grace about their time in Malaga – minus the accusations of infidelity. Ellen explained that Charlotte was Lucy's daughter.

'I think I should meet this Charlotte. If Abigail is friends with her sister and you are friends with her mum, maybe the two of us would hit it off?'

'No.' The word was out of Ellen's mouth before she could stop it. She tried to soften it. 'I mean, I don't think that's a good idea. You're very different.'

Grace laughed. 'I was only joking, Mum. Although, I can't help wondering why you're so opposed. Are you ashamed of me?'

'No. Of course not. It's just... well she's got a very busy job which takes up all her time. And, to be honest, Lucy and I are not particularly close any longer, she did keep rather a huge secret from me about your dad. And I'm not sure that her other daughter will be a particularly good influence on Abbie. I'm grateful for everything Charlotte has done, but I think we need to create a bit of distance between us and them.'

Shifting back in his chair, Robert looked at her in surprise. 'Really? I think we have a lot to be grateful for. And you and Lucy were so close at university. I don't think you can hold this against her. Give it another chance.'

Old jealousies crackled in Ellen's stomach. 'What about the fact she lied about the school she went to? Don't you think that's strange?'

Robert shrugged. 'We were kids. And, anyway, Charlotte might have it wrong. Or she might have gone to a state school for a short while. In the grand scheme of things, it's not really important, is it?'

Not in the light of what was going on right now it wasn't important, no. But it was a pretty strange lie to tell. And to sustain for the whole three years they'd studied together. She thought again of Lucy and Ian. How they had looked down their noses at everyone.

Before she could reply, Grace's mobile buzzed on the table in front of them and a picture of her and Max lit up the screen, before she snatched it up. 'I'll just take this in the hall. Won't be a minute.'

Grace pulled the door closed behind her, but they could still hear her side of the conversation. 'Hey. Hello. Are you on your way? My parents are here. Maybe you can come and say hello and meet them?'

Robert raised his eyebrows at Ellen. Were they about to meet the infamous Max at long last? She wasn't sure this was the right time, but they were here now. It would be impossible to leave without making it obvious. And she was intrigued to see him in the flesh.

Although it turned out from the rest of the conversation that this wasn't going to happen. Grace's voice became more and more disappointed with each word. 'Why?... But you said you had something booked for us... I know that, but... well, I can come and spend the day with the three of you... I see... Yes... No, it's fine... I understand... I love you, too.'

There were a few moments between the end of the call and her return. Clearly, she needed to compose herself. Ellen wasn't a violent woman, but she could have kicked this man for leaving her daughter hanging like this, letting her down at the last minute. And the kick would've been hard.

Grace's face was like thunder when she came back. 'Well, I don't know if you could hear all that, but Max has cancelled. His bloody ex-wife has decided to go away and he has to have the children on short notice.'

Again, Ellen wondered whether the 'bloody wife' was an 'ex' at all. But this wasn't the time to go into that again. 'I'm sorry, love. I know you were looking forward to it.'

In reply, Grace clapped her hands together and her dark expression cleared. 'So I can come and see Abbie with you after all.'

TWENTY-EIGHT

The M2 was full of lorries on their way down to Dover and their car felt very small in the middle of them. They'd travelled this road so many times over the years since graduation, for family trips to Whitstable and Broadstairs, that it was as familiar as their own street. Under any other circumstances, Ellen would have relished a trip to see Abigail with Grace in the back seat of the car. But it was tough to stay upbeat when most of the conversation was about how they were going to break the news, punctuated with the buzz of text messages going back and forth between Grace and Max.

One of the things they'd debated was where to tell her. A restaurant would be too public if she – inevitably – got upset. The shared lounge in her accommodation wouldn't be suitable for the same reason and her own bedroom was too small: they'd be standing there like sardines in a very sad tin. In the end, Ellen suggested a walk.

That made Grace laugh. 'A good old family walk, do you remember, Dad?'

Robert grinned at her in the rear-view mirror. He was in the passenger seat, Ellen had insisted that she drive. 'I certainly do. Every Sunday afternoon.'

'It'll be good for us.' Grace used the high-pitched upper class accent she always used when she was imitating Ellen, even though it sounded nothing like her. 'We shall walk every Sunday as a family.'

'How long did that one last?' Robert asked her.

'Okay, you two. Very funny.' They all liked to mock the many times she'd come up with a plan for them to do something together every week – Saturday badminton, Friday film night, Sunday walks – and then be the first one to forget to do it by about week three. 'Anyway, scrap that idea, I don't think you should be walking anywhere at the moment, Robert.'

That sobered the mood in the car pretty quickly. With no better suggestion, she did reluctantly agree to collect Abigail from the campus and drive to a nearby country park on the strict understanding that they would find a bench somewhere quiet to talk to her.

When Abbie got in the car, she looked pale and lethargic. It was likely a case of burning the candle at both ends, but it made her seem so vulnerable, that Ellen dreaded her reaction to what was coming. 'It's good to see you, sweetheart.'

'You, too, Mum. I'm sorry again about shouting down the phone.'

Abbie had sent a text to apologise the very next day, and so much had happened since, that Ellen had quite literally forgotten about it. 'Don't worry about that. It was my fault, too. All forgotten.'

The park they'd chosen was less than a ten-minute drive away and Grace did a sterling job of keeping the conversation on safe topics until they'd reached the park and found a bench beneath a large tree, secluded from the view of the main path.

As before, Ellen let Robert break the news, but this time she stayed right next to Abbie, with Grace behind her. Robert was

WE BOTH HAVE SECRETS 167

on the other side and took hold of Abbie's hands as he explained as simply as he could what was about to happen and why.

When she gasped, Ellen reached an arm around her trembling shoulders. Her voice was no more than a whisper. 'Are you going to die, Dad? Please don't die.'

'Hey, hey. It's going to be okay. I'm going to come through this.'

As she started to cry, Ellen pulled her close. How frail her body seemed as it was wracked with sobs. Grace reached out, too, and then Robert wrapped his strong arms around them all.

Abigail was quiet all the way home. When they got indoors, and she was hanging her coat up on the peg, Ellen noticed again how pale she looked. 'Are you okay, sweetheart?'

She avoided Ellen's eye. 'I'm fine. I'm just worried about Dad.'

That was, of course, understandable and to be expected. But Ellen's maternal instinct told her there was something more. 'I know, love. But are you sure there's not something else on your mind, too?'

Flushing pink, Abbie scowled, and tears burst from her eyes. 'Can't I just be worried about Dad? This is terrifying.'

As she ran up the stairs, Ellen started to follow her, but Grace caught her arm. 'Leave her for now. I'm going to call Max and then I'll go in and chat to her.'

Ellen watched her follow her sister up the stairs. Like they'd entered a time tunnel, it felt such a short time since this was normal, that they were both home here, in their bedrooms next door to one another. Sometimes the nostalgia for when they were young was almost a physical pain in her chest.

Tea. That's what she needed. In the kitchen, as she waited for the kettle to boil, she ran her eyes down the whiteboard list of things she had to do. *Call Katie. Book car valet. Buy nail polish remover*. Inconsequential things that filled her life with a million tasks that didn't matter.

By the time she got back to the sitting room, Robert was shifting through piles of papers and flicking through a ring binder. Pushing a few pages to the side, she slid his mug onto the table. 'What are you doing?'

On a lined pad, he wrote something down. 'I'm just making a list of all the bills that aren't covered by direct debits. And the dates for the car MOT.'

She thought he'd stopped with this. 'Please will you stop doing that?'

'I need to.'

His voice was so sharp, it made her freeze for a moment. When he spoke again, it was softer. 'I need to, Ellen. I have to have something else to think about.'

She sank down on the couch beside him. 'It's going to be okay tomorrow.'

When he looked up at her, for the first time she saw raw fear in his eyes. 'It feels real, you know. Now that we've told the girls, it feels real.'

She'd felt the same thing coming home in the car this afternoon. Glancing in her rear-view mirror, she'd seen Grace distracting Abigail by telling her a funny story from a night out. Abbie tried to go along with it, but she'd looked as if she might collapse at any moment. 'I know, love. I'm scared, too.'

He covered his face with his hands, pulling his palms down as if he could wipe the fear from his face. 'I'm not ready, you know. I've still got so much life to live. We've got so much life to live. Together.'

In the last few days, every time Ellen had thought that she might lose him, she'd pushed it from her mind. Now, with only hours to go before she needed to drive him to the hospital tomorrow morning, there was no getting away from it. There was a possibility that he would go into that operating theatre and not come out.

She had to try and stay positive. 'The odds are still really good, Robert. And you've got no choice. We've got no choice.'

He nodded. 'I know that, but it doesn't make it any easier.'

Was there any point trying to be a cheerleader? 'I do understand, though. I feel like we've wasted so much time.'

That made him smile. 'I'm not sure our parents would agree with you. I don't think we could've got pregnant and married much earlier than we did.'

It was like he'd pressed a bruise. 'Do you regret it? Starting a family so young? Getting married when we did?'

He shook his head. 'Not for a minute.'

It was stupid of her to ask. What was he going to say? Of course he'd tell her what she wanted to hear. 'There are other things that I wish we'd done differently. I wish we'd got round to the things we said we'd do. Those holidays we'd said we'd take when the girls were grown, the meals out we promised ourselves. We did none of it.'

'I know. I guess it always felt like there were other things that needed doing. Work or maintenance on the house.'

'Dinners with colleagues you didn't even like. Parties we didn't want to go to. All the stuff I thought I *should* do meant that we didn't do the things we wanted to do.'

He nodded, then something seemed to occur to him. 'Did you really think I might be having an affair with Lucy? Or Charlotte? Seriously?'

She was embarrassed to think of it now. 'I don't know. I know it sounds crazy, but I was so confused about what was going on. And you've really been pulling away from me the last few months.'

'I know, I think I was just up in my own head about it. Trying to work it out, trying to find a solution, a way to minimise the damage on your life and the girls' lives.'

'We're a team, we should've worked it out together.'

He reached for her hands. 'I'm sorry. About all of this. The keeping it secret and the fact you've got to go through all this worry. And the girls…'

His face creased and she tightened her grip on his hands. 'None of this is your fault.'

For a few moments, they sat there in silence. Then his voice was so quiet that she could barely hear it. 'I know that you don't want to talk about it, but if the worst happens tomorrow and I don't make it—'

'No!' She'd said that word more in the last two days that in the previous year, but she couldn't even begin to think about that happening. 'Please don't say it, Robert. I can't bear it.'

He took a deep breath. 'Well, I won't say that. But I will say that I want you to have a friend. And Lucy and you were such good friends. She'd be there for you. I know it.'

Would she? 'Maybe. I'll consider it. But for now, I just want to focus on you.'

He smiled at her. 'I think I want to focus on a chicken Madras.'

That she could do. 'I'll get the menu. I need to plug my phone in before the battery dies, too.'

The menus were pinned up inside a cupboard in the kitchen. She unpinned the one for their local Indian restaurant and then rifled through the drawer for a phone charger. Just as she plugged it in, it rang in her hand. It was a UK mobile number that she didn't recognise. 'Hello?'

'Hi Ellen, it's Lucy. I'm back in the UK, how's things?'

She didn't really want to go into everything, but Lucy had been kind. 'Okay. We've told the girls.'

'That must've been hard. I messaged Robert earlier and he mentioned that the operation was tomorrow.'

For all of Robert telling her that Lucy was her friend, it seemed very much as if it was Robert she was more interested in speaking to. 'Yes. Our girls are both here tonight. We were about to order some dinner.'

'Good. I was wondering if you'd like some company tomorrow? I know that you'll be looking after everyone else and I thought I could come and look after you?'

That surprised her. 'That's very kind. But I have the girls here. I'll be fine.'

Lucy didn't give up. 'I'll be honest with you, Ellen. Robert asked me to keep an eye on you and check you were okay. I won't be in your way, but I can come and make dinner or something. Just help out.'

And, just like she had done all those years ago, Ellen gave in to Lucy, did things her way. Muscle memory making her revert to being the follower. 'Okay. Thanks. I'll text you my address.'

As soon as she ended the call, she sent the address through before she forgot. Maybe it would be a good thing to have Lucy here tomorrow. Someone else in the house might force her and the girls not to wallow in fear and worry.

Still, it wasn't lost on Ellen how ironic it was that Lucy would be here on a day that might change their whole lives. Because hadn't she been there when Ellen's life had been upended the first time?

TWENTY-NINE

Robert had to be in early the following morning. Both Grace and Abigail had insisted they get up to see him off. In her pyjamas, Abbie still looked white faced and anxious. Grace hadn't had much luck in getting her to open up last night. Maybe it actually was Robert's operation and nothing else. Nobody could blame her for that.

She'd certainly attempted to be upbeat at dinner the night before. Robert had ordered enough food for about eight people. 'Well, this is nice. Having everyone home.'

Grace had done her best to keep the mood buoyant too. 'Yeah, it's a bit extreme though, Dad. You could've just said you wanted to see us.'

Ellen had tried, really tried, but – with all the people she loved most in the world around the dinner table – all she could think about was how much she had to lose. More than once, she'd escaped to the kitchen to have a little cry. The third time, Grace followed her out there and caught her with a tissue at her eyes. She held out her arms and they cried together.

Now Grace was putting a brave face on it, her arm around Abigail who was distinctly wobbly. 'I love you, Daddy.'

WE BOTH HAVE SECRETS   173

'Hey, hey, Abs. I'm going to be fine. Come here.' He enveloped both the girls in a hug, his own eyes screwed tightly closed to prevent his emotions from escaping him.

Ellen clutched the car keys so tight that they dug into her hand. 'We need to go.'

Never a fan of hospitals, Ellen's stomach started to tighten from the moment they stepped inside. This was a private hospital with doors that hushed closed and carpet tiles that softened footfall, but there was still the air of disinfectant which hit the back of her throat. She was able to accompany Robert to his room and stay with him while the anaesthetist and a nurse came to introduce themselves, before Mr Grayson and Charlotte arrived. Then Mr Grayson went through the procedure with Robert one more time before turning to Ellen. 'You are very welcome to stay here as long as you like, but it will take a while so, if you want to go home, we can call you as soon as he's out.'

They'd already agreed that she would stay home with the girls. 'I'll wait until Robert goes down and then I'll leave, thank you.'

He nodded and placed a hand on Robert's shoulder. 'I'll see you down there.'

Charlotte hung behind to speak to them briefly. 'I won't be in the room. Because I know you, Mr Grayson didn't think it was appropriate. But I'll be here so, if you want to know anything, Ellen, you can just call me.'

Her kindness raised a lump in Ellen's throat. 'Thank you. I appreciate that.'

'Oh, and my mum said just call her when you're on your way home and she will come over. She said not to get any food for lunch because she'll bring it.' She turned to Robert. 'An orderly will be down to collect you in about five minutes. See you on the other side.'

He nodded. 'Thank you.'

With a little wave, she was gone. Ellen rose from the seat

she'd taken and stood in front of Robert. In his hospital gown, he looked so vulnerable. The fear she'd been fighting all morning threatened to get the better of her. 'You'd better come through this, Mr Cooper.'

'I'll do my very best, Mrs Cooper.'

'Do you promise?'

'Of course. When have I ever lied to you?'

She buried her head in his neck and let the tears come. Please let him be right. As far as she knew it was true that he'd never lied to her before.

She only wished she could say the same.

When she got home, there was a red sports car she didn't recognise parked outside. For one horrible moment, she thought that Grace's Max had chosen this moment to reveal himself – it was the kind of flashy expensive vehicle she would assume he'd choose – so she was almost relieved when Grace opened the front door and told her who it belonged to. 'Your friend Lucy is here.'

Resisting the instinctive urge to scold Grace for answering the door to strangers, she followed her through to the sitting room where Grace was holding a mug of steaming coffee and talking to Abbie. 'Lucy? Didn't we arrange that I would call you?'

Even in a cold autumnal England, Lucy carried an air of continental glamour. A black cashmere dress emphasised her willowy frame. 'I know. I'm sorry. But I was so worried about Robert that I didn't know what to do with myself, so I thought I might as well come. I brought pastries.'

She nodded towards a plate of croissants and cinnamon swirls as if they were a good enough reason for her to come so early. 'Thank you.'

'It's been lovely to meet your girls. Abbie has been very loyal and not dished any dirt on my erstwhile progeny.'

Abbie blushed at this. 'Emily has been really great. Honestly.'

Lucy patted her knee before turning back to Ellen. 'How was Robert going in?'

'Upbeat. Positive. Sure he was going to be fine. You know Robert.'

She said this more for the girls' sake than for Lucy's, but Lucy nodded. 'I do. Now, come and sit with your daughters and I'll make you a drink. I'm here to wait on you all today. Whatever you need.'

Before she could argue that her hands were itching for something to do, Lucy had disappeared into her kitchen, so she did as she was told and flopped down on the couch next to Abigail. Grace perched on the arm of the opposite sofa. 'How was Dad? Did the doctor say it was all going to be okay?'

'He said he was confident that your dad was in the best possible hands. It might take a while, but we'll hear in a few hours.'

Abigail snuggled in close to Ellen's side and she snuck an arm around her. She'd always been the more cuddly of the two girls. Maybe because she was the baby. Her fear right now made her voice as a soft as a small child's. 'I'm really scared, Mum. I've been looking online and this is a really serious operation. More serious than Dad made it sound yesterday.'

How could she be cross that Abbie had gone against their advice not to research Robert's condition when she had done the same thing?

Lucy reappeared from the kitchen with a cup for Ellen. It was so strange to have her here; like the past and present had collided. 'You need to eat something, too. Keep your strength up. When Robert comes out he's going to have you all running around after him, so make the most of it now.'

Her positivity was welcome.

'When will we have to be tested?' Grace had slipped onto the sofa now and was dangling her legs over the arm. 'I'll need to book another day off work.'

Her company had been very kind when she'd called them this morning to explain what was going on. She didn't want to think about their scans on top of worrying about Robert. It might tip her over the edge. 'There's no rush. The doctor said that you're too young for it to have an effect yet, even if you do have the same condition.'

Abigail peeled herself away and frowned at Ellen. 'But surely it's better to find out as soon as possible?'

Grace nodded. 'Yes, I agree. Don't you always say it's better to know what you're facing?'

Ellen chewed her lip. That was hard to argue against. 'I just don't want to put you both through that when you've already got your dad to worry about.'

'Why? Is it going to hurt?'

For a tiny moment. Ellen considered employing the same underhand tactics as when she'd told a twelve-year-old Grace that having your ears pierced was agony in the hope it would stop her from asking for them. But that would've been cruel. 'No. It's a blood test and a scan. I meant mentally.'

'To be honest, I think it would be better for me to know the truth one way or the other. What about you, Abs?'

Abbie nodded at her sister. 'Yes. I'd rather know the truth.'

Unasked for, Lucy nodded. 'It's always better to know the truth.'

The way she stared at Ellen as she said it made her suspicious. What was she trying to suggest?

For the next hour or so, the four of them stayed in the sitting room chatting and trying to distract themselves from what was happening at the hospital nine miles away. It wasn't until almost midday, when both the girls had drifted away – Grace to speak to Max again and Abbie to text her friends – that Ellen and Lucy were alone. Lucy was preparing lunch in the kitchen as Ellen leaned against the counter and remembered to ask her the question that'd bothered her since the day before.

'Did Charlotte mention that we saw her yesterday? At the surgery?'

'Yes, she did.'

'She's a lovely girl. You must be very proud.'

When she spoke about her children, Lucy's face took on a softness. 'We are. She's very driven too. I think she's got a great career ahead of her in medicine.'

'She said something strange, actually, which surprised me.'

Lucy raised a perfectly shaped eyebrow. 'Oh yes?'

'It was about you. About your school.'

If Ellen hadn't been scrutinising Lucy for a reaction, she might have missed the microscopic pause before she returned to hollowing out the avocado with a dessert spoon. Her voice – well-spoken, almost accentless – gave nothing away 'That's a strange thing to talk about out of the blue.'

'Yes, it just came up because I was talking about being grateful for the old boys' network in terms of Robert being seen so quickly. Ironic really when you think how much the concept irritated me when we were at university.'

Avocado in the palm of her hand, Lucy was working at excavating the stone from the soft green flesh. 'Yes. I remember.'

'And the thing is that I made a mistake saying that you'd been to school with Mr Grayson and when Charlotte corrected me, she said that you'd been to a state school. Which obviously confused me.'

The avocado stone was released and dropped onto the chopping board with a woody thump. 'I'm not sure that that even matters anymore, does it? School was a very long time ago for both of us.'

She was right, it didn't matter, but Ellen was curious. 'So you did go to a state school? Not a private one?'

Picking up a square of kitchen roll to wipe her hands, Lucy looked at Ellen. 'Yes. I attended my local school.'

This was so weird. 'But I always assumed you were like the others. Clarissa and Petra. Robert. Ian. You knew people that they knew. You had stories in common. You said you'd been to private school.'

She was too embarrassed to admit that this one of the reasons she's always been jealous of Lucy. That she'd assumed Lucy had much more in common with Robert than she could ever have. Lucy just shrugged. 'A good imagination. And I knew someone who'd been to the school. She was the daughter of a client of my father's who we'd seen frequently enough to become friends before they moved to New Zealand. She'd talked about the school and her friends a great deal, so it was very easy to pretend that I'd been there, too. Does it matter to you?'

Ellen started to laugh. All those years she'd felt like the only one. An outsider. And all that time, Lucy was just... making it up? No, it didn't matter. Back then it had felt so important. But now, in the grand scheme of life, it was the most insignificant thing in the world. 'I would never have guessed. You should've got an Oscar. How did you keep it up? And why did you do it?'

Before Lucy could answer, the door to the sitting room swung open and a tearful Abigail flew in. 'Oh Mum, I've done something really stupid,' and she burst into tears.

THIRTY

Lucy stayed in the kitchen to give them some privacy while Ellen led Abigail into the sitting room and onto to the sofa. She brushed her hair away from her swollen red eyes. 'What is it, sweetheart?'

Abbie had a fistful of tissue, which she picked at as she spoke. 'I made such an idiot of myself, Mum. I was drunk and...'

She collapsed into tears again and fell against Ellen who held her close, hoping so hard that this wasn't going to be as bad as her mind thought it could be. Though it only took about a minute for Abigail to regain enough control to speak, it felt more like an hour.

Wiping at her face with the tissue, she began again. 'There was a special offer on shots of Tequila Rose. You know that one that tastes like milkshake?'

Ellen didn't, but that clearly wasn't the important part of the story. 'Yes, I think so.'

'Well, we were with these boys, there were three of them, and they were spending so much money on trays of these shots and – literally – it was like drinking strawberry milkshake and I didn't really realise how alcoholic they were.'

180   EMMA ROBINSON

This was exactly the kind of thing Ellen had been worried about. She didn't want to hear any more – this was going to end badly – but she forced herself to ask. 'What happened, sweetheart?'

Abbie sniffed. 'It hit me all at once. To begin with, I wasn't drunk at all – well, maybe a little bit tipsy – but then it was like I'd run into a wall. Bang. I could barely stand up.'

From the look on Abbie's face, there was worse to come. A cold fear trickled down Ellen's spine. 'What happened?'

'My memory is really patchy, but I was outside and there was one of the boys and we were... I don't really know how to say it... we weren't having sex exactly but his hands were everywhere and... there were people there, walking past. People saw me, Mum. Other students, people in my classes. And then he called a taxi, I think.'

By now, Ellen's heart was racing in her chest. Her mind pulling ahead to the worst possible outcome. She wanted to support her daughter, was trying not to look shocked or worried or anything else that might make her suspect a judgement that Ellen didn't feel. But she did feel physically sick, and angry and violent and a whole host of other emotions. 'Did you go home with him?'

She shook her head. 'Emily just grabbed me. I don't know where she came from. But she pulled me away from him and, I think she yelled at him, and then she bundled me into the taxi and took me home again.'

Breathe. Had she not taken in any oxygen for the last minute? She could come back down from the ceiling now that she knew that the worst hadn't happened. 'Thank God for Emily.'

'She is a good friend, but Mum, I feel so stupid and... humiliated. I don't know who saw me. They might be people in my classes. And I don't know what state I was in. I can't bear it.'

As if it were an emotional muscle memory, Ellen knew

everything her daughter felt. 'It's okay, baby. I know it was a horrible experience, but you don't need to be ashamed. I bet no one knew it was you and, even if they did, they'll forget by the next day. I'm more concerned about dealing with the boy who took advantage of you when you were drunk.'

She shook her head. 'He was drunk too, I think. I don't know that he was any more in control than I was.'

Except he was sober enough to call a taxi, Ellen thought. But she didn't want to make Abbie feel any worse right now.

'Well, you had a lucky escape. I'm just so grateful that Emily was there.'

She nodded. 'I want to tell her mum that. I know she makes jokes about Emily being wild, but she's a really good person. I want to tell her that.'

Placing a cool hand on Abbie's hot face, Ellen smiled. 'Well, you can tell her, she's in the next room.'

Abbie wrinkled her nose. Now the worry had lifted a little, her beautiful innocent face was as open as a flower. 'Can you tell her for me?'

She was still so shy. Gently, Ellen nudged her. 'I can.'

Grace opened the door to the sitting room gently. 'Have you told Mum?'

Abbie nodded. 'Yes.'

'And did she think you were the worst person in the world?'

Abbie looked up at Ellen and smiled. 'No.'

'See, I told you.'

Ellen wrapped her arms around her baby girl and kissed the top of her head. 'You can always tell me anything.' She reached for Grace who slipped in next to her and joined the hug. 'Both of you.'

Her heart swelled in her chest. It was so wonderful to have her beautiful clever girls here together. And she loved that Grace had been a listening ear for Abigail. That she'd steered her towards opening up to Ellen.

182 EMMA ROBINSON

Grace's head rested on Ellen's shoulder. 'We know that we can tell you anything. And what I want to tell you right now is... why do you not have any snacks in this house?'

Abigail sat upright. 'Yes. There's nothing. This has become an ingredients house.'

'What the heck is that?'

'All the food is ingredients. You have to make it into something. You can't just eat it.'

'I've got apples. And bananas.'

Abigail rolled her eyes. She was back to herself again. 'Fruit doesn't count.'

'Well, your dad and I have been trying to eat healthily, so we haven't been buying snack food.'

Grace snatched up Ellen's car keys from the coffee table. 'We definitely need some sugar and complex carbs. If you're okay here with Lucy, Abbie and I can go for a drive and get some?'

She could tell that Grace was itching to do something. 'Good idea. Get something for me.'

Now Abbie kissed her cheek, too. 'I'll just go and grab my phone.'

'Don't bother. You'll just be checking it to see if anyone else saw you that night. Give yourself a break from it.' Grace waved her own phone at Ellen. 'You can call us on mine if you hear anything about Dad.'

'Will do.'

As soon as the front door closed, Ellen rested her elbows on her knees and let her face fall into her palms. The very thought of what could've happened to Abbie that night made her cold with fear. This was exactly the kind of thing she'd lain awake worrying about the week before they'd taken her to Canterbury. Robert had told her not to worry. But Robert was one of the good guys. Had always been one of the good guys. He didn't know what could happen. He didn't know.

WE BOTH HAVE SECRETS   183

All around the living room – on the sideboard or hung from the wall – photographs of the girls at every stage from toothy toddler through self-conscious teen to young woman smiled out at her. Every stage had had its own joys and its own difficulties. Knowing that they had both become such wonderful people made her proud and grateful.

There was a tentative knock on the door and then it was pushed open to reveal a mug, followed by Lucy. 'I did consider a glass of wine but I figured it was too early, so it's just more tea, I'm afraid.'

Ellen accepted it with a smile, the heat from the mug almost burning her icy hands. 'Did you hear any of that?'

Lucy shook her head. 'I was calling Joe. Giving him an update. He's at the house in Malaga.'

It felt like an age ago that she and Robert flew out there to stay with them. So much had changed since then. 'Abbie had a bad experience. With a boy. She was drunk. But your Emily was a hero. She got her out of there.'

A smile tweaked at the corners of Lucy's mouth, even though her eyebrows raised in disbelief. 'Really?'

Ellen sipped at her tea. It was hot and bitter and welcome. 'Really. Abbie says she's a really good friend.'

She'd meant it as a compliment. Something for Lucy to be proud of. But her face creased into an expression that was difficult to read when she repeated Ellen's words. 'A good friend.'

Her response was so strange that Ellen must have misunderstood. 'Yes. That's a good thing, isn't it?'

Ever since she'd known her, Lucy had carried herself with confidence. Whether it was being the first person at the bar to command service two decades ago, or the effortless way she'd ordered hors d'oeuvres for them all in Spanish a few days ago. Head held high and spine straight, she practically glided into a room.

But now she stood awkward and unsure, her elbows drawn

into her sides, her shoulders up to her ears. 'I should have been a better friend to you.'

Where had that come from? Was this about her school? 'I don't care what school you went to. You're right. It doesn't matter. Listening to Abbie just now, it reminds me how young we were. If you felt like you needed to pretend you came from somewhere else, then it is what is. Who am I to judge?'

But Lucy shook her head, her face sharply set and determined. 'That's not what I'm referring to. I mean that Emily saw what was going on with Abigail so she was a good friend and she stepped in. I should've done that for you.'

For the second time that hour, Ellen felt the cold breath of fear on her neck. What did Lucy know? 'Are you... Do you mean...'

She wouldn't, couldn't, finish that sentence. But she didn't need to. Lucy met her eyes with her own dark knowledge.

'I saw you that night, Ellen. I saw you go home with Ian. And I didn't stop it.'

THIRTY-ONE
1999

Ellen had walked around campus for over an hour, trying to find Robert. Her mind and stomach chewing on their argument. Eventually, she decided to go back to the bar, in the vain hope he was also looking for her. Or to continue drinking with that girl who talked about horses. But he wasn't there either.

It was the largest bar on campus and it took her a while to confirm that they weren't there. Just as she'd accepted the fact that they hadn't returned, she felt a hand on her shoulder, turned and bumped into a familiar face. 'Hello, Ellen. What are you doing here on your own?'

Ian was the last person she wanted to see. She could tell he disliked her, both as Lucy's best friend and as Robert's girl-friend. Her face didn't fit in his exclusive group. But his tone was surprisingly kind and she replied in the same manner. 'I'm just looking for Robert.'

Having never been alone with Ian, Ellen hadn't understood the experience of being the centre of his focus. His eyes were so deeply blue, they were almost indigo, and they had a way of boring into her soul. He patted the chair next to him to tell her to sit down and then passed her one of the two bottles of beer on his table. 'Are you sure you're okay?'

He'd never been bothered about that before, either. In fact, she'd often assumed he found her a nuisance, an annoyance, someone that got in the way between him and Lucy.

She shook her head. 'Not really. I think I've ruined everything with Robert. He was talking to a girl and I pretty much accused him of fancying her. He probably thinks I'm way too clingy and possessive.'

Ian smiled and scratched at the back of his head. He had thick dirty-blond hair in a mussed-up surfer style cut. 'Yeah, not really an attractive look to be accusing him of something he hasn't done.'

She groaned and closed her eyes. 'I'm such an idiot.'

Ian took a deep swig of his beer, leaned back in his chair, his long legs stretched in front of him. 'You're not an idiot. He knows that. He's lucky to have you.'

She hoped the large gulp of her own beer would hide her surprise at his words. She hadn't heard him say anything nice to anyone, least of all her. Drinking in the afternoon was not a good idea, her head was already fuzzy from the pint of snakebite and black that Robert had bought her, but she didn't want to be rude. 'I don't know about that.'

He fixed her with those eyes again. Before today, she hadn't understood what Lucy had seen in him. He was arrogant, opinionated and didn't even treat her particularly well. Whether it was the beer or the rawness of her feelings, she could see how it must feel good to be desired by this man.

'Maybe you need to make him realise that he's lucky. Stop chasing after him. Let him come and find you.'

If only. 'I was the one in the wrong. I need to apologise.'

He waved away her argument. 'Apologies are for weak people. You need to know your worth. If Robert did, he'd be here instead of me.'

She took another gulp of her beer. The sooner she finished it, the sooner she could make her excuses and leave. She could feel herself slipping into dangerous territory here. As she drank, she glanced around the bar, hoping that Ian was right, that Robert would come to find her. But she couldn't see him in the sea of faces around her. 'Maybe he's back at my room?'

In the third year, both she and Lucy had opted to move back onto campus. She'd done it to save money, Lucy because she was sick of the two girls they shared with and couldn't be bothered to find anyone new. Ellen had wondered if she regretted now not moving into the serviced apartment with Clarissa and Petra when they'd offered at the beginning of the second year. They barely saw them now. They were history students and their building was in another part of the campus.

Ian drained his beer. 'Drink up, then. And I'll walk you back there.'

'I'll be fine.'

She stood up as she spoke, and her head swam, making her wobble. Ian reached out and held her elbow to steady her. 'Really?'

She shouldn't have drunk alcohol in the afternoon; it never agreed with her. Especially when she hadn't eaten all day to save money. 'Okay, but only if you don't have somewhere else to be.'

'Not somewhere I'd rather be.'

But she'd felt worse as they walked and all thoughts of finding Robert had to be put on hold. She needed to get to bed and lay down.

The next thing she remembered was waking up in bed with Ian beside her, the sheets damp and clammy against her naked skin. Her stomach lurched, she wanted to throw up and it wasn't just the alcohol. How had that happened? Why had she had a beer with him? Why had she let him stay?

As she slipped out of bed, her head throbbed in pain. She needed water almost as much as she needed to get dressed and get him out of there. Picking up her clothes from the floor, vowing to throw them away as soon as he left, she willed him to wake up and leave. Wasn't that what boys like him were supposed to do?

Once she was covered up, she reached out and shook his arm. He stirred and moved on to his side, watched her through bleary eyes. 'Are you going already?'

Feeling too ashamed to be annoyed with him, she just wanted to get him out of there. 'This is my room. You need to go. I've got work to do.'

Her voice was so thin and plaintive, it sounded as if she was begging. He laughed and stretched his arms above his head. 'You work too hard.'

Panic prickled in her gut. She had to get him out before anyone saw him. 'Really, Ian. You need to go. I'm sorry. But I have to get ready and...'

She trailed off as she watched him shake his head slowly, his face twisted into mock-sadness. 'Ellen, Ellen, Ellen. Are you saying this isn't true love? You just want to use me and then abuse me?'

He flopped backwards on the bed, laughing at his own joke. But there was nothing funny here. What if he told Robert? If Robert hadn't already decided that he was sick of her after her performance at the bar, this would definitely finish them off. 'Look, Ian. I don't want to be... well, I think that...'

He was obviously enjoying her discomfort. 'Let me guess. You don't want your best friend and your boyfriend to find out you spent the night with me?'

She winced at the bald truth of it. 'I just don't think it's a good idea.'

He laughed as he swung his legs out of bed and leaned down to retrieve his jeans from the floor. 'Don't worry, petal. Your secret is safe with me.'

THIRTY-TWO

'I saw you go home with Ian and I didn't stop it.'

After ripping away the curtain from the darkest night of Ellen's life, Lucy sank down onto Robert's favourite armchair and faced Ellen on the sofa. Her eyes were such deep pools of guilt that Ellen was frightened to look into them.

The shame and humiliation of that night, and the following morning, had stayed with her forever. Drunk beyond all knowledge, she still had no idea whether she'd consented or not. She did know that she'd spent half her life hiding the fact that she'd cheated on Robert. But had had no idea that Lucy had kept her secret, too. 'How did you know?'

'I'd been searching the bar for him. We'd had another row and I was hoping to make up, idiot that I was. I saw you leaving together. He had his arm around you. You were all over the place. I'd never seen you so drunk.'

Ellen could hardly breathe. 'Why didn't you say something?'

'I was mortified. I knew he'd cheated on me. Why do you think Clarissa and Petra didn't hang out with us all any longer? He'd hit on both of them. But I never imagined it would be you.'

Ellen had had no idea about any of this. 'Lucy, I am so, so sorry. I was completely drunk. I had absolutely no idea what I was doing. That's no excuse, but it's true. And nothing ever happened again.'

Hunched in on herself, Lucy looked the shadow of the woman she'd been only an hour ago. 'I think I was more hurt that you didn't tell me afterwards. That you weren't honest with me. I knew that he was a liar. But you were my friend.'

Robert hadn't been the only person Ellen had betrayed. Suddenly, it all made sense. The change in their friendship back then. Ancient grief tightened her chest. 'I was so ashamed of myself. I was trying so hard to block it out and pretend that it hadn't happened.'

Lucy's eyes searched her face. 'And you never told Robert, either?'

She was almost as ashamed of the deception as she was of what she'd actually done. 'I was terrified that he'd leave me.'

There was no surprise on Lucy's face. 'I was tempted to tell him myself a couple of times. A petty act of revenge.'

Ellen was so grateful she hadn't. 'Thank you for not doing that.'

Lucy flushed. 'I didn't keep quiet for you. I did it for Robert. He's a good man and he didn't deserve to hear it from me. Have you never told him since? In all the time you've been married?'

Guilt that she'd carried for all these years pushed down hard. 'No. There was never a right moment.'

Lucy opened her mouth to speak but was interrupted by the shrill ring of Ellen's phone. It was the hospital. She almost dropped the phone in her hurry to pick up the call. 'Hello?'

'Hello. Mrs Cooper? It's Mr Grayson. Just letting you know that Robert is out of theatre.'

A rush of relief brought tears to her eyes. 'And did it all go well? Is he okay?'

'The procedure went as planned. Once he's fully recovered

from the operation, we'll be able to run some tests and see where we are.'

'Thank you. Can I come in?'

'He should be back in his room in the next ten to fifteen minutes. You are welcome to visit, but he will probably be very sleepy for a while.'

There was nowhere else on the Earth she'd rather be than by his side. 'Thank you. I'll leave now.'

Holding the phone to her chest, she closed her eyes and sent up a silent prayer of thanks before turning to an expectant Lucy. 'He's out of surgery. I can go in and see him.'

Lucy's relief was as palpable as her own. Like a mask she slipped back on, she turned back into her usual self. 'That's great news. Do you want me to drive you?'

They'd need to pick up this terrible conversation another time. Right now, all she could think about was getting to Robert. 'Thanks, but I'll be fine. The girls will want to come. I'll call them now.'

Not wanting to call Grace while she was driving, she called Abbie's phone first. It wasn't until she heard it ringing upstairs that she remembered that Grace had told her to leave it behind. When she tried Grace's phone, it went straight to voicemail. Maybe it was buried in her bag. 'Hi love, it's Mum. The hospital have called to say that Dad is out of surgery. I want to go straight away, so why don't you meet me there? Call me when you get this message.'

She clearly wasn't thinking straight because she'd hung up before she realised that Grace had her car. She turned to Lucy. 'Actually, can I take you up on that offer?'

Lucy picked up her bag. 'Of course. Ready when you are.'

It was only a twenty-minute drive to the hospital. Once Lucy had punched the address into her sat nav, they were on their way.

Ellen had never been in a sports car before. Robert had

toyed with the idea once a couple of years ago, but the girls had been so merciless in mocking a possible mid-life crisis that he'd let it go. It suited Lucy with its cream leather interior and sleek dashboard, but Ellen didn't feel particularly safe this low to the ground.

Lucy pulled out of the road into traffic. 'You must be really relieved that the operation is over.'

'I am. Although I'll feel better when he's awake and I can actually see him. Talk to him.'

She checked her phone again for a message from Grace. Had she not heard the voicemail? She tried again, but there was still no answer. She left a second voicemail. 'It's me again. Mum. Did you get my message? Can you just get Abbie to send me a text from your phone or something?'

Lucy flicked down her indicator. In this luxury car, even that sounded deep and expensive. 'They're a nightmare with their phones, aren't they? They are welded to their hands unless you're trying to contact them and then... nada.'

She was right, but surely Grace and Abigail would be listening out for a call about their dad. 'Maybe she's driving. I think they were only going to the supermarket for snacks.'

'It's nice that they get on so well.'

'Yes. It's great. What about yours?'

'So-so. It's definitely better now they're older.'

'It's funny that we've both ended up with two girls with similar age gaps.'

'Mmm.'

They'd reached a junction so there were a few moments of silence while Lucy waited for both lanes to clear so that she could turn right. Once they were moving again, she glanced at Ellen. 'When did you say that the girls are having their tests to see if they have the same condition as Robert?'

Ellen stared out of the passenger side window, watching the houses go past. She didn't want to face Lucy or this subject.

'We haven't booked anything yet. Mr Grayson said it wasn't urgent.'

'But they want to find out as soon as possible, surely?'

She swallowed. 'I guess so.'

There was silence for a few beats. 'You don't want Grace to be tested, do you?'

Ellen's heart plummeted to her boots. 'What do you mean?'

'Ellen. Look at me. Tell me the truth. Is Ian Grace's father?'

Ellen could barely breathe. This was the question she had dreaded for the whole of Grace's life. 'I honestly don't know.'

THIRTY-THREE

Ellen knew how stupid she sounded. How could she not know who was the father of her twenty-six-year-old daughter?

'I know you probably won't believe me, but I didn't even consider that he could be her father when I first found out I was pregnant. It wasn't until I went to the midwife and she got out that circular card thing to try and work out the conception date that the possibility even occurred to me.'

It did sound like a lie, but she'd been so consumed with whether or not she was even capable of going through with a pregnancy, then so relieved that Robert had been so great about it, that the dark night two months before hadn't even figured in her calculations. It wasn't until she was sitting in the midwife's room, answering questions about the date of her last period, that the dark shadow of possibility had crept over her.

Lucy looked dubious. 'Come on, Ellen. I know you were pretty naive back then. But you weren't stupid.'

She'd run this over in her mind so many times that even she no longer knew what was true. Rather than a sequence of events, she just remembered the feelings. Shock, fear, trepidation and then a tiny ray of hope. Whether or not she had, deep down, wondered about the night with Ian, she couldn't risk everything by revealing it to Robert. 'I did think about telling him. Of course, I did. But I was terrified, Lucy. And it was easy to convince myself that the chance of me carrying Robert's child was far far higher than the chance it was the result of one night with Ian. I wasn't even sure that we'd slept together. I couldn't remember anything about that night.'

Something crossed Lucy's face, but she said no more about it. She turned right into the entrance to the hospital and found a space almost immediately. 'Another benefit of a private hospital You can actually park your car.'

At the end of a manicured path, automatic doors swept open releasing the warmth of the entrance hall. They were almost at the reception desk when Ellen's mobile rang. It was Abbie and she sounded strained. 'Mum? Where are you? What's going on?'

'I'm at the hospital. Where are you? Is Grace not with you?'

'Yes, she's right here. We're back at the house. How's Dad? Is he okay?'

There was definitely something off in Abbie's tone. A kind of breathlessness. 'I haven't seen him yet, but the doctor says the operation went well. I left you a voicemail on Grace's phone. Dad's out of surgery. Lucy brought me straight here and I said on my message to meet me at the hospital.'

The tinkling music being piped into the reception area was obviously intended to be calming, but Ellen was more than a little irritated. Weren't they as worried as she'd been about Robert? In which case, why weren't they listening out for her call?

There was a silence and a muttering at the other end of the line. 'Ah, yes. Er... Grace's phone isn't working.'

That was clearly a lie. 'What are you talking about?'

More muttering. 'She broke it.'

There was something strange going on here. 'What do you mean she broke it? How?'

'She lost her temper at something and she threw it but it doesn't matter. We're leaving now. We'll meet you at the hospital.'

And she hung up.

Ellen was already on high alert worrying about Robert. Add in the conversation with Lucy in the car and the mystery of why her eldest daughter had been so upset that she'd thrown her phone hard enough to break it and she might lose it altogether. At least some of this must have shown on her face because Lucy touched her elbow. 'Is everything okay with the girls?'

'I have no idea. I mean, they're fine but something has clearly happened.'

'Are they coming?'

'Yes. At least I hope so.'

Lucy was in organisational mode. 'You go and see Robert. I'll wait here in Reception for them and let them know where you are.'

For all her reservations, Ellen was pleased that Lucy was here. Still, she felt uneasy knowing that Lucy now had a lot of knowledge about her. 'Our conversation... about what happened.'

Lucy fixed her with an honest stare. 'It's not my place to say anything to anyone.'

It was a temporary fix, but it would have to do for now. 'Thank you. Could you text me as soon as the girls arrive?'

'Of course.'

Having already been to Robert's room, the receptionist let her straight through. But when she pushed open the door, he wasn't there. She stuck her head out of the corridor and caught the eye of a young nurse. 'Hello. I'm here to visit Robert Cooper. He's supposed to be back from recovery by now.'

The nurse smiled. She looked barely older than Abbie. 'I'll just find out for you.'

Ellen sat on the plastic chair by the side of Robert's bed, legs crossed, marking out the seconds the nurse was gone by tapping her foot in mid-air. Until she saw him herself, it was impossible to settle. It would be such a relief to see his handsome face. They'd been apart for only a few hours yet it'd felt like a life-time. Having come this close to losing him, she would never ever take him for granted again.

When the door clicked closed, the room was so silent that all she could hear was the buzzing in her ears and Lucy's voice in her head. *Have you never told him? In all the years you've been married?* She'd never lied to Robert about anything else in their marriage. But what relevance was that when she'd kept this gigantic secret for so long? When they were in Spain, it'd been him she'd doubted. His honesty. His loyalty. What a hypocrite she'd been.

There was a soft knock on the door before it was pushed gently open. But it wasn't the nurse who'd returned; it was a woman in a white coat. 'Mrs Cooper?'

She scanned the woman's face to work out if it was good or bad news that a doctor had come to speak to her, but the professional veneer of calm gave nothing away, so she had to ask. 'Is Robert okay? Is he still in recovery?'

'I'm Doctor Reynolds. Please, take a seat.'

She hadn't realised that she'd stood when the doctor came in, but she did as she was told and returned to the plastic chair. 'What is it? What's happened?'

Doctor Reynolds held up her hands to halt the questions. 'The surgery went well, but there's been a complication and Robert has been taken back into theatre.'

She heard the sharpness of her own gasp. 'But Mr Grayson said he was fine.'

The doctor nodded. 'He was. We think there is a minor tear that needs to be repaired. Mr Grayson is in there with him. He's in the best possible hands.'

Ellen brought her own hands to her face. This was her fault. She'd persuaded him to have this operation. If this went wrong...

The doctor looked concerned. 'Are you here on your own? Can I call anyone?'

She could barely form the words. 'My daughters are coming. My friend is in the waiting room. Lucy.'

The doctor looked relieved that she'd be able to pass her onto someone else. 'I'll go and get her for you.'

Within a couple of minutes, Lucy was there. Ellen explained the situation and Lucy looked as shocked as she felt. Quicker than Ellen, though, she regained control of herself. 'He's going to be fine, Ellen. Charlotte says that the surgeon is the best there is. Robert will be fine.'

Panic swelled in her chest like a wave surging from a long way out. 'I can't bear to think about life without him.'

'Don't. Don't think about that. Think about anything else but that.'

Now it crashed over her like a rip tide. 'Is this my fault, Lucy? Do I deserve this because I lied to him? Am I going to lose him? This is all my fault, isn't it?'

'No.' Lucy shook her head. 'This is not your fault.'

There was no escaping the threat of it pulling her under. 'How can you say that? You know what I did. I slept with someone else and never told him. I told him I was carrying his child when there was a possibility that it was someone else's. And I've kept that secret. From him. From Grace.'

Lucy gripped her forearms, held her still. 'Stop this, Ellen. It's not helping. This is a different situation.'

She could feel herself losing control. She was drowning in

the guilt and fear of what she'd done. 'It's my fault, Lucy. It's all my fault.'

Still holding onto her arms, Lucy shook her. 'No.' Then she paused, took a deep breath. 'I need to tell you something, Ellen. Something I should have told you a long time ago.'

THIRTY-FOUR

The small hospital café contained only six tables and a small counter selling hot drinks, biscuits and cakes. Ellen had chosen a table near the window. She'd wanted to stay in Robert's room, but Lucy had persuaded her that they'd be far better off here at the front of the hospital 'where we can keep a look out for the girls when they arrive'. She'd also insisted that Ellen drink something hot and sweet for the shock and Ellen had to admit that she was grateful for the sugary tea in her hands. 'What is it that you should've told me?'

Lucy took a deep breath. 'I need to go back to the beginning. Before I really knew you. I arrived at the university before you did, remember? And I met Robert and a couple of the others. I liked him straight away. He was exactly the kind of guy I'd hoped that I'd meet there.'

It was such a strange thing to say. Even meeting someone – let alone a specific kind of someone – hadn't been further from Ellen's mind when she'd prepared herself to start college. She'd been far more concerned about her course and living alone and making friends. 'I was late starting because I had my grandma's funeral.'

Lucy nodded. 'I remember. I thought that was the reason you were quiet when you first came. Robert and I had spent two days and a relatively chaste night together before you got there. But it didn't go anywhere. For him.'

She looked at Ellen meaningfully. Robert hadn't wanted anything more with Lucy? But she'd been stunning. And fun and exciting and all the things that Ellen knew she wasn't.

Lucy gave her a moment to take that in and then continued. 'And then you arrived and we all became a group. I did really like you. You came from the same kind of family as mine. Had been to a similar school. But I couldn't tell you that because, by then, I'd decided that the only way to become one of them was to pretend that I already was.'

'But why did you do that? I still don't understand.'

'I wanted better, Ellen. I wanted a bigger life. And I was eighteen. I knew nothing of the world, had never been abroad, it was the only way I could see me really becoming part of that world that I wanted so much. And then, of course, Robert fell in love with you.'

Ellen's heart squeezed with a fleeting memory of a young Robert, looking at her with those big honest eyes and telling her that he loved her. Then she pictured Robert lying on that surgical table maybe only yards away from where they were now and sent another silent prayer for his safe return to her.

Lucy sipped at her black coffee. She, too, seemed lost in her memories. 'I was always jealous of how Robert was so clearly infatuated with you. I couldn't understand why it had never worked out between him and me. I'm not proud of this, Ellen, but I hoped that it would run its course and I would have a second chance with him.'

This version of events was so different to what she'd known that Ellen was having a hard time processing it. 'But you were on and off with Ian in that time?'

WE BOTH HAVE SECRETS 203

Lucy nodded. 'I know. He was my back-up plan. He was charismatic and generous and he made life a lot of fun.'

Begrudgingly, Ellen had to admit that she was right. Despite his caustic wit and arrogance, he would always be the one to buy drinks for everyone at the end of term when she was scratching around in pennies waiting for her next grant cheque. Of course, he could afford it, but that didn't mean he had to do it. He and Lucy had seemed a good match in many ways. They were both the central characters in whatever was happening. 'You two were the power couple of our group. Not that I would have called it that back then.'

Lucy's laugh was hollow. 'I can understand how it seemed like that. I sometimes wonder if that's why he kept going with me. He could see that we would make a good double act. With the benefit of hindsight, I also believe that he could see something in me. A need. Something that meant that I would put up with things that other women wouldn't. In his own way, I do think he needed me as much as I thought I needed him.' She lowered her gaze and stared into her coffee. 'Because then you got pregnant and I knew that there was no chance that there would be anything between Robert and me.'

Shocking though it was, this made a lot more sense of the way that Lucy had reacted to Ellen telling her about the pregnancy. How she'd couched her advice in such a way that had made Ellen seriously consider a termination. 'That's why you didn't want me to have the baby. Why you said I shouldn't even tell Robert.'

For perhaps the first time in all the years she'd known her, Lucy blushed to the roots of her hair. 'I'm not proud of the way I was back then, Ellen. And I am really very sorry for anything I said to you. I felt... desperate. You were getting what I wanted more than anything and you hadn't had to try, or pretend or do anything other than be yourself. You were my friend, but there was a part of me that... that... hated you.'

The shock of that winded Ellen. 'You hated me?'

Lucy shook her head. 'I don't know. Maybe that's too strong, but when you told Robert you were pregnant and he was so calm about it all and then you were both so happy about it, it sent me a bit crazy for a while. I didn't want to be around you. Not that you came out with us much after that.'

'I couldn't be in smoky areas with loads of drunk people when I was pregnant. And I was throwing up most mornings. It was all I could do to hold it together to get to my lectures.'

Also, as soon as the pregnancy had started to show, she'd scuttled from her classes back to her room, hating the stares and whispers from other students that she was 'that girl who got pregnant'.

She'd preferred being back in her room with Robert anyway. Once the shock was over, and they'd got through the pain of telling their parents, they'd started to enjoy planning for the baby's arrival. He'd been so sweet to her, rubbing her aching calves, cooking healthy food, making sure she took her pregnancy vitamins. Though she'd urged him to still go out with his friends, enjoy his last few months of college, he'd been adamant that the only place he wanted to be was with her.

'Once I'd been pregnant myself, I understood it. Back then, it felt like I was losing everything. You were the only real female friend I had, Ellen.'

That was another shock. 'What about the other girls in the group?'

Lucy shrugged. 'I couldn't let my guard down for a minute with them. Anyway, once you and Robert were out of the picture, Ian was my only hope. It wasn't the worst thing. You know how wealthy his family were, we had a great time together, travelling around Thailand and Vietnam, planning our next steps. Then I got pregnant too but his reaction was very different to Robert's.'

Ellen didn't like to ask her whether she'd got pregnant on purpose. 'What happened?'

'He wasn't ready for a child, didn't know if he ever wanted one. Unsurprising really. But then his family found out about the pregnancy and their only response was to offer me money to have a termination. And my own mother told me I was a stupid fool who was throwing away the chance of a better life than she'd had.'

Even after all these years, there was a wobble in Lucy's voice when she said that. Her experience had been so different to Ellen's. Her own mother had cried and her father had looked disappointed, but they had told her from the very beginning that they would support whatever she wanted to do. Robert's family had been much the same. And, once Grace was born, she'd been the apple of everyone's eyes – they'd all adored her. 'I'm so sorry it was hard for you, Lucy.'

'Well, they actually did me a favour. Ian had a very difficult relationship with his family – boarding school at eight, father who had multiple affairs, mother who spent whole days in bed – so their reaction made him go the other way. He offered to set up home with me in a flat.'

How had Ellen not known this? Had she been in such a bubble with Robert and Grace that she hadn't even noticed that she hadn't heard from her closest friend. 'I'm sorry that I didn't—'

Lucy waved away her apology. 'I'm sure you sent me emails that I ignored. We're both equally responsible.'

'What happened once you moved in together?'

Lucy leaned back in her chair, feigning a nonchalance that she clearly didn't feel. 'Well, when I was around eight months pregnant, he slept with another girl. I found out when she came looking for him at the flat. He denied it of course and I didn't have the energy at that stage to push too hard for the truth. Not

206   EMMA ROBINSON

long after Charlotte was born, I found out he was sleeping with a different woman every week.'

Ellen's hands flew to her face. 'That's awful, Lucy. I'm so sorry you had to go through all of that.'

Lucy smiled. 'Hold on to your sympathy. It gets worse. That first girl told me that she believed Ian had spiked her drink with something because she didn't remember anything. But I didn't believe her. Something I will always be ashamed of. One of the other women he slept with also turned up at our flat and said the same.'

Ellen frowned. 'But spiking drinks wasn't a thing back then.'

Lucy held out her hands. 'Apparently it was. I've done my research. Just not as widespread as it is now. And Ian was a very talented chemistry student. All of those girls...' She shuddered. 'I had no evidence that he was using drugs, otherwise I honestly think I would have gone to the police. But I did leave him.'

The wheels of Ellen's brain were moving slowly. 'So do you think...'

Lucy nodded. 'I do think that this is what he did to you, too. It wasn't your fault, Ellen. You didn't choose to sleep with him.'

THIRTY-FIVE

Ellen stared at Lucy. Cogs of memory turned slowly in her brain. That was why she hadn't remembered anything. Hard as she'd tried for weeks afterwards to piece together the events from walking home with him to waking up the next morning, it'd been a deep black hole from which she couldn't retrieve anything.

Across the table Lucy watched her intently, as if to gauge how this information had landed. Was this really true? It changed everything. 'Do you really think that's what happened?'

Lucy nodded. 'I do. He wouldn't have cared that you were Robert's girlfriend or my best friend. It was a game to him. It was about control. I've had enough time to think about it to realise that.'

It was almost too much to process. All these years of hating herself. Of anger directed at her weakness. Even now, she could close her eyes and be back in her university bedroom that morning. The shame sinking beneath her skin like tattoo ink. Indelible. Permanent. 'So you're saying it was not my fault? That I didn't choose to sleep with him?'

Lucy's eyes looked directly into hers. 'That's exactly what I'm saying. You can't remember a thing about it because your beer had been laced with Rohypnol or whatever it was that monster used back then.'

Ellen slumped in her chair like a deflated balloon. When you've lived with shame for so many years, it becomes part of you, like extra weight you can never lose. Freedom from the belief that she had knowingly cheated on the man she loved made her almost dizzy.

But the relief was short-lived. She may not have been in control of her body when she spent the night with Ian. But she had kept the truth from Robert. She had still lied.

And that was the part that was most unforgivable. She knew that.

Thinking about Abigail now – only two years younger than she had been – she had sympathy for her twenty-year-old self. Young and naive, she'd been so scared of telling Robert about that night. Terrified of losing him. And then, once she found out she was pregnant, that was a whole other level of fear. She'd meant every word of what she'd said to Lucy, she really had thought that the chances of the baby being the result of her night with Ian were miniscule. But that didn't make it okay.

She looked at Lucy now. 'This is so hard to take in.'

'I know.'

Over the years, there had been times when the guilt had gnawed at her, but there had always been a reason not to tell Robert. The longer they were married, the more she couldn't stand the risk of losing him.

Would she have judged a woman who'd done what she'd done? Who'd kept this secret from her husband and daughter? Possibly. But having lived it, having been that scared pregnant student, that young overwhelmed new mother, that thirty-year-old wife with two girls who loved one another, that woman in her forties facing a house emptied of the two lights

WE BOTH HAVE SECRETS 209

of her life. When would she have told him? When could she have risked tearing apart the life they'd built together with something that might – if Grace was Robert's biological daughter as she hoped – be completely incidental to their life together.

She reached across the table for Lucy's hand. 'Thank you for telling me this. I'm sorry that you had to go through that with him, too.'

'I should have contacted you before now, but I let jealousy get the better of me.'

Maybe not on the same scale, but this was another surprise. 'Jealousy? Of me?'

Lucy nodded. 'Yes. You had everything I wanted. Robert. A happy family life. I looked you up on Facebook a couple of years ago I couldn't get past your security settings, but I could see your profile pictures over the years. How happy you were.'

Ellen had done the same thing two weeks ago after she'd spoken to Lucy's daughter Emily in Canterbury. 'But your life is so glamorous. *You* are so glamorous. I'm not sure that anyone would understand that someone who looks like you would be jealous of someone who looks like me.'

Shaking her head slowly, Lucy laughed. 'It's not about looks.'

'I know but, seriously, when I saw you in Malaga I felt ashamed of myself. How I'd just let myself go. You always look amazing.'

'I know I do. But that isn't by luck. I work at this every single day.'

This made Ellen feel even more embarrassed. 'I know, but it's done the trick.'

'No, that's not what I meant. The truth of the matter is that I'm terrified to let myself look older. If I don't look good, what else have I got to offer? You've seen Joe. He has women throwing themselves at him and he travels so much, he could be seeing any number of women and I would know nothing about it.'

Ellen thought back to Joe's comment about their 'understanding' and it made her feel sick. Why was a woman like Lucy attracted to men who treated her so casually?

'You are lucky, Ellen. You've had such a long and stable marriage. Robert still looks at you as he did when you were young and thin and beautiful.'

Ellen tried not to be offended by the implication that she was no longer any of those things. Lucy was right. She was lucky. But that luck might be about to run out when she told Robert the truth about what happened all those years ago. Worse than that, she was going to have to tell Grace what had happened and Grace would have to have a DNA test.

As if thinking about her had summoned her into being, Grace and Abigail appeared at the door to the canteen. Abbie got to her first. 'The receptionist told us that you were in here. What's happening? Where's Dad?'

Grace was close behind, but there was something hooded in her expression. Was it anger? 'Sit down, both of you.'

Lucy stood to offer Abigail her chair. 'I'm going to go. But call me if you need anything. I've booked a room in a hotel not far from here.'

Ellen looked her dead in the eye. 'Thank you. I'll call you later tonight with an update.'

Grace pulled a chair over to join Abigail. There was definitely something wrong with her. 'What's going on, Grace? Why are you angry?'

Her face flushed, Grace shook off Ellen's question. 'It's nothing. I'll tell you later. What's happening with Dad?'

Ellen took a deep breath, kept her voice soft and calm. 'As far as I know, the operation went well, but then there was a complication and he had to go back in to surgery.'

WE BOTH HAVE SECRETS   211

Abigail gasped as her hands flew to her face. 'Is he going to be okay?'

Ellen glanced at the large clock on the wall, it'd been about forty-five minutes since she'd spoken to that doctor. 'I was just about to check with someone.'

The efficient receptionist put a call through to the theatre reception. While she was waiting, Ellen watched her daughters. There was clearly something going on between the two of them that had nothing to do with Robert. Grace's hands were gesticulating wildly until they both glanced over in her direction and she restrained herself. Was there any chance that she already knew Ellen's secret? Had she overheard somehow?

The receptionist began speaking to someone on the other end of the line and Ellen's ears craned to piece together what was happening from her side of the conversation. When she put the phone down again, she smiled at Ellen. 'Mr Grayson is just on his way to talk to you. He said he'd meet you in your husband's room.'

'Thank you.'

Heart thumping, Ellen relayed the information to the girls and they made their way to Robert's room in silence, fear resting on their shoulders. Halfway down the corridor, Abigail slipped her hand into Ellen's.

The room felt emptier than when she'd left it with Lucy. Trying not to read too much into Mr Grayson's request to speak to her here – in private – Ellen tried her best to be upbeat for Grace and Abbie. 'I'm not sure your dad will be too impressed with that picture.'

On the wall opposite the bed, an oil painting of a lake scene, possibly a Scottish loch, was framed in a distressed gold frame. The still waters were possibly intended to engender a sense of calm. All Ellen could think about was how deep that water might go.

There was a soft knock on the door, and Mr Grayson

appeared with a smile that made Ellen's heart rise in hope. 'Okay to come in?'

In both senses of the word, she was anxious to see him. 'Of course. How is he?'

His smile was as reassuring as his words. 'It was a small tear, but it's been repaired and all is well. He's going to be fine.'

Holding Grace and Abigail close, their arms and tears entwined, Ellen sent up a prayer of thanks. Their family was still together. For now. She could only hope that, once she told Robert her terrible secret, that would still be the case.

THIRTY-SIX

'Come on, then. Out with it.'

From his position on the lone armchair, Robert raised his eyebrows at her. She still couldn't believe that – less than a week after heart surgery – he'd been allowed home with nothing more than a couple of bottles of pills and strict instructions to rest. That said, in the last two days she'd had to chase him back from the kitchen twice and threaten him with divorce if he even tried to go into his email to 'just keep a check on a few potential orders'. He wasn't the most patient of patients.

His enforced rest had obviously left his mind free to observe. Though she'd agreed with Lucy that she had to reveal her secret, now was not the time. After keeping quiet for twenty-seven years, dropping the bomb on him in the weeks after he was recovering from major heart surgery would surely just be compounding her sin. She kept out of his sightline by reaching behind him on the chair to reposition his pillow. 'I don't know what you mean.'

They were alone in the house. Two days after Robert's surgery, they'd persuaded Abbie to go back to university and Grace was at work. Ellen's attempts to get to the bottom of why her eldest daughter was upset had come up empty. She was due to come for dinner tomorrow night, so she'd try again with her then.

Obligingly, Robert leaned forward to allow her to plump up the pillow that had been fine the way it was. 'Oh, come on, Ellen. We've been married long enough for me to know when you've got something you want to tell me. Just hit me with it.'

The time for lying was over, but – despite what Mr Grayson had said about him being a 'new man' – she was genuinely concerned for the effect on Robert's heart. 'It's nothing that can't wait until you're better.'

Mock indignant, he pointed towards himself. 'What are you saying? That I don't look fighting fit.' He laughed. 'I'm fine. I actually feel worse trying to work out what it is you're keeping from me. My mind is going in all manner of directions. Are you having an affair with Mr Grayson?'

His customary humour in the face of great stress wasn't actually helping today and she couldn't reflect a smile back at him. 'No, it's not that.'

He frowned at her serious tone. 'Just tell me, Ellen.'

This was it. The moment she'd been dreading for twenty-seven years. It could be the end of everything. In the last week, she'd played it over in her head so many times. Particularly the last two nights, lying awake next to Robert, watching the rise and fall of his chest in the same way she'd watched Grace breathing in her sleep as a newborn. Why was it so difficult to find the words? 'I'll tell you. But you have to just listen until I get to the end.'

He nodded. And she told him, haltingly, the same story she'd recounted to Lucy a week ago, this time adding the new information that Lucy had shared with her. It was physically painful to see the changes on Robert's face. Confusion, fear... disgust?

'You slept with Ian?'

She'd heard that question many times in nightmares and yet it pierced her painfully hearing it for real. 'I think so. Yes.'

'You think so?' Robert's face contorted with pain. 'Surely you must know?'

'I don't remember anything. I never have. And now I know why. It'd be like asking you to remember what happened on the operation table. But I did wake up next to him. I did... I was... I think we did have sex.'

Even saying the words brought back those feelings. Disbelief at waking up next to him, the disgust that she'd pulled over herself like a heavy quilt, cold with damp.

'I just can't believe it. With him of all people. He wasn't even nice to you. You hated him.'

Trying to explain what'd happened when it felt as if someone had hold of her throat was so hard, but she needed to make him understand. 'I did hate him. I do hate him. It was never my choice, Robert.'

He couldn't even look at her. 'But you must have walked with him back to your room. You must've invited him in?'

Hot tears coursed down her cheeks. 'I must have. But I don't remember. I think he spiked my drink, Robert. I have no idea what state I was in when I left the bar.'

Robert's face flushed with anger. 'Why didn't you tell me? I could have done something. I could have...'

'No.' She reached out to touch him, but pulled back when he flinched. 'I didn't want you to know. I was ashamed. So ashamed.'

There was a battle being waged inside Robert, she could see it on his face. What was going on in his head? What was he thinking about her? Would he – could he – ever forgive what she'd done?

When he spoke again, his voice trembled. 'And all this time? All these years? You've never thought about telling me?'

She'd thought about it a million times. 'I was so scared.'

Tears spilled from his eyes. 'I'm scared, too, Ellen. I just don't know... I need some time to think about this.'

Carefully, he pushed himself out of the chair. Panic coursed through Ellen. This is why she hadn't wanted to tell him until he was fully recovered. 'Where are you going? You can't leave the house. You need to rest.'

Having reached the door to the hallway, he paused but didn't turn to face her. 'I'm just going upstairs for a while. Don't come up. I want to be on my own.'

As the door clicked closed behind him, Ellen bent forward and wept. What had she done?

For the next hour, Ellen stayed frozen on the sofa, terrified about what was going to happen next. If Robert couldn't forgive her for this – and who could blame him – how would she cope? Like a festering wound, this secret had been hidden for so long that she was almost used to the pain of it. But tearing off the bandage and exposing it to the air had been agony. What had she expected Robert to do? Just accept it and move on? He was a good man, a wonderful man, but this deception might be more than he could deal with. Because it wasn't even just a one-night infidelity. It was the whole question of whether or not he was the father of their eldest daughter.

Though he'd asked to be left on his own, she had to go and check on him. He was only a week out from major heart surgery and she'd rather risk his anger than the possibility that he might be in pain. But when she went into their bedroom, he wasn't there. The bathroom door was open so he wasn't there either. Anxiety crackled at the edges of her chest until she pushed open the door to Grace's bedroom and saw him sitting on her bed, a framed photograph of the four of them in his hand.

Ellen pressed a fist to her chest to ease the pressure there. 'Can I come in?'

WE BOTH HAVE SECRETS 217

When he lifted his face to look at her, the anger had gone, but the sadness that had replaced it was palpable. 'Yes.'

Not wanting to push herself onto him, she took the chair at Grace's dressing table. It squeaked as she turned towards him. 'I'm so sorry, Robert. I know that I've done a terrible thing keeping this secret from you.'

His voice was quiet, she had to crane her ears to hear him. 'I think, on some level, I knew.'

Now it was her turn to be surprised. 'How is that possible? What do you mean?'

He sighed deeply. 'I knew something had happened that night we had the big argument. You were so strange afterwards. I knew what Ian was like. I mean, not the part of it that Lucy told you, but I knew how he was with women. And I didn't call him out on it. The way you were around him, there was always a suspicion that something had happened, but I guess I didn't want to face it. There was a moment – only a fleeting one – when you told me you were pregnant, that I wondered if, for sure, the baby was mine, but I pushed it down. I wanted so much for it to be our baby that I refused to think that anything else was possible.'

Listening to his side of this, her good, kind, loyal husband, brought tears to her eyes. 'I'm sorry, Robert. I'm so, so sorry.'

He reached out for her hand. 'It sounds like it wasn't your fault. If Lucy is right and that bastard spiked your drink.'

She shook her head. 'I don't just mean about that. I mean about the lie. About not telling you. I was just so desperate for it not to be true. And then there never seemed a right time to tell you about it.'

He squeezed her hand. 'I can understand that.'

She couldn't believe how calm he was being about it all. 'You must be angry with me?'

'If this had come out six months ago, maybe I would have reacted differently. But this health scare has changed me. Made me realise how precarious life is. And how precious. It hurts like hell to think that there's a possibility that Grace is not biologically my child, but she *is* my daughter. She will always be my daughter. Nothing will ever change that.'

A sob escaped from Ellen as she leaned into Robert's arms. Relief, guilt, fear, love: it all poured out of her as she cried in his arms. She didn't deserve to be as lucky as to have a man like him. When her tears subsided, she stayed there, not wanting to leave the security of his arms, his chest, his warm beating heart. There was more that she wanted to ask him, more reassurance that she needed to hear, but that was selfish. This was about him now. Him and Grace.

He must have been thinking about their daughter, too. With her head resting on his chest, his voice seemed to come from his heart. 'We have to tell her.'

Of course, he was right, but the thought was unbearable. 'I don't know what I'm going to say.'

'We'll tell her together. One upside would be that she wouldn't have to be scanned for the heart condition.'

His wonky smile brought fresh tears to her eyes. 'That's the only part of you I don't want her to have. Everything good about her comes from you.'

He kissed the top of her head. 'Yeah, you're right there.'

She pulled away and looked at that impish smile that she knew – and loved – so well. 'I'm so lucky to have you, Robert. I was so scared that I was going to lose you.'

She felt the tears come again and he brushed them away with his thumb. 'You will never lose me. I love you.'

Again, the question she wanted to know – would you have still married me if you'd known back then? – was too much to ask of him. 'I love you, too.'

'Is Grace still coming for dinner tomorrow? We can tell her then.' His voice cracked. 'I just hope that, if the worst is true, she doesn't feel any differently about me.'

'She won't. I know it. You'll still be the dad who played tea parties with her and drove her to school discos and listened to her practise the violin over and over and over.'

He nodded. 'I loved that little girl so much. She was my world. She still is.'

Unable to speak, she nodded. Desperately hoping that this was going to end well.

THIRTY-SEVEN

Every mother must think their children are beautiful, but Ellen knew it to be true of both her girls. Abbie had a delicate beauty, rarely wore make-up and – at eighteen – could pass for much younger. Grace was striking. She'd never met a shade of lipstick she didn't like and was no stranger to the world of fake tan.

That evening, though, when Ellen opened the door, Grace looked pale and tired. If she hadn't known better, she'd have thought she was ill. 'Are you okay, sweetheart?'

She shook her head and her face crumpled into tears. Ellen opened her arms and took her into them. 'What is it? What's wrong?'

Robert was still in the shower, so she led Grace through to the sitting room and kept her arm around her once they were on the sofa.

'It's Max.'

Of course, it was. From day one she'd known that man was going to break her daughter's heart. But if she wanted Grace to tell her everything, she'd need to let her speak. 'What happened?'

'You know the day of Dad's operation? Last Monday? Well,

WE BOTH HAVE SECRETS

when Abbie and I went to the shop, I tried to call him and he didn't answer. So I left him a voicemail and asked him to call me back.'

She paused to blow her nose on one of the tissues that Ellen had passed her from a box on the coffee table. It was horrible to see her so upset. 'And did he?'

She nodded. 'About five minutes later. He said that he was in the middle of a meeting at work and had just popped outside the room to call me back so that he could check I was okay and that everything was going well with Dad.'

'He knew about the operation?'

'Of course. He's my boyfriend. He *was* my boyfriend.'

Ellen was pleased about the 'was' but not about how upset Grace was. 'So that was okay, then?'

'Yes. That was okay. Better than okay. I thought he was really sweet for coming out of an important meeting just to check on me. I even told Abbie that he and I were going to be getting really serious. And I am a complete and utter idiot for that.'

She started to cry again and Ellen rubbed her back. 'You are not an idiot. It was a nice thing to do.'

'Except, he wasn't in a meeting at all.'

Now Ellen was confused. 'How do you know?'

'Because, about three minutes later, he called me again. Except he didn't mean to call me. He must have butt-dialled me.'

Ellen knew what that meant. She could see where this was going. 'Oh.'

'Exactly. And I heard him talking to a woman. I couldn't get every word, but it definitely wasn't about business. I could hear glasses clinking and her giggling and the kind of small talk you only make when you're chatting someone up.'

Poor Grace. 'And that was why you looked so cross when you arrived at the hospital on Monday?'

Grace nodded. 'I didn't want to say anything because obviously Dad's operation was so much more important than whatever Max was getting up to, but it was hard not to feel awful about it.'

'Of course it was. Have you spoken to him since?'

She was the last person who wanted to side with this creep but she wanted to make sure that Grace wasn't jumping to conclusions. She did have form in changing her mind pretty quickly.

'Yes, I spoke to him that night, once we knew Dad was okay. He tried to shrug it off and said that I must have misheard, but I knew I hadn't. We arranged to meet up and talk about it and he told me that he'd never cheat on me and what did I need for him to do to prove it to me?'

Ellen almost didn't want to hear the answer to that. 'What did you say?'

'I told him that I wanted to be a part of his whole life. I wanted to meet his children.'

'And?'

'And he said the same old things he always says. His ex-wife won't let him introduce the children to anyone new blah blah blah.'

To be fair, that part could be true. 'So you ended it?'

'No. Worse.'

What could be worse?

Grace screwed up her face. 'I'm not proud of myself, but I know where the house is that he used to live in with his wife. One of the secretaries told me. I know he was supposed to collect the children on Saturday so I waited nearby the house to see him come out with them. I was going to follow them to the park and then pretend that it was a coincidence that I was there.'

That was a truly terrible idea. 'Grace, that's not fair on the children.'

WE BOTH HAVE SECRETS 223

'I know that. It was stupid. But I was so desperate, Mum. I wasn't thinking straight and, don't worry, I got my punishment.'

'What do you mean?'

'I saw Max coming out of the house, I saw the two children and I saw his wife. And he had his arm around her and kissed her before they left the house. And, before you ask how I knew it was his wife, it was because the children called her mummy.'

As Grace started to cry again, Ellen pulled her close. In her gut, she'd known he was still married. What an absolute pig of a man. How dare he use her daughter like this? Lie to her. Break her heart. 'Honey, I'm so sorry. I hate that he's done this to you.'

Unfortunately, Robert chose that exact minute to come into the sitting room, hair still wet from the shower. The smile on his face froze when he took in the scene of his daughter sobbing in her arms. 'Have you told her already? I thought we were going to do it together?'

Ellen's heart sank. Grace pulled herself back up out of her arms and looked between the two of them. 'Told me what?'

Robert looked panicked, realising what he'd done. She tried to smooth it over. 'Grace has had some bad news about Max. Turns out he's not separated from his wife after all.'

She gave him a wide-eyed stare that this was his cue to swerve the conversation they'd planned to have with her. Thankfully this was a cue he picked up on. 'Sweetheart, I'm so sorry.'

But Grace was nobody's fool. 'Told me what?'

There was no way Ellen wanted to compound the pain Grace was already going through, but her mind was a blank. She looked to Robert for help and he tried his best. 'Your mum and me were thinking about booking a holiday. When I've recovered. For all of us.'

Grace shook her head. 'That's not it. You're scaring me, now. What is it? Is it Dad's heart? Is there a problem?'

What could they do but tell her the truth? 'No, it's not

Dad's heart. He's doing really well. We do have something to tell you but it's a lot to take in and I don't think that now is the right moment.'

There was never going to be a right moment, that was the problem. And they couldn't just leave it there. Grace wiped away her tears with a ferocity that made her face red. 'Just tell me. You can't make me feel any worse than I do right now.'

How wrong she was, but there was nothing else for it. Robert nodded at her and she began to explain the story to Grace that she had recounted to Lucy only a week before.

To begin with, Grace looked confused as to why her mother was recounting a night with another man at university, but as the significance of that night became clearer, her eyes widened and her mouth fell open with shock.

Ellen and Robert had discussed whether to add the final piece of the puzzle – Lucy's revelation that Ellen's drink was probably spiked – and had decided that Grace was old enough to hear the full truth. Now, as Grace covered her face with her hands, Ellen wondered if she should have held back.

She looked from Ellen to Robert and back again. 'I can't believe this.'

Ellen reached out for her hand. 'I know it's a lot to take in.'

Grace pulled her hand away as if Ellen had burned her. 'You lied to me all these years. And to Dad.'

She deserved that. 'I did. And I'm not trying to excuse that. I was wrong. But you have to remember that I was young and pregnant and scared.'

'But you kept lying. I'm twenty-six, Mum. Are you saying you never had the opportunity to tell Dad the truth? To tell me the truth?'

Everything she said was right, Ellen had nothing with which to defend herself. But Robert tried on her behalf. 'Your mum was doing what she thought best, love.'

She turned on him then. 'How can you forgive her so easily?

WE BOTH HAVE SECRETS 225

How can it be doing her best to lie to us? It's the same as Max. Just lies.'

Tears sprang to Ellen's eyes but she wouldn't let them fall. This was not about her pain. This was about Grace. 'It might be totally irrelevant, Grace. There's only a tiny chance that he could be your father.'

That seemed to make her worse. 'Only a tiny chance that a nasty piece of work who spikes girls' drinks is my biological father? Thanks so much, Mum. I don't believe this, I just can't... I need some time on my own.'

Robert reached for her arms as she walked past him. 'Gracey.'

'No, Dad. You might be able to forgive this instantly. But I can't. I'm going up to my room, don't follow me.'

They let her go. Robert moved over to the sofa and put his arm around Ellen as she cried. 'She just needs some time to process it. She'll be okay.'

His love and kindness only made her cry harder. Because Grace was right. She didn't deserve to be forgiven.

An hour later, Ellen took a cup of hot chocolate up to Grace's room. Though she'd moved out over eighteen months ago, everything had been left the way it was when she'd last lived under their roof. When Ellen knocked softly on the door and heard a muffled 'come in' she pushed open the door to see Grace curled up on her bed with her old teddy bear tucked under her arm.

'I brought you a drink.'

'Thanks.'

Ellen slid the cup onto the bedside table, then sat on the floor with her back against the wardrobe. 'I don't expect you to forgive me, Grace. I don't forgive myself. I never have.'

Just like Robert, Grace was calmer now she'd had the time

to process everything. 'I understand that you were scared when you were young. I know things were different in those times.'

Ellen almost smiled at the 'those times' which made her sound as if she'd been born in 1920. 'I was just scared that I'd lose your dad. I loved him very much.'

Grace's face creased in pain. She must also be thinking about her own heartbreak. 'I understand that part. It's just that I don't understand why you never told him.'

'Because I was a coward, I suppose. I loved my life. Loved my family. It felt like too big a risk.'

'But you always insisted that we tell the truth. Always said that you could fix anything if we were honest with you.'

She had said that to them. Many times. 'I'm also a hypocrite, then. I guess the only way I can explain it – not excuse it – is that I didn't believe I deserved to be forgiven. Your dad... he's an amazing man. I can't believe he has taken this news the way he has. It's made me love him even more. And he loves you, sweetheart. So very much.'

Grace's eyes filled with tears. 'And I love him. So much. But what if I do a DNA test and he's not my dad?'

THIRTY-EIGHT

The DNA test kit arrived the next day and all three of them sent back a sample. Grace decided to stay over with Ellen and Robert and, by the time she got home from work on Thursday, the results were in her email inbox.

Even in these circumstances – maybe especially in these circumstances – Ellen had loved having Grace at home. The evening before, they'd watched a film and she and Grace had curled up on the sofa together. She'd missed having her close. When Robert tired early and went to bed, they'd sat up talking about Max and the situation of having to see him at work every day. He'd made a half-hearted attempt to justify his behaviour, but – thankfully – Grace wasn't having any of it.

This morning, when Ellen had heard Grace's alarm go off, she'd slipped on her dressing gown and come downstairs to make her coffee and a sandwich to take with her to work. Grace had laughed at her. 'I'm a bit old for a packed lunch, Mum.' But she'd taken it all the same.

It'd been a rough day for Robert. He was getting frustrated that he was stuck in a chair for most of the day and the results of the test were obviously on his mind. When Grace got home

228   EMMA ROBINSON

around six-thirty, they were both waiting for her. Despite her suit and heels – her perfectly applied make-up – to Ellen she was no different from that little girl who'd clatter in the front door after school, throw her bag on the floor, kick off her shoes and follow Ellen out to the kitchen, her conversation a stream of consciousness recount of everything that had happened to her since breakfast.

When she saw her coming up the path, Ellen opened the front door to welcome her home. 'How was your day, love?'

Standing on one leg, then the other, Grace eased off her black patent heels. 'Dull. I just wanted to be back here. How's Dad?'

'Driving me crazy.' She smiled. 'He's fine. Waiting to see you.'

'I checked my phone on the train home. I've got the results.'

Ellen scanned her daughter's face for a clue. 'And?'

She shook her head. 'I haven't looked yet. I was waiting to get home in case... well, I wanted to be with you and Dad. If he's up to it?'

Robert's voice called out from the sitting room. 'What are you two whispering about? What's a man got to do round here for a hug from his daughter?'

Grace smiled and Ellen followed her into the sitting room, watched her lean down and wrap her arms around Robert. 'Hi, Dad. How are you feeling?'

Robert didn't answer. Instead he kept his arms around Grace. It took a few moments for Ellen to realise that he didn't want to let her go.

She watched them there, as if that moment was frozen in time. As soon as Grace opened that email, everything might be different. For now, in this tiny slice of time, they were as they'd always been. A lump rose in her throat.

When Grace emerged from Robert's arms, her face was wet

with tears. Robert kept hold of her hand. 'Nothing will change, Gracey. You'll always be my girl, whatever that says.'

Ellen placed her hand on her throat to try to stop it from hurting. Grace nodded at Robert, her own voice not much more than a whisper. 'I know, Dad.'

Ellen didn't know what to do with herself. It was her secret that had put them in this position. Now, the not knowing was unbearable. Still, she was torn between wanting – like pulling a tooth – to open that email and know for sure. Or whether she wanted to leave it, to never know, to carry on as she had for the last twenty-six years, believing that Grace had the father she deserved.

Robert glanced at her, then back at Grace. 'Shall we, then?'

Grace nodded. She relinquished Robert's hand and perched on the sofa opposite, thumbing through her phone to get to the email.

How could something so momentous in their lives be decided by an electronic message on her phone? Robert reached out for Ellen's hand and she took it. Watching Grace's face as she read from her screen. *Please let Robert be her father. Please.*

But when Grace looked up, the colour drained from her face, it was clear that it was not good news. She shook her head, her hand fluttered to her face to catch a sob.

Maybe she had it wrong. 'Can I see?'

Grace passed the phone over. On the screen, a table which compared numbers across three columns: Mother, Child, Alleged Father. At the bottom of the table, the summative statement which had caused Grace's reaction.

Robert tried to peer over Ellen's shoulder. 'What does it say?'

In an act of penance, she read it aloud. 'The alleged father is excluded as the biological father of the tested child. The probability of paternity is zero per cent.'

Robert closed his eyes. It was so unusual for her to hear him cry, that she thought he was coughing. Grace was out of her seat in a second. 'Oh, Dad. Don't cry, please don't cry.'

He held out his arms and she fell back into them, the two of them united in their shared grief. Ellen was frozen, looking at the screen. She'd really believed that Robert was Grace's father. They were so alike. They enjoyed the same films, had the same sense of humour, she even smiled the same as he did. This must be wrong? But it was there in black and white. *The probability of paternity is zero per cent.*

'I'm so sorry.'

Initial shock over, sobs shuddered through her own body and Robert reached for her, holding her as she wrapped one arm around Grace and another around him. It was impossible to see where one of them ended and another began. He whispered into her hair. 'It's going to be okay. It's all going to be okay.'

She wasn't sure how long they stayed like that, but eventually they let go of one another. Robert searched their faces. 'I meant what I said before. This changes nothing. It's just biology. You're my daughter, Gracie.'

'And you're my dad. I know. I just wanted...'

With his forefinger, Robert reached out and caught the fresh teardrop on her cheek. 'I know. Me, too.'

Ellen's whole body ached with guilt and grief.

'And I don't want that person, the one who did that to Mum, I don't want to be related to him. I don't want to be connected to him.'

Ellen felt exactly the same. She hated Ian more than anyone else on Earth. Even more so since Lucy had told her what kind of man he'd continued to be. She didn't want him to have any kind of claim on her precious girl. 'You're not connected to him. I can see nothing of him in you.'

Robert nodded. 'I think your mum's genes must've done a number on his. You're all your mum.'

They all knew this wasn't true, but she loved Robert for

WE BOTH HAVE SECRETS   231

saying it. Grace chewed on her lip. 'But I want your genes. I want to be yours.'

'You are mine and, let's face it,' he pointed to his chest, 'my genes aren't necessarily the best. I'm very glad that you haven't inherited this from me.'

That was another set of results that they'd have to worry about. Grace would no longer need to be tested for Robert's heart condition, but Abigail would.

Grace sniffed. 'I'm going to go and wash my face. Take my suit off.'

'Okay, love. I'll make you a cup of tea, shall I?'

At the same time, Robert and Grace said, 'Have you got any biscuits?' Then they looked at each other, and laughed at how similar they were, before Grace began to cry again.

Ten minutes later, she'd disappeared upstairs and Ellen had returned from the kitchen where she'd put the kettle on. Robert was still in his chair, staring into the middle distance. She was almost scared to interrupt his private thoughts. 'Are you okay?'

He turned his kind blue eyes in her direction. 'Bruised not broken.'

It was a phrase they'd used with the children when they were small. A shorthand way to ascertain the seriousness of a fall or collision or accident. He held out his hand and she took it, perching herself on the arm of his chair.

Though she'd said it many times, there was no other word for the way she was feeling. 'I really am so sorry. I know that this is all my fault.'

Robert brought her hand to his lips and kissed her knuckles. 'You need to stop apologising. It is what it is. We're going to be fine. Better than fine, we are going to be great.'

There was another question that she hadn't been able to purge from her mind. Perhaps it was selfish to ask, but she needed to hear his answer. 'Do you think we'd still have got married if I hadn't got pregnant when I did?'

His eyebrows raised in surprise. 'Of course. From the moment I met you, I knew you were the one for me, Ellen.'

Her throat threatened to close up. 'And what about if you'd known that the baby wasn't yours? Back then, I mean. When we were twenty and hadn't even graduated?'

Robert studied her face. Clearly, he knew that she didn't want a pat answer: she wanted the truth.

He kept his gaze on her as he spoke, his voice gentle. 'Honestly? I can't say what I'd have done in that moment. I was a kid. We were both kids. But if I hadn't married you, it would've been the biggest mistake of my life, Ellen. I was meant to be with you. You have made me who I am. Our girls have made me who I am. Without the three of you, my life would have been far the poorer.'

Fresh tears flooded her cheeks. For over half of her life, she'd lived with the guilt and felt not good enough. If only she hadn't held this secret like a cold pebble of fear in her chest all of these years. 'I love you so much.'

He smiled. 'And I love you.'

The door opened and Grace, looking about fifteen in her pyjamas with her face scrubbed clean of cosmetics, appeared around the door. Ellen stood to hug her close and she kissed her. 'I'm on my way to get the tea and biscuits.'

'I'll come out with you to make sure you don't try and fob us off with the non-chocolate ones.' She winked at Robert and he held his hand up for a high five. They were going to be okay. She was sure of it.

In the kitchen, Grace leaned against the worktop while Ellen dropped a tea bag into each cup. 'I was thinking. The girl that helped Dad out with his heart thing – Charlotte is it? She's my half-sister.'

Probably because she'd been so convinced that the DNA

report would show Robert to be Grace's father, Ellen hadn't actually made that connection. It made her feel more than a little uncomfortable. Biologically, Grace would be as closely related to Charlotte as she was to Abigail. 'I suppose she is, yes.'

Grace reached up to the cupboard where the yellow plastic Tupperware containing the biscuits lived. 'I think I'd like to meet her.'

THIRTY-NINE

Just over a week later, Ellen invited Lucy, Joe and Charlotte to dinner.

Ellen had spent the last two days cleaning the house from top to bottom. An hour before they came, she was still plumping cushions and straightening photo frames. They had a nice home and Ellen loved it, but it was not a patch on the place Joe and Lucy had in Spain and she spent the whole day trying to make it look as nice as possible.

Robert had laughed at her. 'They're coming to see us. Not buy the place.'

He was right. And there were much more important things to be achieved tonight than for Lucy to think she had a nice carpet. 'I wonder how it will be for the girls? It's a big deal.'

Over the last week, she'd had a chance to get her head around the idea that Grace had another sister. No one had told the other two sisters yet. It was the kind of thing that couldn't be done over the phone and they'd reasoned that, right now, it was more important that they enjoy their first few weeks at university. Abigail, especially, could do without another bombshell. Ellen worried briefly that this was another secret but both

Grace and Robert had assured her that this was different. They would tell Abigail as soon as they saw her next. Lucy agreed and said that they wouldn't tell Emily until then, too.

She and Lucy had spoken on the phone several times in the last week. Now everything was out in the open, she was remembering just how much fun they had had together. She felt younger, somehow. It hadn't all been reminiscing and nostalgia, either. Lucy had made her laugh with stories about her neighbours and had been genuinely interested to hear about Ellen's work in the lab: a job she would need to return to next week. Charlotte and Grace had also spoken on the phone and – according to Grace – they had a lot in common. But this was to be the first time that they'd met in real life.

Grace had offered to peel the potatoes while Ellen prepared the chicken by tucking garlic cloves under its skin. Ellen wondered if this unusual helpfulness was because she just wanted to be kept busy. 'Are you nervous, Grace?'

Tilting her head, Grace considered the question. 'More curious. She sent me some pictures of herself, but I'm intrigued to see if we have any mannerisms or habits that are the same. It's a weird thought, having such a close relation that you've never met.'

Ellen drizzled olive oil over the chicken. It *was* a weird thought. Even weirder that their shared DNA had come from someone else they'd never met. 'Has she said anything about him? Ian?'

His name was unpleasant in her mouth, but she wasn't for a second going to refer to him as their father. Robert and Joe were their dads.

The colander clattered as Grace dropped a peeled potato into it. 'I asked her if she'd ever considered looking him up – Ian – and she said she'd never wanted to. She said if he wanted to be in her life, he would be. She wasn't about to go chasing after him.'

'That sounds reasonable.' Though she was scared of the answer, she had to ask the same question. 'Do you want to look him up?'

Grace looked appalled. 'No. Absolutely not. I feel sick at what he did to you. At what he's done to other women. To be honest I'm sick to death of all lying men right now.'

She did that funny, turned-down smile she'd done since she was a baby that pulled on Ellen's heart strings. 'Not all men are lying. Your dad is a good one.'

'It's okay, Mum. I'm not going to turn into a man-hater. I just think I need a break from them at the moment.'

'Well, you've got plenty of time to worry about that.'

Grace twisted a lock of her hair between two fingers. 'Do you ever regret having me so young. I mean, especially now you know that—'

'No.' Ellen was back across the room in two steps to cut her off. She didn't even want her to finish that sentence. 'I have never ever regretted having you for one single second. It was tough being a young mum, but you brought so much more than you took. You were – you are – our absolute joy.'

Grace smiled again. This time the edges turned upwards. 'Good.'

Charlotte and Grace seemed to hit it off almost immediately. Ellen had positioned them next to one another and they were soon laughing and finding out a million more things that they had in common.

Before the dessert was served, Grace turned to Ellen on her other side. 'I don't think I'm ready for dessert. Actually, Charlotte and I wondered if you'd mind if the two of us ducked out for a bit? Just for quick drink at the Foxhound. We'll only be half an hour and then we'll be back for dessert.'

The Foxhound pub was about four minutes' walk from their

house. It was small and quiet and ideal for an intimate conversation. Ellen could understand that there might be things that the two of them would want to talk about away from their parents' eager ears. 'Of course, We'll save you some.'

Once they'd gone, the four of them stayed at the table, talking about Joe's latest project, Robert's recovery and Ellen's imminent return to work. After an hour or so, she pushed away her chair and stood up. 'I'll just clear these plates away and bring the dessert out. That way it'll be there when we want it.'

Joe stood and began to collect the plates from his end of the table. 'I'll help you.'

The last time she and Joe were alone, he'd been showing her around the house in Malaga and she'd been imagining all sorts of things between her husband and his wife. Some of the things they'd discussed that day came back to her now and she felt the need to apologise again. 'I'm sorry about how strange I must have been when we stayed with you.'

Joe slid the pile of plates onto the counter. 'Please don't apologise. Completely understandable in the circumstances. You and Robert must come back again as soon as he's up to it. Bring the girls.'

He was such a kind and affable man, that she decided to risk speaking to him about something that had been worrying her. 'I know we don't know each other that well, but can I ask you a question. It's personal.'

Joe smiled. 'Well, I think we've been through enough in the last week or so for you to do that. Go ahead.'

'You and Charlotte are really close aren't you? I mean, I know you're her dad, but... well, I suppose what I want to know is, is it different? Charlotte and Emily. Do you feel differently about Emily because you're her biological dad?'

Joe didn't say anything and she worried that she'd offended

him. But then he nodded. 'I suppose the difference is that Charlotte wasn't a baby when I met her. She was this tiny but fully formed human with a personality and a stare that could freeze you in place. I hadn't even considered becoming a father before I met Lucy. I mean, I was only in my early twenties. But I fell in love with Lucy and she made it clear from the very beginning that Charlotte was part of the package. I was worried that I wouldn't be up to it. That I wouldn't like being a parent. I had no idea what I was taking on.'

He paused again and gazed at the corkboard of photographs on the kitchen wall as if he was picturing Charlotte back then and Ellen worried that she'd made him feel bad. 'I can imagine it was a lot. It was a lot for us to have Grace so young.'

He smiled. 'The thing is, I didn't need to know what I was doing, because Charlotte did. She taught me to be a dad. I grew up with her. I grew up because of her. It's given us a special relationship. It's different to my relationship with Emily, but I love them the exact same amount.'

That's how she felt about her girls. She loved them the same but different. 'I get it.'

'And you don't need to worry about Robert. Him and Grace, anyone can see how close they are. Lucy said the same thing to me on the way here. There's nothing of that man in her. She's completely yours and Robert's.'

Tears pricked at Ellen's eyes. 'Thank you.'

He was about to go when she remembered something else. 'When I hear you talk about Lucy and the girls, I can help but wonder about this "open marriage" between you and Lucy. I know it's none of my business, but...'

She trailed off at the look of bewilderment on his face. 'What do you mean?'

She felt flustered. 'You said that you had an understanding. That she gives you the freedom to do what you want.'

Joe threw back his head and roared with laughter. 'Our

understanding isn't about other women. It's about houses. I buy.
I sell. We move a lot. She lets me do it.'

Now Ellen felt terrible. 'I'm so sorry. I think I was in a
different headspace when we were out in Spain. I was seeing
things that weren't there.'

She could cringe now for remembering that she'd thought
that there was something going on between Robert and Lucy.
Worse than that, between him and Charlotte.

Joe was still chuckling to himself. 'How could I want
another woman when I have her?'

The simplicity of his question almost made Ellen cry
again. She remembered Lucy's honesty about her own insecu-
rities, her need to always look perfect, be perfect. Why do
women always feel not good enough? 'I think you should tell
her that. In those exact words. Come on, let's take this dessert
through.'

Robert and Lucy were laughing about something when they
returned to the table. And her heart felt full. 'It's so nice to have
you all here.'

Robert raised his glass of lemonade to chink it with Joe's
wine. 'Speaking of which. Where have those girls got to? They
said that they were only going out for one drink.'

Lucy leaned down to the side of her chair and reached
inside her bag for her mobile. 'I'll send them a text, see what
they're up to.'

At the same time, Ellen checked her phone to see if there
was anything from Grace. That's when she noticed the message
with a picture attached. She'd written 'Look who we found'.
And then there was a picture, a screenshot from Facebook, of an
award ceremony in central London. Once she saw the name on
the Facebook account, she looked up in horror, meeting the
same reflection mirrored back in Lucy's face.

'How did they find him?'

Robert had been showing Joe one of the architecture videos

he'd been watching while he was stuck at home, but he looked up at the panic in Ellen's voice. 'What's going on?'

Lucy was shaking her head from side to side. 'They must've just searched for him online.'

Ellen shuddered, then passed her phone to Robert. 'It's Ian. They've found his Facebook account. I can't bear to think about Grace even looking at a photograph of that man.'

She didn't want to see him herself. It was bad enough remembering him as an arrogant entitled twenty year old. She didn't want his face in her mind now.

'It's worse than that.' Lucy turned her screen around so that Ellen could see the replica screenshot that Charlotte had sent to Lucy. Except her message was longer. Lucy leaned over so that she could read it more easily. 'They've gone to speak to him.'

FORTY

Joe was the first to his feet. 'What? We have to stop them.'

The rest of them were standing now, unsure of which way to turn.

'Have they gone already? If only we still had Grace on the tracker app.'

It was a stupid thing to say about a twenty-six-year-old woman. But Ellen wished she could still keep a hold of her daughter.

'I'm calling Charlotte.' Lucy already had her phone to her ear. 'This is madness.'

'And I'll try Grace.'

'What do you think they're planning on doing?' Robert looked so concerned that Ellen worried about his heart.

Joe was probably thinking the same, because he changed his tone to one of studied calm. 'We need to all sit down. Once Lucy and Ellen have spoken to them, they'll probably turn around and come straight back.'

After five rings, Grace's number went to voicemail. Then Lucy tossed her phone down onto the table. 'Charlotte isn't answering. They know we'll try and stop them.'

Ellen left a voicemail for Grace to call her. Then looked to Lucy. 'What now?'

Lucy had already scooped her phone back up and was thumbing the screen. 'We'll have to find the bastard on Facebook. Ha. Of course his account is not locked down. He'd want everyone seeing everything, wouldn't he?'

She'd found that pretty quickly. 'Have you looked him up online before?'

Lucy shook her head. 'I've had no interest whatsoever in knowing what disgusting things he's up to.'

Ellen felt the same. She'd done her best to not even think about him for the last twenty-six years. To look at him online would've only been like reopening an old wound. Worse than that, she had the superstitious feeling that looking him up might conjure him back into her life.

'I think I've found it.' Lucy frowned. Then brought the phone closer. Then swore under her breath before reaching into a bag for a pair of reading glasses. Without looking up from the screen, she pointed at Joe. 'Do not say a word.'

Joe laughed and then mimed zipping his lips.

Robert leaned towards Lucy. 'What does it say? Where is he?'

Lucy was scanning the post. 'It looks as if it's some kind of conference in a hotel in central London, maybe an award ceremony. Oh my God, they're giving him an award for something to do with his career. If only they knew.'

Ellen had a sick feeling that they might be about to find out. 'We need to get there.'

Robert was out of his seat again and looking around him. 'Where are my car keys?'

He was still under strict doctor's orders to take things easy. 'No way, you're not going.'

'But I'm the only one that hasn't had anything to drink.'

It was true. Charlotte had brought Lucy and Joe in her car.

WE BOTH HAVE SECRETS

She was staying sober because she was due at work early tomorrow, so Joe had already had three glasses of wine. As had Lucy and Ellen.

But there was no way Robert was getting into some kind of car chase less than two weeks after heart surgery. Lucy was swiping at her phone screen. 'I'm already booking an Uber. It's five minutes away. Ellen and I will go. Joe, you can stay here and keep an eye on Robert.'

Joe frowned. 'I'm not sure I'm happy about you both going on your own.'

'I feel the same,' Robert agreed. 'And I don't need babysitting. Joe can come with you.'

'Please.' Ellen's heart was racing, she needed to get to Grace as soon as possible. 'I'm worried enough about Grace. I don't want to worry about you here on your own.'

'I agree.' Lucy slipped her bag onto her shoulder. 'Ellen and I have got this. You two stay here. We're just going to find the girls and make them come back with us.'

Robert's face darkened. 'I don't want you to have to see him. After what he did, I want to...'

She reached out and held his arm. 'I know. And that's exactly why you can't come. Please, Robert. I need you to relax.'

After a strong look from Lucy, Joe retook his seat. 'Yes, come on mate. I think we've been told on this one.'

Lucy waved her phone. 'The Uber is here. Wish us luck. If either of the girls call you, tell them we're coming.'

Once she'd given the Uber driver the hotel address, Lucy sat back and raised an eyebrow at Ellen. 'This is not how I expected tonight to go.'

That was the understatement of the year. 'Me neither. But it has been nice having you all in our home. I was thinking this afternoon, why did you invite us out to Spain? Really.'

This time Lucy told her the truth. 'I was going to tell you that I knew, that I suspected, what had happened between you and Ian. I was even going to ask you if Grace was really Robert's child.'

'But you didn't.'

'No. When you first came, I was determined to show you what a great life I had. That I had made it despite what had happened to me. But when you came, it was you, my oldest friend, and I wanted to protect you from what you were about to find out about Robert. I don't know if this will surprise you, but I don't find it that easy to make female friends.'

She pulled a face and, for the first time, Ellen saw that girl from over two decades ago. Young, fierce, determined to make her way in the world. 'I don't think I would have enjoyed my time at university half as much if I hadn't met you.'

Lucy smiled. 'Really? I feel the same. The time I spent with you was the closest I got to being myself.'

'You should be yourself. I like yourself.'

Lucy laughed. 'You might be the only one.'

'I spoke to Joe earlier. In the kitchen. I'd misunderstood something. I put a couple of things you said and a couple of things he said together and came up with five. I thought... well, it doesn't really matter what I thought. But he really loves you, you know. He told me that he would never want anyone except you.'

Tears filled Lucy's eyes. 'Robert said something similar about you.'

'We're very lucky.'

'We are.' Lucy winked. 'And so are they.'

Despite the fear in her belly, Ellen laughed. 'They are.'

Lucy checked Google Maps. 'We're about six minutes away. I hope we get there before they find him.'

It was a public place and they were together, but still Ellen's

WE BOTH HAVE SECRETS 245

stomach squeezed at the very idea of those two girls in front of that man. 'I don't want to see him, either.'

Lucy shook her head. 'Nor me. I'm surprised that Charlotte has gone. I've always told her that she can contact her father if she wants to. I've even offered to help her. But she never has.'

'Grace can be quite impulsive. And I think she's still getting over the shock of finding out her boyfriend is still very much married. Plus the worry about Robert. She's had a lot to cope with these last couple of weeks. What do you think they're going to do?'

Lucy looked up from the map on her phone. 'I really don't know. What would you do if you were them?'

That was impossible to answer. 'Not this. I've been trying to pretend he no longer exists.'

Lucy nodded. 'They're very different from us, aren't they?'

The taxi pulled up by the side of a hotel. 'Here you are, ladies. Door to door.'

'Right, then.' Ellen looked at Lucy. 'Let's go find our girls.'

FORTY-ONE

The hotel foyer was almost empty. Its rich velvet furniture and thick carpets absorbing all sounds except the classical music playing through hidden speakers. As they approached the reception desk, Ellen spotted a large white noticeboard on an easel.

Chemistry Today Winter Awards Ceremony. The Wellington Room. First Floor.

She pointed it out to Lucy who got directions from the young man on reception.

The lift seemed to take an age to come. 'Do you think they're in there? The girls?'

She'd sent another two texts to Grace from the Uber, but hadn't had a reply. Lucy rattled the button to the lift in impatience. 'I don't know. But I'm hoping they haven't found Ian yet. Let's take the stairs.'

The staircase was wide and carpeted in the same dark-blue velvet as the reception area. By the time they got to the top, Ellen was a little out of breath. 'Where now?'

Lucy pointed to a large wooden door bearing a brass name-plate: The Wellington Room. 'In there.'

WE BOTH HAVE SECRETS

Ellen had never gatecrashed an event in her life. But this was for Grace. 'Let's go.'

On the other side of the door, the room was full of round tables seating maybe eight to ten people. All the men were dressed in black tie, the women in silk or sequins. Whoever *Chemistry Today* were, they liked to put on a party.

Ellen had felt good in the calf-length ruby dress she'd worn for dinner with Lucy and Joe, but felt decidedly underdressed in this company: even the waiting staff wore bow ties. They kept to the very edge of the room as they scanned the tables for the girls, but they were nowhere to be seen. She whispered to Lucy. 'Maybe they changed their minds?'

A couple of people around the tables at the back had turned to look at them. Any minute now and someone was going to come and ask them what they were doing here. Lucy seemed oblivious to this as she started to wander up the side of the room, checking the tables. Ellen followed, trying to ignore the glances they were getting. There were people meandering around, waiters pouring drinks, and a hubbub of chatter and laughter.

'There!' Lucy pointed to the side of the temporary stage that had been erected at one end of the room.

Relief swept over Ellen. They'd found them and Ian McCready was nowhere in sight. Just as they were about to walk across the room to them, a tall thin man in an expensive dinner suit tapped the microphone. 'If I can have your attention again, ladies and gentleman, we are about to present our final award of the night.'

Ellen and Lucy froze in place on their side of the room, trying to get the girls' attention without drawing any to themselves.

The man on the stage continued, 'Before I introduce this year's recipient of the Chemistry Today Award for Significant

Contribution to Research, I have had a last-minute request, which I think the recipient will enjoy.'

When he then looked over at Grace and Charlotte with a smile, Ellen's stomach clenched. What was going on?

As both girls took the three steps up to the podium, Lucy grabbed Ellen's arm. She could barely hear her voice over the polite applause. 'What are they doing?'

Whatever it was, they were too late to stop it.

Charlotte stepped up to the microphone first.

'Hello, everybody. I hope you've had a nice dinner. Thank you for letting us come to speak to you this evening on a night to honour Ian McCready.'

Ellen followed the direction of Charlotte's hand to a table at the very front of the room and that was the first time she saw him. Ian.

Her gasp made a woman sitting close by turn and frown at her. There he was. Looking a little older, but really not much different than he had when they were young. Lucy leaned in close to her ear. 'The bastard hasn't even had the decency to age.'

She was right. Much as she hated him, he was a very attractive man. The arrogance was still there: tilted back in his chair, jacket unbuttoned, elbow resting on the table, the familiar sneer on his lips. He still believed he was better than everyone.

Even he looked confused at the two young women on the stage pointing towards him. He had no idea who they were. Grace, she could understand, but Charlotte? He'd known her. He'd lived with her. Had he not taken any interest in following her online at least?

Now Charlotte was addressing the audience again. 'You may be wondering why we are giving this introduction tonight. Well, it's because we both wanted to pay tribute to this man before you. My name is Charlotte Meads and Ian is my father.'

Ian had frozen in his chair, oblivious to the shock on his

face, murmurs of surprise and pleasure rippled around him. The other guests must be expecting a sweet speech of love from these two girls. How wrong they were.

'As you may know. my father studied chemistry at Canterbury University where he met my mother. Some might say that they had instant chemistry.'

Her smile was so saccharine as she waited for the polite laughter at her joke. She had them in the palm of her hand. Ian stuck a finger in the front of his collar and pulled at it as if it was too tight. Was he worried? Ellen really hoped so.

'I was born a year after my parents graduated. Mum was hoping for a girl, Dad was hoping for a termination.'

The atmosphere in the room changed, but there were still a few uncertain laughs, maybe thinking that she was still joking. The look on Ian's face was thunderous.

'Still, they did make a go of it and he lived with us for – about a year or so, I think? He came home *most* nights, apparently. And I think it was only three times that my mother was absolutely sure that he had screwed someone else.'

Now the room was absolutely silent. No one was still under the misapprehension that this was some kind of joke.

The man who had been on stage when they arrived was ashen, Ian called out to him. 'Are you not going to stop this?'

But when the man moved, Lucy stepped in front of him. 'Don't even think about it.'

Charlotte's tone was still so upbeat that people were looking from her to Ian as she continued her speech. 'Can you imagine my surprise when I found out that I had a sister that I knew nothing about and – even more curious – she was a year older than me?'

Charlotte took a step to the side and nodded at Grace. Ellen's stomach lurched. Was she really going to do this?

Within a heartbeat, she discovered that, not only was she going to do it, but she was going to make sure everyone heard

250   EMMA ROBINSON

her, loud and clear. 'My name is Grace Cooper and I have never met my biological father before today. In fact, I don't know that he even knows that I exist.' She stared Ian down in way that made Ellen's heart swell with pride. 'Hello, Dad.'

Ian opened and closed his mouth, shocked into silence.

'The reason I haven't met him is that Ian spiked my mother's drink so that she was unconscious when I was conceived.'

That made him move. He stood so quickly that his chair clattered to the floor behind him. 'What is going on? Somebody needs to stop them. Where is security?'

Frantically, he looked around him for help. Seeing him so rattled was more pleasurable than Ellen had expected. But no one came to his aid. She wouldn't mind betting that there were several people in this room tonight who were pleased to see him get his comeuppance.

Grace – articulate, confident, strong – kept going. 'We have only just realised that we are sisters. And we're wondering – Daddy – whether there are any more half-sisters or half-brothers out there? Just in case, we're going to make it our business to try and find all the other women whose drinks you spiked so that you could rape them.'

Shocked gasps peppered the room at the use of that word. Had they not been listening? Did they think there was a difference between drink spiking and assaults in the park? Were they more shocked at the words of these young women than they were at the actions of the man who sat among them?

Charlotte put a hand on Grace's shoulder and swept an arm to encompass the room. 'There are plenty of people filming this right now and I would imagine that some of those videos are going to make it on to the Internet before the night is over. When you post them, please add the hashtag IanMcCreadyS-pikeStory and make sure you tell the press that we're available for interviews and comments.'

'That's enough!' Ian leaped forward as if he was going to

climb the stage, but wasn't fast enough to stop Ellen and Lucy getting in his way, standing between him and the girls.

Lucy's voice was pure hate. 'No you don't, arsehole.'

He recoiled as if she'd struck him. 'What are you doing here?' His eyes widened as he saw Ellen. 'Ellen? Is that you?'

Her name on his lips made her feel sick, but if her daughter was brave enough to do what she'd just done, then Ellen wasn't about to be the weakest link. 'Yes, it's me.'

Old habits die hard and he looked at her as if she was dirt on his designer shoes. 'I'd hardly recognise you. The years have not been kind. What the hell are you doing here?'

Lucy almost went for him, but Ellen held out her hand to keep her back. He wasn't going to make her feel small any more. 'Since the night that you raped me, I've had to live with a guilt that doesn't belong to me. I'm here to give it back to you. Because, you know what? Despite what you took from me, I've won. However awful your actions, I got Grace from it. And I got Robert. And then Emily. And I got a wonderful life with my family. We are safe. I don't know what kind of life you've built for yourself, but you might want to start saying goodbye to it. Because we're not keeping secrets any longer.'

For a moment, she thought he might hit her. But then he sneered at her. 'I don't think so. You'll be hearing from my lawyer in the morning.'

By this time, Grace and Charlotte had made their way down from the podium. Grace put her arm around Ellen's waist. 'That's good. Maybe he can also sort out your appointment for a DNA test.'

When did her daughter become so quick and confident? Ellen held her close. On her other side, Lucy reached her right arm around Charlotte and her left across the top of Ellen's back.

They stood there, watching him. Four strong, confident women standing firm in the truth.

Ian McCready, face like stone, turned and walked away.

FORTY-TWO

'The video has already been uploaded all over Instagram and TikTok.'

Grace almost squealed with pleasure as she scrolled through the images on her phone. The girls were almost drunk on their success, the atmosphere in Charlotte's car was electric. Lucy was beside her daughter in the passenger seat. Ellen was in the back with Grace. She had hold of her hand and wasn't planning on letting her go for the rest of the evening.

'You adding the hashtag was genius,' Charlotte called over her shoulder. 'It'll be so much easier to find everything.'

Ellen still didn't really understand how this had all come about. 'When did you decide to do that?'

Grace put down her phone for a moment and looked at Ellen, her face flushed with their success. 'We'd talked on the phone about whether or not either of us ever planned to track him down. I mean, we both knew we didn't want him in our lives, but I was so curious. Then Charlotte found him on Facebook and we got more and more cross as we saw him out and about at various bars and clubs. We thought, what if he is still doing it? What if there are girls out there who he might be doing this to even now?'

The same fear had occurred to her, but she hadn't been brave enough to face it. The way Lucy reached out to put a hand on Charlotte's shoulder, her thumb rubbing her arm, suggested she was thinking the same thing.

Charlotte threw a smile in her mother's direction before taking up the story. 'We didn't decide to do it until we were in the pub tonight and we looked him up and he was there. Even in the car on the way there, we hadn't properly formulated a plan. We just knew that we wanted to show him up for what he really was. In front of everybody.'

Ellen swallowed a lump in her throat. 'I am so proud of you, Grace. And you, Charlotte. You were both amazing up there.'

Grace grinned at her. 'I know. It felt so good. Like I had the power to really do something.'

For all her ebullience, Ellen was still conscious of the gravity of what had transpired. Charlotte had known about Ian's existence her whole life; for Grace it'd all happened so fast these last few days. She and Charlotte seemed to have formed this instant bond that had carried them through this evening, but what happened next week, next month, when it all sunk in for real?

She squeezed Grace's hand. 'How did it feel? Seeing him like that?'

Grace paused to consider. 'Surreal, I think. That's probably the best word.'

Ellen was also worried about other implications for the two girls. 'What if he does get his lawyer involved?'

'Let him.' Lucy turned to look at her. 'It's all true. What can he do?'

She and Lucy had already called Robert and Joe to tell them what had happened – and that the girls were safe – but

254   EMMA ROBINSON

something else occurred to her. 'What about Abigail and Emily? What if they see the video?'

'Good point. We'll call them when we get home.'

Robert must've been looking out for them, because he had the front door open as soon as Charlotte pulled onto the drive. Grace was out of the car in moments and straight into his arms.

Both girls were so wired by the events of that evening that they were able to recount – with help from the videos that were being shared online at an alarming rate – the whole thing to Robert and Joe, who both looked stunned. Ellen was a little concerned that the excitement might not be the best thing for Robert's recovery, so she was a little relieved when Grace and Charlotte decided to relocate themselves to Robert's study so that they could respond to all the reposts on his computer as well as their phones.

Joe and Lucy had insisted that they made the coffee and were in the kitchen. Clearly, they needed a moment alone and were giving Ellen and Robert the same thing. The two of them were on the sofa.

Robert held her hand in his. 'How was it for you? Seeing him again. I was worried it would bring things up for you.'

She'd considered that, too, but in fact the opposite had been true. 'I think seeing the girls' reaction to it, the way they were so brave and honest. It made me realise that keeping this a secret, pushed down inside myself, had just given it more power. Bringing it out like that, it took that power away.'

He smiled. 'I'm glad. I really am.'

She didn't want him to think she was making light of the impact it had had on him. 'I'm not trying to absolve myself of responsibility, though. I'm still guilty of keeping the secret from you all these years.'

'I know. But we have to get past that. We're still here. Our family is still here. Nothing – and no one – can ever touch that.'

Judging by the watery look to Lucy's eyes when she and Joe came back in, they'd had a similarly emotional conversation. Before they could discuss it, though, Grace barrelled into the sitting room, followed by Charlotte.

'Mum, look at this.'

Ellen took Grace's phone and peered at the direct message that she was pointing to. What she read took her breath away. 'I hope you don't mind me contacting you. I think Ian McCready did the same thing to me.'

She passed the phone to Lucy and watched her reading it, before she looked up at Ellen with a bittersweet smile on her face. 'He's finally going to get what he deserves.'

FORTY-THREE

Malaga in December was nowhere near the same temperature as Malaga in October, but Joe had brought out the patio heaters and the four friends were enjoying the orange light of the late afternoon.

The table was laden with food. A huge terracotta pot with the last of the Andalusian stew had been pushed to the side to make way for a platter of cheese and rustic bread. Though they were a week away from Christmas, Lucy had decorated the white cloth with small pots of Poinsettia, ruby glasses and emerald-green candles. It was – as always – utterly perfect.

Robert leaned back in his chair. 'I don't think I'm going to need to eat again until the New Year.'

Joe refilled Robert's glass with Rioja. 'We've got all night.'

Lucy was – as always – utterly perfect, too. Her magenta sweater and black wide-legged trousers gave her the look of a Chanel advert. At no point during the last two months had Ellen seen her look anything less than chic and sophisticated. Her plum varnished fingernails wrapped around the bottle of Cava as she topped up Ellen's glass. 'We need to keep up with these two.'

WE BOTH HAVE SECRETS 257

Ellen sipped from the delicate coupe, the dry zesty bubbles making her nose tingle. 'That's delicious.'

The difference was that she no longer resented Lucy's perfection. In fact, she'd begun to admire her for it. Even asked her opinion sometimes on what to wear or cook or buy. Not that Ellen had changed a great deal. No, she was still the same on the outside. Her changes had been within. She felt lighter, happier, freer. She hadn't realised how heavy the burden of her secret had been until she let it go. There was no fear anymore. No fear that Robert would find out the truth. No fear that he'd only married her because she was pregnant. No fear that he needed her to be anything other than the woman she was.

Joe rested his arm on the back of Lucy's chair. 'When do you have to go back to work, Robbie?'

It still felt strange hearing them calling Robert by his old nickname, but she'd grown to enjoy that, too. No one else used it: it was their special thing.

Robert glanced at her for confirmation. They'd only just decided this week what he was about to tell them. Not even the girls knew. 'Actually, I'm not going back.'

Lucy looked from Robert to Ellen and back again. 'What do you mean? Everything's okay isn't it? Charlotte hasn't said... I mean, I know she wouldn't tell me, but... everything is okay?'

Robert smiled and snaked his own arm around the back of Ellen. There'd been a lot more of this in the last two months. It was as if they'd found one another again. 'Everything is great, actually. So I don't want to spoil it by returning to work.'

If he was going to be enigmatic about it, Ellen would need to put them out of their misery. 'We found a job. Online. It's a research project. Terrible pay. Well, no pay, actually, just expenses. But, well, Robert is going to take his pension early and go for it.'

Joe reached across the table with a grin and his hand out to shake. 'Well, done, mate.'

258 EMMA ROBINSON

Lucy clapped her hands. 'I knew it! I knew you'd do something amazing one day.'

Robert laughed and glanced at Ellen, that look that still made her stomach flip. 'I'm not sure about amazing, but I'm pretty excited about it.'

And that wasn't all. She leaned across the table. 'And we're going to travel. Together. We're going to do city breaks and mountain treks and safaris and see the world.'

She was so excited about this. Now that the girls weren't at home, they had the freedom to go wherever they wanted. Finally, those trips they'd planned laying in Robert's bed at university might come to fruition. Although they might swap the youth hostel they would've had back then for a decent hotel.

Lucy gasped. 'I'm so pleased. I really, really am.'

Ellen could see from the brightness of Lucy's eyes that she meant that. Over the last two months, they'd managed to put their friendship back together a piece at a time. There was something very special about a friendship that began in your youth. Being with Lucy made her feel young again. As if all the roles and habits they'd acquired in their twenties and thirties had dissolved away and they were back to being the girls with their heads full of plans and no responsibilities to hold them back.

Joe was clinking glasses with Robert. There was something different about him that she hadn't been able to put her finger on since they'd arrived this morning. He seemed less frantic, less occupied. 'What about you, Joe? How's your work? Where's your new project?'

With the intensity she'd grown to feel comfortable with, he leaned forward conspiratorially. 'Actually, I've taken a leaf out of Robert's book. I've hired someone to oversee all the current projects so I don't have to be away from home. He's my man on the ground and I manage it remotely.'

Lucy raised an eyebrow. 'Not that he's actually let the poor chap do anything without running it past him first. Joe may not be there in body, but...'

Despite her comment, her pleasure in having Joe around more was evident. He leaned towards her and kissed the top of her cheekbone where it met her hair. 'I'm getting there. And, anyway, I need to be here in case you decide to have an affair with one of our houseguests in my absence.'

He presented a mock innocent face to Ellen and she threw her napkin at him. 'Very funny.'

It no longer embarrassed her that she'd jumped to such idiotic conclusions. Those few days in October had become a part of their friendship lore, to be referred to in jest whenever the mood took them.

Joe winked and blew her a kiss. 'Seriously, though. If you're both going to be taking more holidays, maybe we can come with you?'

Now it was Robert's turn to hold up his glass. 'That would be great.'

The three of them raised their glasses to meet his. Just as the girls clattered out onto the patio. Grace stood behind Robert, placed her hands on his shoulders. 'Are you still eating? We're ready to go to the beach.'

If she'd been worried about Grace and Robert's relationship back in October, it was no longer something she even considered. If anything, they were closer, more loving, as if they wanted the other to know just how much they meant.

October had been quite a rollercoaster. Abigail's scans had come back clear of Robert's condition, which was a huge relief to all of them. But their joy had been tempered by her upset at finding out about Grace's DNA results.

Many tears had been shed, but much love had been professed and – Ellen was so grateful – their family was stronger than ever. Grace told her that Abigail had made her promise that she would always be her favourite sister. Once she'd done that, she was very happy to meet Charlotte and make her welcome.

This meant that their family had kind of expanded. Though Grace was the only person with a blood relation to Charlotte, they'd all grown to love her. They'd also got to meet Emily and learned that her heart was as big as her thirst for adventure.

Now the four girls stood in front of them, determined to make sure that they keep their promise to go for an evening walk on the beach, even if they'd drawn the line at a dip in the December sea.

'Come on, Dad.' Now Emily was pulling at Joe's arm. 'You promised to film us running into the water.'

Lucy was already getting out of her chair. 'Yes. Let's go. It'll be great for Instagram.'

Emily rolled her eyes. 'You are so embarrassing, Mother.'

At the end of November, Grace and Charlotte had started up a charity to support women and girls who'd been affected by drink spiking and to increase awareness of it. Lucy was helping them. Since their public outing of Ian, there'd been three more women who'd come forward in response to the video being shared online. All of the information was with the Metropolitan police and they were waiting to hear whether they had enough information to press charges. It was looking very promising.

Charlotte waved a set of keys. 'I haven't been drinking. I'll drop the girls down there then come back for you four.'

Twenty minutes later, the eight of them were on a deserted beach. Beside Robert, watching the girls shrieking as they were splashed by the icy waves, Ellen couldn't remember when she'd been happier.

'Those girls are absolutely crackers.' Lucy shook her head behind her large sunglasses.

Joe laughed. 'I blame their mothers.'

Lucy turned and grinned at Ellen. 'Yeah, I think that's pretty fair.'

The two couples made their way down the beach in the direction of their brave and beautiful daughters, ready for their next adventure.

A LETTER FROM EMMA

Dear reader,

I want to say a huge thank you for choosing to read *We Both Have Secrets*. If you did enjoy it, and want to keep up to date with all my latest releases, just sign up at the following link. Your email address will never be shared and you can unsubscribe at any time.

www.bookouture.com/emma-robinson

I can't quite believe this is book number 16.

It was great fun setting a story in Malaga, Spain. Visiting somewhere on a research trip makes you look at it with different eyes and I would thoroughly recommend it!

I also loved thinking back to university days to write the flashback scenes for this book. Though I'm in denial about how long ago I was there, it made me think about the friendships that are formed in our youth and how some stick and some fade away. This book is dedicated to a friend I have known since I was in secondary school. Both our lives have taken twists and turns, but she has always been a great support and a wonderful pal. I hope that you have friends in your life like that, too.

I hope you loved *We Both Have Secrets* and if you did I would be very grateful if you could write a review. I'd love to hear what you think, and it makes such a difference helping new readers to discover one of my books for the first time.

I love hearing from my readers – you can get in touch through social media or my website.

Thanks,

Emma

www.motherhoodforslackers.com

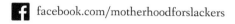 facebook.com/motherhoodforslackers

ACKNOWLEDGEMENTS

For tightening my plot and my prose, grateful thanks to my brilliant editor, Laura Deacon. For PR magnificence, thanks to the lovely Jess Readett and the rest of the PR team and to everyone at Bookouture – thanks for all that you do and for letting me write more books with you!

A big thank you to Alice Moore for the fabulous cover and to Donna Hillyer and Deborah Blake for ensuring that the book inside the cover is equally well polished. For picking up the pesky mistakes that make it through five rounds of edits, thank you to Carrie Harvey.

I had a fabulous weekend in Malaga as research for this book (it's a tough job sometimes!) and I would have been completely lost without help from Lesley McLoughlin – thanks so much! Thanks also to the Trauma Fiction group on Facebook for helping me out with ideas for Robert's heart condition: any mistakes are mine.

Lastly, as always, to my family. My son has his final GCSE exam on the day this book is published and I'm prouder of him than I can ever put into words. (If my daughter is reading this, I'll mention you in the acknowledgements of the next one.)

PUBLISHING TEAM

Turning a manuscript into a book requires the efforts of many people. The publishing team at Bookouture would like to acknowledge everyone who contributed to this publication.

Commercial
Lauren Morrissette
Hannah Richmond
Imogen Allport

Cover design
Alice Moore

Data and analysis
Mark Alder
Mohamed Bussuri

Editorial
Laura Deacon
Imogen Allport

Copyeditor
Donna Hillyer

Proofreader
Deborah Blake

Marketing
Alex Crow
Melanie Price
Occy Carr
Cíara Rosney
Martyna Młynarska

Operations and distribution
Marina Valles
Stephanie Straub
Joe Morris

Production
Hannah Snetsinger
Mandy Kullar
Ria Clare
Nadia Michael

Publicity
Kim Nash
Noelle Holten
Jess Readett
Sarah Hardy

Rights and contracts
Peta Nightingale
Richard King
Saidah Graham

www.ingramcontent.com/pod-product-compliance
Ingram Content Group UK Ltd.
Pitfield, Milton Keynes, MK11 3LW, UK
UKHW041256120825
7359UKWH00025B/92